CONSUMED
ABBIE
RUSHTON

ATOM

ATOM

First published in Great Britain in 2016 by Atom

A CIP catalogue record for this book
is available from the British Library.

ISBN 978-0-349-00203-3

Typeset in Palatino by M Rules
Printed and bound in Great Britain by
Clays Ltd, St Ives plc

Papers used by Atom are from well-managed forests
and other responsible sources.

MIX
Paper from
responsible sources
FSC® C104740

Atom
An imprint of
Little, Brown Book Group
Carmelite House
50 Victoria Embankment
London EC4Y 0DZ

An Hachette UK Company
www.hachette.co.uk

www.atombooks.co.uk

A̶ ̶w̶a̶s̶ ̶b̶o̶r̶n̶ ̶a̶n̶d̶ ̶b̶r̶o̶u̶g̶h̶t̶ ̶u̶p̶ in a small village near Newmarket, Suffolk. She has a degree in English Literature with Creative Writing from the University of East Anglia, and currently works as an editor at a leading educational publisher.

While working as a part-time bookseller during her studies, Abbie rediscovered a love of children's and young adult books. In 2010 she was a winner of Undiscovered Voices, a writing competition run by the Society of Children's Book Writers and Illustrators.

Abbie lives near Newbury, Berkshire. She is a keen traveller and is never happier than when planning her next adventure.

34 4124 0009 5816

For Reena

1

Myla

Where am I? God, where am I?

There's a sharp, white pain behind my eyes. I open them. It's night. A fat moon hangs heavily above me. The star-specked sky rolls for a few moments, then stops.

I'm cold. So cold my limbs have stiffened with it. I'm on my back, my pulse thud-thud-thudding in my ears, the taste of blood at the back of my throat.

I turn my head. Something prickles my cheek. Marram grass. Does that mean ...? I curl my fingers, feel the scratch of sand beneath my nails. I strain to hear above my rapid breaths. Then it reaches me with a roar: the sea.

My feet are bare. Where are my shoes?

There's something lying in the sand. I blink a couple of times, try to focus, then squint through the moonlit gloom. A Smarties tube. Crushed in the middle.

Asha. Asha was here. Where is she now?

The sand around me has been rucked up. Why did she leave?

I feel something else now, besides the cold. A throbbing in my shoulder.

I bite my lip to stop myself whimpering.

I have to find Asha.

I sit up. Too fast. The dunes lurch and slip in and out of focus. I draw in a long breath, blink a couple of times.

'Asha!' I yell, desperately searching for my sister in the almost-darkness. 'Asha!'

There's no response. I slam my fists into the cold sand, feeling the burn of tears in my eyes.

Then I hear it. This low, grating noise. Like rasping breaths. A crackly, wet cough. That sound. It burrows through my pores and slips into my bloodstream, turning everything to ice.

He coughs again.

He's close.

I stumble to my feet, try to grab something to steady myself, but my fingers slip through the air.

The throaty noise is right in my ear now. Fingers claw at my clothes. No! I twist away.

I run. The rattling wheeze is close behind me. Spears of grass slash at my skin and the sand sucks in my feet with every step.

I reach the sea. Moonlight dances across the waves like a flame. A beacon. I plunge into the icy black, the cold stealing my breath, sending my heart into a wild canter. As I gasp and cry, I swallow gulps of water, then clamp a hand over my mouth to stifle my spluttering.

2

Is he following? I can't tell.

I wade deeper and deeper. I carry on until my feet lift and I'm swimming.

Something grabs my ankle. I scream. Seaweed. Just seaweed. Did he hear that? Is he coming?

I pause. Tread water. Listen.

Asha, where are you?

My eyes snap open. I'm in my bedroom, my body tangled in damp sheets. I'm screaming, screaming my sister's name.

But she doesn't come.

She never does.

2

Jamie

My chin jerks up again. I yawn, shake my head. How many stops did I sleep through? The old girl opposite smiles at me. Crap. My T-shirt sleeve is damp. Must've been drooling.

'You all right?' she asks. 'You look exhausted.'

'Yeah.' I look out the window so she doesn't see me blushing.

'Polo?' She stretches over the table to hold out the packet.

I stare at it. 'Nah, I'm all right, thanks.'

'Go on, be a devil!' She winks.

'Um, thanks,' I mutter, taking one.

I wait till she goes back to her iPad, then shove it in my pocket.

Outside, trees and fields and sheep blur past. It's so empty. There's just . . . nothing.

I should get off at the next stop, catch a train back to London. Go home. Imagine *his* face if I turned up. Thought he'd got rid of me; thought he'd have a whole summer with Mum to himself. I can see the curl of his lip, the way he'd stalk off to their bedroom and slam the door.

The pale smudge of my face looks back at me in the window. It's thin. Thinner than the last time Ness saw me. What if she's forgotten what I look like and I end up stuck in a creepy station in nowheresville on my own?

It was a few years ago, the last time I saw her. At someone's wedding. Ness rocked up late, tried to slip in at the back, but caused a fuss when she stood on someone's toe. She's not small. Least, she wasn't back then.

I'm about to close my eyes when the old girl pipes up again, 'Where are you off to?'

Dunno. Can't remember the name of the place.

I try to speak, but my voice grates out. I clear my throat. 'Somewhere near Cromer.'

'Stratten?'

'Er, yeah.'

'Me too. You're not Ness's nephew, are you?'

'Yeah. How did you know?'

She beams. 'Oh, everyone knows everyone else's business! None of us have any blinking secrets. But Ness and I are friends so I heard all about you. I'm Lil.'

I try to smile. 'Jamie.'

'Well, it's nice to meet you, Jamie.'

I look at Lil properly. She's got grey hair, older than Ness, but doesn't look like your typical nan. She's got a solid, almost square body, and her eyes are much younger than her face, which is covered with make-up – splashes of bright colour on her eyes and lips.

Lil chats a bit, tells me which chippy to avoid (apparently they refry yesterday's fish), which beach is the best (only the locals use it) and that I should tell Mr Whatshisface at the bakery that I'm with Ness (otherwise I'll get charged the 'tourist price').

Ten minutes later, Lil gets up. 'We're almost there. I've got to dash – my son's picking me up. You'll be all right. No doubt Ness will be late.' She rolls her eyes, then grins. 'I'll be seeing you, Jamie!'

She heads off before I can say bye.

I heave my bag down from the rack. Jesus, it's heavy! I head for the door, but almost trip over this canvas shopping bag which has fallen out from under the table. It's got a picture of an ugly cat on the front. Lil must've forgotten it. I look over the heads of the people queuing in the aisle, but can't see her. Must be at the door already.

I grab the bag, wait for everyone to get off, then try to find Lil on the platform. She's almost at the exit so I have to run after her. I'm outta breath in seconds, shaking and sweating. Feels like everyone's looking at me.

I catch up and tap her on the shoulder. 'Er – Lil?'

She turns.

'You . . .' I drag in breaths between words. '. . . fc
your . . . bag.'

'What a fool!' she shrieks. 'I don't know. You'll get old one
day. Thank you, Jamie.'

I nod once, then watch her leave.

My stomach growls. I ignore it. In my bag, squashed
against my games console, there's a sandwich that Mum
snuck in there. Found it after I'd got on the train: posh, thick
slices of ham – none of that wafer-thin junk – and doorstep
wedges of bread. It's not just a sandwich, though. It's a fat
pile of guilt, wrapped up in foil and sent as far away as possible. Along with me.

She can't just forget about me.

Can't pretend that she didn't choose *him* over me.

The station is poky – just two platforms and not even a
shop. A couple of people march straight down some steps
to the car park. Should I wait there, or here? An Asian
bloke in a swanky suit hangs around for a couple of minutes. He looks at his watch, then his BlackBerry, then back
to his watch. A brunette in a hippy sundress walks up. The
businessman smiles and chucks his arm round her waist as
they walk off.

That's it. I'm alone. I sink onto a cold metal seat. Mum
tried to give me Ness's number before I left, but I wouldn't
take it. Was too busy giving her the cold shoulder. I'm not
phoning Mum to ask for it. No way.

There's the rumble of an engine in the car park, then a

screech of brakes. Maybe that's her. I get up, my stomach twisting. I dunno what to say to her.

Ness meets me at the bottom of the steps. She looks flushed and a bit harassed. I manage a half-smile but don't get a chance to say hello before she pulls me into a hug, squashing me against her chest. 'Jamie,' she whispers in a voice that's frighteningly close to tears. 'Sorry I'm late. I'm so pleased you're here! I've got your room all ready.'

She lets me go and I drag in a huge breath, my face flaming. 'Er . . . hi,' I say. 'Thanks.'

I'm not really sure what else to add.

'Let's get you home.'

Ness grabs my suitcase as if it weighs nothing and wheels it away. She's fast! Faster than I'd expect for . . . someone her size. I try to keep up as she heads off, wobbling beneath a bright, flowery dress. There's a hole in the back of her tights and one of her shoelaces is trailing through the puddles.

Ness's old Volvo estate is sprawled across two spaces. There's a dent and a couple of scratches in the bumper and the rear number plate is hanging on by one screw.

A dog is steaming up the back window, which is covered with wet marks from its nose. It's already started to bark and wag its tail before Ness opens the boot. Then it licks her arm as Ness shoves my suitcase in. It's one of those sheepdogs and it looks – and smells – like it's been in the sea.

'This is Ian,' Ness says.

Before I can help myself, I crack a smile. What the hell kind of name is that for a dog?

Ness catches my eye and grins. 'Don't ask!'

I open the door and stare into the footwell, wondering if I'm s'posed to tread on all the crap down there. There's a polystyrene cup with a bit of tea still in the bottom, a tin opener, a cupcake wrapper and a rubber chicken. The seat is just as bad, but Ness sweeps everything off to join the other junk on the floor.

The rubber chicken makes a comedy squeak when I step on it. Ian barks.

'That's Alonzo,' Ness says, starting the car. 'He's Ian's favourite.'

Ness's driving is mental. She's so close to the kerb the tyres bounce off it a couple of times, and she never leaves second gear. When she brakes, she *really* brakes, making the seatbelt cut into my shoulder.

'I work in the post office a few days a week, so you and Ian will have the house to yourselves. It would be great if you could walk him. He does get lonely when I'm not around.'

'I can try. Never walked a dog before.'

Ness's eyebrows shoot up, but she says nothing.

Damn, it's hot. Ian is panting in the back, filling the air with doggy fumes. My stomach rolls. Am glad it's empty.

I try to wind down the window.

'Oh, that hasn't worked in years,' Ness says. She starts to

wind hers down. 'And mine always sticks about . . . ' It moves a couple of inches. ' . . . here!' She chuckles, then looks at me. 'So how are you? How are you feeling?'

I flap my T-shirt away from my sticky body. 'OK, I s'pose. Tired.'

'Yes, but how are you feeling about coming here? Are you worried about how we're going to get along? Wondering what you're going to do all summer? Anxious about making friends?'

Well, yeah. All of that. But what's with the questions? I stare straight ahead, breathing through my mouth to avoid the stink of dog.

'Well, you don't need to worry about the friend thing.' Ness looks well pleased with herself. 'My friend has a daughter: Shamyla. Half-Mauritian. Very pretty girl.'

Jesus! Sounds like she's setting me up.

Ness carries on. 'She gets it from Jav, her mum. Jav looks incredible. I swear you'd think she's in her thirties, but she's forty-three, almost the same age as me. Anyway . . . ' She raises her eyes and smiles, like she's laughing at herself. ' . . . I said you'd visit her.'

I scrunch my nails into my palms. 'You said *what*?'

Ness shakes her head, looking dead serious. 'That family, they've been through an awful lot.' She pauses, then sighs. 'I might as well say it now, get it out of the way.'

God, what's she gonna tell me?

'Two years ago, Myla's sister was murdered.'

The car suddenly seems very cold. I swallow heavily, struggling to find the words. 'What happened?'

'She was abducted from Heartleas Cove, right in front of Myla,' Ness says softly. 'They found the body on the same beach two days later.'

I almost grab the wheel when Ness takes both hands off it to wipe her eyes.

'The police thought Asha had been held captive somewhere before she was killed. God only knows what that poor girl went through.'

'Did they catch who did it?'

Ness nods, her mouth set in a grim line. 'Si Ashworth. Nasty type. Really nasty. A wife-beater. Someone found one of those phone charms behind a cushion in his house. It was in the shape of an "A". When the family confirmed it was Asha's, the police searched the whole place and found fingerprints and a hair. Awful business. You just don't expect it in a place like this, Jamie.'

We sit in silence for a moment.

How do you even begin to deal with that? What would I say to her?

'She's very fragile, but such a sweet girl. I know you're going to be good for each other.'

'So, what?' I ask. It comes out like a bark – much harsher than I meant it to. I take a breath, try not to snap out my next words. 'I'm s'posed to cheer her up? I'm hardly the best guy for that.'

'No. Well, yes, if you can. But really it's to give her some company. She's obviously very troubled. She has panic attacks and all sorts. Poor thing must be lonely.'

'Why?'

Ness sighs. 'She won't leave the house. That's why I said you'd go round. Myla hasn't left the house for the last two years.'

3

Myla

'You had no right! What do you think I am? Some kind of charity case? You're so embarrassing!'

'Myla, will you just stop squawking for a second and listen?'

'Listen? Did you listen to me when I said I was fine? I don't need a babysitter.'

'Don't be ridiculous. He's new to the area, doesn't know anyone. This isn't just about you.'

I cross my arms. 'I have friends, Mum.'

'Do you mean your "online" friends?'

She actually uses air-quotes.

'Yes, I mean them. And Lauren.'

Mum's eyes soften. 'Lauren hasn't been round for over two months,' she says gently.

'She's busy. We still text. Everything's fine.'

Mum's twisting a tea-towel in her hands. She won't look at me. 'I just worry about you, Myla.' The towel is wound as tight as it will go, the material rigid with tension. Mum bites her lip to stop it from quivering.

I let out a shaky breath, take a step closer and put one of my hands over hers.

We stand for a moment in silence. I pretend not to see the tear that Mum wipes away. I twiddle a loose button on my jumper. Mum frowns at it. She hates sewing.

'When's he coming?' I mutter.

'In an hour.'

'An hour!' I yank the button clean off and smack it down on the work surface. 'An hour.'

Mum nods meekly.

'And what does Dad think about this?'

'It's fine. We've discussed it.'

'Oh, I'm glad. So I don't get a say.'

'I'm just trying to help,' Mum says. Then she sighs, picks up the button and leaves.

I feel a stab of guilt. She's only doing her best. And now I don't know who I'm more angry with: her or me.

There's only one thing that will make this better. Cookies.

I mix the ingredients by hand, pummelling the butter and sugar together, smashing the eggs against the bowl in brisk, efficient strikes. It took me months to perfect this recipe. I made it over and over again – a little less vanilla, a couple more chocolate chips, just thirty seconds longer in the oven. It's now the most viewed page on my blog.

I watch the chocolate soften in the oven, wishing my anger would melt away with it. I run my finger across the edge of the bowl then lick off the mixture as I stare out at the garden, wondering what this boy might be like. I don't remember the last time I saw a boy face-to-face.

Oh, God! What if ... No, surely they wouldn't be trying to set us up. It's just too horrific.

I need to talk to Eve. She'll know exactly what to say. She always does.

I peer around the corner to check that Mum's not still hovering. I don't want another fight. She hates me talking to people online, but short of disconnecting the Internet and confiscating my laptop and phone, she can't do much about it. Every couple of weeks, I get a lecture about Internet safety, followed by an interrogation about who I've been talking to and whether I've been sending them any photos or money.

I pick up my phone and type my username – Saffy42 – into Messenger. Although Eve knows my real name, she likes calling me Saffy. It was Asha's nickname for me. Sometimes it hurts to hear someone else using it. But I try to think it's nice that it didn't die with Asha.

I got the nickname on my tenth birthday. We had this tradition where Mum would make a biryani on special occasions. It would take her most of the day to cook the curry, bake it with the rice on top, make the whole range of garnishes. The smells were incredible – the spiced, yoghurty curry mingling with the sharp tang of burnt onions and the nutty warmth of toasted almonds.

I was in charge of the saffron drizzle to go on the top. It's just warmed milk and saffron – nothing fancy – and is more about colour than flavour.

I'd done some research about saffron for a blog post. There's a window of only a few weeks when the saffron crocuses blossom. They have to be harvested in the morning before they wilt, and the stigma inside the flowers must be removed with tweezers. And for all this effort, it takes 75,000 crocuses to make just one ounce of saffron.

I was weighing out the spice, wondering if all the effort was worth it, when I caught the bowl with my elbow. The yellowy liquid splattered all over my dress. I thought about all those farmers working nineteen-hour days to collect the saffron and I burst into tears.

Asha gave me a hug and helped me to clean up. She was always the level-headed one. I was the silly, emotional sister who got too caught up in things. She used to call me Saffy when she thought I was being a drama queen.

I feel like I'm always being a drama queen these days. Losing a sister will do that to you.

I shake myself, blink back tears, check my phone. Despite everything, my lips curl into a smile when I read Eve's last message:

Night. Sweet dreams xxx

I type a quick note:

Mum's invited this boy over. Ness's nephew. She's totally sprung this on me. Didn't even ask. Can you believe her? ☹

I put my phone on the counter and start to clear up, listening for a response. Sometimes Eve comes back to me instantly; other times it's a couple of hours. She's always here for me, though. Has been since—

The doorbell makes me jump. I tell myself to breathe. It's OK. Just Ness. I brush a spattering of flour off my top, push some stray hairs from my face.

'Myla, that'll be Jamie,' Mum calls as she comes down the stairs.

I don't reply so she knows I'm still mad.

Mum opens the door and the noise of the street floods in: a car roaring past, a dog barking, someone tinging a bike bell. I gasp and shrink into the furthest corner of the kitchen.

I'm fixing Mum with my best glare as she leads the others into the kitchen, then she suddenly steps to the side as she introduces Jamie. He's standing behind her so he gets the full brunt of my glare. Jamie's eyes widen and he takes a hesitant step back, bumping into Ness.

Damn! I didn't mean for that to happen. I try to catch his eye, to smile, but he's looking away. I take a quick moment

17

to size him up. He's tall and pale, with red hair and freckles. Nice eyes. Really thin, though he's trying to hide it beneath a T-shirt that totally swamps him.

'Myla,' Ness says, beaming. 'This is Jamie.' She thumps two hands on his shoulders and practically propels him into the room. I stiffen. He's the first stranger to come in the house for ages.

Mum gives me a pointed look. I do a stupid half-wave thing in Jamie's direction.

'All right,' he grunts.

I hate it when boys do that. What's the appropriate response? Yes, I'm fine, thank you. How are you?

Mum's pointing at my forehead and mouthing something. 'What?'

Ness chuckles. 'You've got chocolate on your face, Myla.'

Oh. Great first impression.

'I know you two are going to get on wonderfully,' says Ness, grinning as if she's imagining our dark-skinned ginger-haired babies.

Jamie blushes and shuffles a few steps away from her, focusing on his shoelaces.

'Come on in, Jamie,' Mum says. 'Myla has been baking.'

My cookies! I spin around and rush to the oven. They were supposed to be chewy on the edges and gooey in the middle. Now they're going to be dry and hard and horrible. I take the tray out and slam it on the hob, swearing as the heat passes through a wet patch on the tea-towel.

Mum tuts. 'Myla!'

'What? I almost burned myself!'

'Myla's a great cook, Jamie. Would you like to try one?'

Jamie's eyeing the cookies as if he's afraid of them. He doesn't answer.

Mum smiles. 'Well, there'll be plenty more. Myla bakes three or four times a week.'

Ness shakes her head. 'It's a wonder you stay so slim, Myla.'

'Good genes,' Mum replies, unable to resist a smug smile.

Ness looks enviously at Mum's petite frame.

'Myla's got her own blog, Jamie. I'll give you the address. Over five hundred followers now.'

Silence.

Mum and Ness share a look. Ness nudges Jamie, who glances up and mumbles, 'Thanks.'

Ness is trying to hide a grin. Her eyes dart from me to Jamie like we're the cutest thing she's ever seen.

She might be a busybody, but I like Ness. I like how her hair is this straggly sort of bush that looks like it's never been combed. I like how she doesn't bother with make-up, how she always has clay under her fingernails, or streaks of paint on her arms, and I like how easily she smiles, how much her blue eyes twinkle.

'So, how are you settling in?' Mum asks Jamie. 'Did Ness actually clear some space for you, or are you sleeping on a pile of newspapers she's kept from 1979?'

Ness starts to protest, saving Jamie from answering.

My phone pings. I seize it, quickly scanning the message from Eve. I frown. Not what I was expecting. I thought she'd sympathise, but all she said was:

What's he like?

I start typing a string of adjectives. I get to 'weird' when Mum hisses, 'Myla!'

I stop, hit send, and put the phone down.

'Take Jamie into the living room,' she says in a low voice.

'I'd best get going,' Ness says. 'I've got my still-life class. Jamie, don't forget the bread.'

Jamie nods, then follows me into the other room while Ness and Mum say goodbye.

I sit on the furthest end of the sofa, pulling my knees to my chin and wrapping my arms around them.

Jamie drops down at the other end. He looks tired, wilted. His eyes search the room, looking for something to fix on. Anything, as long as it's not me.

My phone pings. My fingers twitch, desperate to reach for it.

Jamie has grabbed a corner of the multi-coloured throw from the back of the chair and is poking his fingers through holes in the weave. He asks, 'How long have you lived here?'

'All of my life.'

Silence. So that conversation is pretty much a dead-end.

There must be something I can ask him, but the things I tend to wonder about don't exactly count as small-talk. I can obsess for hours over things like – What feels better, dipping your finger into the cream on top of coconut milk or running your hands through a bowl of pistachio shells? Or, would you rather pick sand out from between your toes or peel dry glue off your skin?

Jamie sighs, shifts in the seat. 'Look. Sorry about . . . this. It was just kinda dumped on me.'

I raise an eyebrow. Not exactly flattering, but at least it's something we have in common. 'Me too.'

He manages to meet my eyes and offers a brief smile. I smile back. There is something kind of sweet about his shyness.

My phone goes off a second time. I pick it up, twirl it in my fingers. That's two unread messages from Eve now. God, I wish she was here. It's so awkward.

I switch the phone to silent and put it back on the armrest.

'Popular,' Jamie says lightly.

'Not really.' I sounded cutting, harsh. I didn't mean to.

Jamie has actually picked a hole in the throw now. I ignore the look of horror on his face and ask, 'So which part of London are you from?'

'Near Camden. You know, the markets?'

'Oh yeah, I know. I mean . . . I've heard of them.'

He looks cross with himself, as if he's said something he shouldn't have.

'Nice house,' Jamie offers.

'Er – thanks? Can't really take credit for it. It's not like I bought it or anything!'

When he glances at me to offer a quick smile, I notice how much the shadows under Jamie's eyes stand out against his pale skin. I wonder why he's so tired.

I hold out my arm, studying my own skin. It's got lighter these last few years – less of a rich brown. I'm lucky to have inherited more of Mum's colouring than Dad's, but I don't want to lose it. On nice days, when light streams in through the windows, I stand there, eyes closed, face tilted, looking at the rosy glow through my eyelids.

I search for something else to say. 'So, you're in Year 10, right? Which GCSEs are you doing?'

Jamie tells me, though I'm struggling to concentrate. My phone keeps lighting up. I flip it upside down, turn away from it so I can focus on him.

Jamie clears his throat. 'So, how does it work – with your GCSEs, I mean?'

'I have a tutor during term-time, then ... ' My eyes have strayed back to the phone. Even though it's upside down, I can see the light beneath it. I know that Jamie's waiting for me to finish, but I'm wondering what Eve's saying. How many messages has she sent?

'Are you always this attached to your phone?'

Jamie's voice is sharp. When I turn round, he looks away, like he's embarrassed about being annoyed.

It's me that blushes this time. 'Sorry. I'm really sorry. What was I . . . ? Oh yeah, I'll sit the exams with an invigilator, right here in my living room. Weird, huh?'

'Yeah.'

Jamie opens his mouth to say something else, but he stops

This is torture!

What else can we talk about? Books? Something tells me he won't be into my kind of books. Films? I'm always so behind because I have to wait for everything to come out on DVD.

'So, are you into music?' I ask.

For a brief moment, Jamie's eyes light up. 'Yeah. Metal, mostly. Some rock.'

'Oh.' I give him an apologetic smile. 'I'm into pop.'

'I like that new Chelsea Logan one.'

I laugh. 'You do not!'

'I do,' he insists. 'It's better than some of the other crap out there. Have you heard the new M-pathik one?'

'No.'

He shakes his head. 'Shocking.'

Neither of us says anything.

'What TV shows are you into?' Jamie tries.

'I watch a lot of documentaries,' I admit. 'And cooking shows. How about you?'

'The usual. *Simpsons, Futurama.*'

'I used to watch those, a couple of years ago.'

Oh my God. That came out wrong. I might as well have called him a baby.

Another silence lands with the weight of a sledgehammer.

Jamie makes one last, desperate attempt. 'How 'bout computer games? You into them?'

I shake my head hopelessly. 'Want to watch TV?' I ask, already reaching for the remote.

An hour later, I catch the sound of Dad's key in the lock. I hold my breath.

Mum rushes in from the kitchen and plonks herself on the armchair next to us. I give her a weird look, but she just smiles. I get it. Dad's fine with Jamie's visit, but only if we're supervised. For goodness' sake!

'Hello, hello,' Dad says in his gentle Irish lilt. As he comes into the room, he musters a weary smile. Dad moves around the back of the sofa, planting a kiss on the top of my head, then kisses Mum on the cheek and perches on the armrest next to her, his stomach straining a little against his shirt.

Dad runs his hand through his sandy hair, which is greying at the temples. 'You must be Jamie,' he says, nodding curtly.

'Nice to meet you,' Jamie mumbles.

If he seemed uncomfortable before, Jamie looks like he wants to dive under the throw and hide now.

Dad gives him a firm, appraising look. 'So how are you finding life in sleepy Norfolk? Must be a shock to the system.'

Jamie shrugs. 'It's all right.'

Nobody says anything. Another dead-end.

Mum smiles at Dad and rests her hand on his arm. 'Good day?'

He starts to complain about all the meetings he had, but then he stops and breathes deeply. 'Is that cookies I smell?'

My face breaks into a smile and I nod.

'What kind?'

'Chocolate chip. They're a bit overdone.'

Dad gets up. 'Well, I'm starving. I'd better get changed for dinner.'

Jamie stands too, taking his cue to leave.

'Good to meet you, Jamie,' Dad says, shaking his hand without a smile. 'Why don't you take a cookie?'

Jamie looks away. 'I'm OK, thanks.'

Dad unclasps his hand and frowns. 'Don't let Myla put you off. She's just a perfectionist.'

'He doesn't have to take one if he doesn't want to,' Mum says quickly.

But why doesn't he want one?

'It's OK,' Jamie says, eyeing Dad. 'I'll take one. Thanks.'

Mum wraps one in a piece of kitchen towel and presses it into Jamie's hand, giving him an apologetic smile. She tries to chat for a bit, unfazed by his muted responses, but Dad's silence makes it clear that it's time for Jamie to go.

As soon as the door shuts, I let out a massive sigh. Mum glares, but I'm not getting into another argument. I want to check my phone. I grab it off the sofa and flick through the messages.

So you don't like him?

What's going on? Are you all right?

Myla, talk to me!

Wow. Why is she being so arsey? She's usually never short with me. Unless . . . wait! She's jealous!

For some reason, a tingly shiver flies up my spine.

I run upstairs. I'll switch my laptop on, write Eve a proper reply, tell her how awful the whole thing was. But once I'm in my room, I find myself at the window, watching Jamie slouch off down the street. He seems weak, like he's dragging something heavy behind him. A few paces after passing a bin, he pauses, turns, and chucks my cookie away.

Bastard! It wasn't my best, but it really wasn't that bad. I swipe the curtains closed and flop down on my bed, arms firmly crossed. That's it, then. I don't care what Mum or Ness says. That's definitely the last time he's setting foot in this house.

4

Jamie

I'm not going back. No way. What was her problem? Could tell she didn't want me there. Staring at her phone like that. If I'd been stuck in the house for two years, I'd be well pleased to have someone to talk to.

Still, she must be pretty messed up. I try to imagine what it would feel like if it was someone close to me, if it was Kai. Jesus.

Should've called him before I came here, but stuff's been off between us for a while. He hasn't said anything, but I know he's pissed that I haven't been round much. He thinks I've got some beef with Nana Bo. Her and Kai are really tight. When he was a kid, his parents weren't around a lot so she pretty much raised him. Now he lives with her.

It's not right, what he thinks. I love Nana Bo. Hanging with her, it's cool. Like I've got a gran again. But the thing is, she's a feeder. The second I'm through the door, she's trying to ram stuff down my throat, going on about how skinny I am. I just can't deal.

I feel bad. Wanna tell him, but every time I try, I end up bottling it.

It's a bit odd, Stratten. All grannies and gift shops. It's a small place – just one main street with weird old-fashioned shops like a butcher and a greengrocer. It's dead quiet, too. No one shouts, beeps their horns, drives around with the windows down blasting out music.

As I walk, I keep an eye out for Ness's pottery. She sells it in a couple of local galleries. The night I arrived, she showed me her workshop. It was a bit of a state, like the rest of her house. Sacks of clay lying about, empty yoghurt pots, some of those wooden forks you get in chippies. There were these old, buckled shelves with all her work on. She makes crooked cottages on cliffs and little fishing boats. She'd even used a piece of driftwood as a base for one of her things.

When I'm looking in one of the windows, I notice someone else behind me. He's got his hood up so I can't see his face, but there's the glow of a fag and a haze of smoke around him.

I move on, watching him in the reflection. This guy, he walks with a hard-man swagger that just spells trouble. He's tall, lean, but he's definitely got some muscles on him. I don't like how close he is.

I try to speed up, but my legs are already aching and I'm feeling rough.

I stop outside the bakery, trying to remember what Ness wanted. In my pocket, I run my fingers over the four coins she gave me. A bit extra so I could 'treat myself'. As if!

I take a deep breath and hold it before going in. It's an old place, with uneven floors, a low ceiling and windows fogged with condensation. Out the back are a couple of small tables where two women are nattering over a pot of tea. The blonde behind the counter has her back to me, reading a magazine or something. I keep my eyes up, refusing to look at the cakes in the glass cabinet. My stomach grumbles, but I feel sick.

I wait, not sure what I'm s'posed to do. Eventually, the blonde flings a bored look over her shoulder, clocks me, and turns slowly. She's chewing gum. Pretty, but a bit too much make-up. 'What can I get you?' she says, looking through me, rather than at me.

I sneak in a shallow breath and the smell of dough and sugar hits the back of my nose.

'Er . . . ' My eyes fly across the loaves on the back wall. Why are there so many? Why can't I just walk in and ask for 'bread', for God's sake?

'Yes?' she asks, finally making eye contact, but only so she can fix me with a look.

Heat swamps my face. Great, now she probably thinks I've got a hard-on for her.

'I'm s'posed to pick up something for my aunt,' I mumble.

She frowns, shaking her head like I'm an idiot.

A burly bloke with a crop of black curls steps behind the counter. 'You must be Ness's nephew,' he says, smiling.

'Yeah.'

'Ness's usual, Steph. Wholegrain multi-seed round cob.'

Steph nods and packages it up for me.

The man rings it up on an ancient till. 'Anything else?'

I shake my head.

He sticks his chest out and rubs his hands together, grinning at me. 'Well, enjoy your stay with Ness!'

I try to smile as I fumble with the coins, dropping them into one of his massive paws.

I'm already charging towards the door when I hear him say, 'Bye now!'

I almost turn back, but my lungs are tight and I need air. I catapult myself outside, where I heave in a massive breath and lean against the window, gasping.

My stomach rumbles again. Yeah! That's willpower. That's control. Walking into a bakery when you're starving, light-headed, and not touching a damn thing. What a rush!

I'm feeling epic, and I wanna tell someone. I pull out my phone to text Kai. Then I pause, sigh. He won't understand. But I wanna say something, remind him I'm still his mate, even if I haven't been acting like it much recently. So I say:

How's it going? It's weird in Norfolk. They all know each other.

He comes back straight away with:

Man, that's cos they're all related!

I snigger, then type:

I'll call sometime. It's boring here.

I put my phone back in my pocket. Then I push myself away from the window and start off down the high street. I pause outside a flower shop. Should I use what's left of Ness's change to buy her some flowers or something? I dunno. I'd probably just embarrass myself or pick the wrong thing or get something she's allergic to.

The door swings open as someone comes out and I catch a figure in the reflection. No way! That man again. He's stopped just behind me and is pretending to look at the flowers. He's blatantly following me. What does he want?

A braver guy than me would whip round, square up to him, ask him what he thinks he's doing. Me? I panic and walk away as quickly as I can.

I'm listening out for him now, can hear the way his footsteps pound the pavement like he's angry with it. Jesus! He must be a psycho! Where do I go? What do I do? I'll look like an idiot if I dive into a shop and start wailing about some stranger following me. I've got my phone, but who can I call? Not the police – he hasn't done anything! And Ness already thinks I'm a headcase.

I make a sudden turn into a side street. Of all the stupid things to do! We're even more alone now. But he has turned with me, so he's definitely following me. I'm sweating, my legs weak. I kinda want to turn round, get another look at him, but I can't. It's like my neck is locked.

I dunno where I am now. I know the high street and Ness's road. That's it. Maybe I can turn left, then left again, find my way back. I'll do that, and this bloke will give up, get bored, go home.

I turn left and walk down the longest frigging road I've ever seen, and there's no link back to the high street – only right-hand turns. So I'm lost now. Amazing. I'm wandering around a place I don't know, with a psycho on my tail.

My heart's going way too fast and my chest is stretched tight. I'm slowing down. I can't keep up this pace. The man is catching up, his shadow stretching out ahead of me. I can't make a run for it. I just can't.

This is what *he* said would happen, when I wouldn't start pumping iron with him. Can't even defend myself.

The man slips into step beside me. 'All right, mate?' he says as he pushes his hood back. 'Fancy a ciggie?'

I stop. Stare.

He's a couple of years older than me. He's trying to smile

but his blue eyes are hard. He's so close I can smell his ashy breath.

I gawp at the packet he's holding like it might be a grenade. He raises an eyebrow and shakes the fags. 'No? Sure?'

'I'm good, thanks,' I say, walking on.

He matches my stride. 'Suit yourself. I'm Finn.'

I try not to stammer. 'Why are you following me?'

He shrugs, then spits on the ground. 'You're new, right?'

'Yeah.'

'You want someone to show you around?'

'What? No.'

'Just trying to be friendly. What you been up to?'

I stop, face him, all my muscles tightening. 'What do you want?

Finn takes a step back, palms up in a gesture of peace. 'All right, I'll level with you. Just want to know how Myla is.'

Without thinking, I take a tiny step towards him. 'What the hell? How long have you been following me?'

Finn prods me in the shoulder, pushes me back. 'Calm down, you idiot. It's not like that.'

'Well . . . well, what *is* it like, then?'

He shrugs, glances up the street at a mum singing into a pram as she pushes it.

'Who are you?' I ask. 'Friend of hers?'

Finn snorts. He's rocking on his heels like he's got all this energy coiled up. 'Something like that.'

'Then ask her yourself.'

He fixes those hard, blue eyes on me. It's like he's swinging searchlights in my face. 'Did she mention Ash ...?' Finn swallows. He has a really big Adam's apple. 'Did she mention her sister?'

I shake my head. Why would she?

Finn swears and kicks an empty beer can, which hurtles across the street. The mum looks up and stops singing. A muscle twitches just below Finn's jaw. I flinch as he moves suddenly, grabbing a fistful of my T-shirt. 'You'd better not be lying to me, you scrawny little tosser.'

'I'm not!'

He glares at me, then lets go.

'Why are you asking all these questions? How did you even know I was there?'

'Forget it!' he snarls. 'Just forget it.'

Finn storms off, yanking his hoodie up as he goes. As he gets close to the woman with the pram, her eyes flick to the other side of the road, like she's wondering whether to get out of his way. But he barely glances at her as he stomps past, his shoulders hunched as if he *really* wants to punch something.

Then he stops, turns. 'Don't tell Myla about this. You keep quiet.'

I don't reply, just stare at him.

'I mean it, Jamie,' Finn bellows. 'Keep your mouth shut.'

What? How does he ...

Blood roars in my ears and – for a moment – I think I might

pass out. I sink down against the wall, my pulse going mental. I put my head between my knees and suck in deep breaths.

He knows my name. And if he knows my name, that means he knows where I live.

5

Myla

The baked sand is hot beneath my body. Seagulls screech and arc in a candyfloss-cloud sky. Asha is stretched out next to me like a cat soaking up the last of the setting sun, her black hair haloed above her.

'Tell me a secret,' I say.

Asha doesn't answer. Her eyes are closed, her chest rising and falling slowly.

'You must have one,' I persist.

Asha breathes out a long sigh, as if even the effort of sighing is too much.

A breeze wafts over and I catch traces of Mum's perfume: citrus and green tea. It's weird that Asha smells like Mum. She's never bothered with perfume before.

Asha opens her eyes and looks at me. 'You already know all my secrets, sister dearest,' she says with a wry smile.

I twirl the bangle on her wrist, mesmerised by the blue topaz catching the fading light. 'I know who you were with last night.'

'What?' she snaps. 'What do you mean?'

'Well, I know you weren't with Cassie.'

'How do you know that?'

'Because she was at the bowling alley. She posted a picture. You weren't in it.'

Asha lets her breath out quickly, laughs and lightly slaps my arm. 'Clever, little sister. I'd just gone to the loo. Mind your own business, though.'

The wind whips up, peppering our bare legs with sand. Goose-pimples wind across my skin.

'We should head home,' Asha says, without moving an inch.

'Can't we stay a bit longer? I want to go for a paddle. Dad's probably not even back yet.'

'You'd better hope not.'

I rattle the tube of Smarties that lies in the sand between us. 'Want the last one?'

'Why, thank you, oh generous one. It's not like you haven't already scoffed most of them!'

She opens her mouth and I tip the Smartie in. 'Orange,' I say. 'See, that's how much I love you. Saved the best flavour, just for you.'

Asha shakes her head. 'You're nuts. They all taste the same.' She sticks her orange tongue out at me.

I poke her in the ribs. Asha squirms and bats my hand away, her chocolatey breath whispering over my cheek.

'Can you imagine not hearing the sea?' she asks.

I close my eyes, listen. When we were little we had this CD called the shusher. It was supposed to mimic the sound in the womb or something, but I always thought it sounded just like the sea. Shush-shush-shush. *The sound that had been a part of our lives for as long as we could remember.*

'No,' I reply. 'It's weird to think it never stops. I mean, even while we're asleep, it keeps on going. It never rests.' I consider for a moment. 'Do you think it gets tired? I'm tired just thinking about it.'

'You are silly. Are you going for a paddle or not? We really need to get home.'

'In a minute. I'm comfy here.'

I wriggle further into the sand. I love the way it wraps around my body, moulding to the shape of me. In the hollow of the dune, with sand rising up all around me, and Asha by my side, I feel sheltered, safe.

I open my eyes. That's my last pristine, pure memory of her. I clutch it as tightly as I can, making sure I stamp it in my mind so I'll never forget.

Part of me wishes I could remember more – remember what happened between leaving Asha to go and paddle and waking up cold and alone on the beach.

But part of me wishes I could press pause after those last blissful minutes with my sister – erase the rest and forget that terrifying night on the beach, the dark figure who still stalks my dreams.

I shudder.

Eve. I need to talk to Eve.

I pick up my phone.

Saffy42: Hello? Are you there?

I wait. Eve's here. I'm sure she's here. She's just playing games. I sigh, try to bat down a flicker of irritation. I look through her last few messages. They're all so intense. She's never been like this before.

Saffy42: Eve, are you mad?

Eve51x: I was worried. Why didn't you reply?

Saffy42: Jamie was there! What was I supposed to do?

Eve51x: You were supposed to tell me that you were OK.

Saffy42: My mum was in the next room. I was fine.

No reply. I sigh. This would be so much easier face-to-face. If only Eve could come over. She lives in Cambridge so could be here and back in a day. But the last time I gathered up the nerve to invite her, she made some excuse about having 'family issues'. Maybe she's just more comfortable chatting online. Maybe she's shy in real life.

I maximise her screen picture, scrutinise it for a moment as I try to imagine what her voice might sound like. She's got a cool diagonal fringe sweeping across her forehead, eyes the colour of Asha's topaz bracelet. She's really pretty. I probably look at this picture way too much, but it's the only one I have.

I was so flattered when Eve sent me a friend request eighteen months ago. She said she'd found my blog and absolutely loved it. I accepted her request straight away. Back then, Lauren was the only one still coming to see me. A lot of my other 'friends' had stopped bothering as it became clear that I was stuck in this house for good.

I have a few other online friends, but nobody understands me like Eve does. She was there for me all through the trial, logging in at the end of each day so I could run through every last detail, starting with the moment – that horrifying moment – when I first saw the man I believed had killed my sister.

Saffy42: I thought I was prepared. I've seen his picture in the papers, but facing him in person was . . . I don't even know how to describe it. All I could think about was his hands around Asha's neck.

Eve51x: God, Saffy. You poor thing. I'm here for you. You can tell me anything. What happened next?

Saffy42: I had to give my evidence first, as they told me I couldn't watch the rest of the trial until I'd done it.

Eve51x: What kind of things did they ask you?

Saffy42: I went through every single detail of her abduction, over and over again. It was excruciating, having to relive it all. And everything was so jumbled in my head. I must've sounded crazy.

Eve51x: Give yourself a break, Saffy. Didn't you say you were concussed and hypothermic when they found you?

Saffy42: Yes, but I still felt like I was failing her.

When they asked me if the figure I saw could've been Si Ashworth, I just looked at him, long and hard, trying to make him fit my messed-up memories.

The thing is, everyone was telling me it was him. Mum and Dad were already convinced. They were so sure. It sounds strange – but part of me *wanted* it to be him, to know that someone would pay for what happened to Asha. I found myself saying, 'I think it could have been him.' Several jury members nodded their heads. A couple scribbled something down.

I listened as Si gave his evidence. The first time police had questioned him about his whereabouts at the time of the abduction, he'd lied. Si had been convicted for beating up his ex and was out on parole. He claimed that he'd lied at first because he was breaking his restraining order by hanging around his ex's house, spying on her and her new partner. But no one could confirm it. He swore he had no idea how Asha's phone charm had ended up on his sofa – that he didn't even know her.

'Liar,' Mum murmured on the bench next to me, her eyes burning into him. 'He's a liar.'

She looked at me, willing me to agree, but I couldn't look back. Suddenly I wasn't so sure . . .

And then, when they were grilling him about his history of violence towards women, I heard Si let out a nervous cough. In that moment, I knew, I *knew* it wasn't him. I don't care how muddled I was, how much gibberish I was talking when they found me. I will *never* forget the sound of those breaths as he chased me – the throaty rasps and that horrible, phlegmy cough.

I leapt to my feet. The entire courtroom turned to stare at me. 'It's not him,' I said to no one in particular. The prosecutor took off his glasses, wiped them and put them back on again. The defence lawyer lifted his wig slightly and scratched his head. One of the jurors pretended to be reading his papers, as though he hadn't heard me.

I said it again. 'It's not him. His cough . . . it's not the same.'

I looked at Mum and Dad. Mum was shaking her head, tears streaming down her face. Dad wouldn't meet my eyes.

The judge called for order.

I left. I couldn't stay there and watch them send away an innocent man.

That night, I had a massive row with Dad. 'It's over,' he yelled. 'Done. She's gone and we can't even start to move on until that man is locked up. All the evidence points to him. All of it.' He took a deep breath, continued in a quieter voice. 'It's all right for you to feel confused. You hit your head and were obviously very traumatised.'

'Don't patronise me! I'm telling you, it wasn't him. Please, will you just call the police station, ask them to re-interview me, take another statement? I'll swear to it, Dad, that it wasn't Si Ashworth.'

But he was already shaking his head. 'Myla, I don't believe the police will appreciate a fourteen-year-old telling them how to do their jobs. The trial is almost over and I . . . we need closure.'

'This isn't closure! This is . . . It's just wrong. Everything about it is wrong!' I stamped into my room and slammed the door.

The next day, I called the police station myself, begging them to reopen the case. How could they let my sister's killer go free? How could they live with themselves, knowing there was even a shadow of doubt that they'd arrested the wrong man?

Our family liaison officer listened patiently, but said the same as Dad. He explained that – given the 'inconsistencies' in my statements and the fact that I'd suffered a head injury – re-testifying probably wouldn't make much difference.

Si Ashworth denied it until the day he was sentenced. And I was the only one who believed him. Well, me and Eve. She had faith in me, didn't judge or think I was mad. She stopped me drowning in those few months.

When another message pings up from her, it makes me jump.

Eve51x: So is he coming round again, this Jamie?

I snort.

Saffy42: No! Definitely not.

Eve51x: Good.

I smile uncertainly, think for a minute, then type fast, my fingers hammering the keys.

Saffy42: I can have other friends if I want, Eve.

Eve51x: But I want you all to myself!

Is it wrong that I feel a little thrill at that?
I start to type a reply, but Dad appears at my door,

knocking softly and nudging it open. 'Hello you,' he says. 'What are you up to?'

I close my laptop. 'Nothing. Just chatting.'

Dad pulls a pen from his shirt pocket and hands it to me with a flourish. 'Brought you something from the office.'

I run my finger over the company logo – some kind of satellite surrounded by stars – and raise an eyebrow. 'Is this part of your promotion? A free pen?'

He gives me a rueful smile, as if he knows that a free pen doesn't make up for the fact that he's hardly ever around any more. 'It's the first step. Once I've been in the job for ten years I get a free trip to Space!'

I laugh.

'Jamie seemed – nice,' he says. 'Bit quiet.'

'You could've gone easier on him!'

Dad's mouth drops. 'What do you mean?'

'Come on! Don't pretend you weren't doing the whole "stern dad" thing.'

He smiles, but it's gone in a second.

Mum comes up behind him – she always seems to glide through the house without making a sound – and wraps a hand around his waist. 'Dinner's ready, you two.' Then she frowns and tugs on Dad's tie. 'Why aren't you changed yet?'

Dad sighs and waves his mobile at her. 'Sorry. Got distracted.'

Dad's skin seems even more sallow next to Mum's rich, dark tone. To me, they look like they completely belong together, but Mum said her Mauritian family had a tough time dealing with her being in a mixed-race relationship.

Dad was on holiday when they met. He was only planning on staying on the island for two weeks, but ended up extending it to a month. They wrote to each other for a while after Dad came home, then Mum used her nurse's qualification to get a job over here.

'I wish they hadn't given you that BlackBerry,' Mum mutters.

'Well, it comes with the job now.'

Mum gives him a sad smile. She's missed him since he started the new job.

'Don't be long,' Mum says, before leaving.

'Have you started your summer reading yet?' Dad asks. He's not even looking at me. He's thinking about work – I can see all the stress etched across his face.

'No, but I did get a tattoo of a rhino on my bum, downed an entire bottle of Goldschläger, then photographed a squirrel dancing the can-can.'

Dad gives a little shake of his head. 'Sorry, what was that? Did you say you'd made a start?'

'Not yet.'

Dad's brows furrow. 'Hmmm. Then I'm not sure you should be chatting to your friends.'

'OK, fine,' I say, picking a book off my bedside table and staring at it until he leaves.

I flop back onto my bed with a groan. What is it with

everyone today? Who are they to say what's best for me, what I need? Do they not think I hate being trapped in this house while all my old friends are out there, having fun? I've unfriended all of them, except Lauren. I know it's selfish and bitter, but I can't bear to see them all doing things that I can only imagine now – picnics on the beach, the prom ... even school trips.

I pick up my phone to finish replying to Eve. Ooh! A new comment on my blog. I open it quickly, hoping it will be someone else telling me how incredible my devil's food cake is.

But my throat closes and a wave of heat roars across my body. It's not a comment on my food blog. It's on my other site – the one that's still under construction. I haven't even posted on it yet. The ID is 'Anonymous' and it says:

You're right about Si Ashworth. We need to talk: freesi@wemail.com.

6

Jamie

I'm stretched out on my bed, staring at the ceiling. There's a crack winding through the plaster like a river, and a damp patch in the corner that looks like an old leak.

If I was at home, I'd be on the South Bank, feeling the breeze from the Thames at the back of my neck. Might stop to watch a couple of break-dancers or a rubbish Michael Jackson impersonator. Or sometimes I look at the boarders in the skate park, wishing I had their stamina, their speed. London is always buzzing; there's always something to do. Best night out here is Ness's bingo.

My phone vibrates on the bedside table. Mum. I just stare at it. Can't deal with her going on about *him*, being so obvious about how they're loving having the place to themselves.

My stomach groans. I'm not giving in, though. It doesn't

own me. I need to distract it. I make myself get up and pace around a bit. I need exercise. I want it. I just don't have the strength.

Ness tried to get me to walk Ian the other day. We managed about fifteen minutes before I gave up and turned around. Ian wasn't impressed. Didn't matter how much I yelled at him, he dragged his arse along the pavement the whole way back.

I walk the six paces from the door to the window, then back again. It's not bad, my room. It's big. Would be even bigger if Ness hadn't piled stuff around the edges. There's this massive stack of old books – like Ness can't walk past a charity shop without buying another tatty romance. There's a mound of clothes shoved in a corner. They won't fit in the wardrobe, Ness says. She's already taken up the wardrobes in her room and mine, and there's stuff stashed under the bed too.

At least there's a TV, even if it is a crappy old one. Ness was well pleased when I said I could play my games on it. Said she knew there was a reason she kept it. She could probably come up with loads of reasons why she keeps all this junk.

Ness doesn't seem to notice it, though. When she showed me the room, she was more bothered about the colour of the walls than all the clutter. 'I know dusky pink won't be your thing, Jamie. You can thank the last people who lived here. I've always meant to change it, but, well, you know how things are. Oh, and look at that clock! It's an hour out. I meant to put it forward in March. Remind me to change it, won't you?'

I shrugged. I was so knackered even the flowery bedspread didn't put me off – I just wanted to collapse. Next thing I knew, Ness had plonked herself at the foot of the bed. She reached out to touch my arm. 'I'm always here, if you ever fancy a chat.'

I nodded. 'Er – thanks, but I'm fine.'

Ness gave me a look. 'I think we both know you're not. You have to be honest with yourself, Jamie. You have to—'

'Have you got that spare key?'

Ness's face dropped.

I felt like a bastard, but I'd literally just stepped through the door!

'I'll leave it on the table,' she said flatly.

It's been weird, these last few days. Trying to get used to each other. Most mornings, Ness wakes me up banging and crashing around the kitchen, or singing when she gets out the shower.

The house phone rings. I wait for Ness to answer it. Please don't let that be . . .

'Jamie,' Ness calls.

'Um – hang on.' It comes out as more of a mumble than a shout. Don't think Ness hears because she starts to thump up the stairs. Then she shoves the door open without knocking. I sigh. She doesn't think much of privacy, either.

'Your mum's on the phone.'

'Can you tell her I'm out?'

'I'm not lying, Jamie. Come on, now. Chop, chop!'

I don't move, don't look at her. I just sit there.

Ness comes in. 'I think she'd love to hear your voice.'

'Well, she should've thought about that before she sent me away.'

'That's not what . . . ' For the first time since I got here, Ness looks pissed off. 'Fine. Suit yourself. I'll talk to her.'

I listen to her move down the stairs, then I creep out onto the landing. ' . . . Sorry, Angela, I don't know what to do with him . . . Well, no, he won't talk to me. I've tried, believe me . . . Yes, I'll ask him to answer his phone next time . . . You OK? You sound . . . All right. You sure? . . . Look, I've got to go, love. Got bingo tonight and the girls will be waiting . . . Yes, OK then. Bye.'

Ness puts the phone down, lets out a massive sigh.

I get it. She's been lumped with this nephew she hardly knows, and now she's having to deal with stuff between me and Mum.

I traipse down the stairs, wondering what to say. But Ness doesn't give me a chance. 'Jamie, we have to talk. I'm trying my best with you, but . . . '

I can't believe it! She's kicking me out. First my own mum, now my aunt.

'Look, you can't just lollop around the house for the rest of the summer. You'll have to find something to do.'

Oh. OK.

'I feel awful for letting Jav down about Myla.'

'What do you want me to do? We didn't get on.'

51

'Give her a chance, Jamie. She needs help. And – whether you're willing to admit it or not – you do too. I think you could be so good for each other, and I don't see what else you've got on that's any more important.'

'Why can't you just leave me alone?'

Ness throws her hands up. 'I'm trying to help you! Isn't that why you came?'

No. This wasn't my choice.

Ness whips her keys off the table and grabs her coat, almost pulling the coat rack down with it. 'I'm late. Let's finish this later.'

After she's gone, I turn on my games console and find the bloodiest game I can. I splatter policemen's brains out, rob a post office, a bank and a supermarket, then joyride in a stolen car. In the game, I can do whatever the hell I want. In the game, I'm in control, and I love it.

Half an hour later, I'm bored of the game. I flop back on my bed. Can't just lie here. If I do, I'll start thinking. I'll start thinking about *him*, about what I've got to go back to at the end of the summer – all the sneaky shitty ways he's gonna put me down.

Every sneering comment, every humiliation, every cruel nickname, they all burrow into my skin like leeches. They keep digging, deeper and deeper until they're all the way inside, gorging on my low self-esteem, sucking up every negative thought, devouring every drop of sadness. And those leeches, those greedy bastards, are still in there, fat and swollen and toxic. I want them out, but it's like they're part of me now and there's nothing I can do about it.

I look at the sandwich that Ness has left outside my door, the bread hardening on top, the cheese starting to sweat. That ... *that* I can do something about.

I wasn't s'posed to be thinking about this.

I pick up my phone and call Kai.

'Jay! How's it going?'

'You know, not bad.'

'So what's it like there?'

'All right. Weird. I dunno. What's happening at home?'

'Not much. Some kid got arrested for knifing that hobo who hangs around the park.'

'Jesus.'

'Me and Isma split again.'

I open my mouth, about to say how much that blows.

'Then we got back together.'

'Moron!' I laugh. 'How many times have you guys broken up? Make up your damn minds.'

He laughs back, then there's a pause. 'You really in Norfolk or are you in some rehab joint where they're force-feeding you cakes? You gonna be two stone heavier next time I see you?'

I cough, try to laugh, but don't answer.

Kai lets the silence ride out for a bit, then he says, 'Jay, dude, you are getting better, right? 'Cos last time I saw you, you looked bad.'

'Yeah, sure.'

'You're eating, right?'

'What are you, my mum?' I snap.

Kai sighs. 'Saw your mum down the shop yesterday, with that guy she's seeing. Damn he's big!'

I mutter, 'Tell me about it. Did you talk to them? He give you any grief?'

'No. Seems all right. Why would he give me grief?'

I snort. 'Nothing. Forget it. Everyone thinks he's "all right".'

'You've been weird ever since he moved in. What's the deal?'

'There's no deal. Leave it, right?'

'OK. Calm down. It's all good, man.'

'It's not all good! I'm sick of being fucking interrogated all the time. My aunt is shoving questions down my throat every time I leave my room. When are you all gonna listen? I don't wanna talk!'

I hang up before he can reply, slamming my phone on the bed. It just sinks into the mattress. That annoys the hell outta me. I fling it across the room. It hits the wardrobe mirror and – Christ, no! – cracks it. Dumb – really dumb. Another reason for Ness to hate me.

I need to get out. Go for a walk or something. Ness has been on at me to try walking Ian again. Guess I could. It won't make up for the broken mirror, but it's something.

In the kitchen, there's a load of old dishes in the sink. I run the tap and leave them to soak. On Ness's table is an open pot of oil paint. I find the lid buried under some bills and replace it. Then I pick a piece of driftwood off the table and stash it in Ness's studio.

The dog comes running the second I pick up his lead. His paws skid on the floor and his tail's going like a nutter. I almost grin. At least someone wants me around. I pick up Alonzo and make him squeak, which just works Ian up even more.

The home phone starts to ring when I'm a foot away from the door. It's Mum. Gotta be. She knew Ness was going out, that I'd be here alone. I listen to it ring. Man, she must be getting frustrated.

I didn't know Ness had an answer machine until it kicks in and I hear her asking the caller to leave a message.

Someone lets out a shaky sigh. It's not Mum. 'Ness, are you there?' Myla. 'Ness, please pick up if you're there.' Her voice sounds all high-pitched, like she's about to cry or something.

I don't even think about it. I pick up the phone and say, 'Myla?'

She gasps. 'Who's this?'

'Jamie.'

A pause. A long pause. Her breath is hitching. Myla repeats my name slowly, in a whisper. 'I'm – I'm sorry to call. Is Ness there, please? It's really important.'

'Er, no. She's out.'

It's easier to talk to her on the phone. I'm not even blushing.

'Oh.'

She starts to say, 'Never mind,' at the same time I say, 'What's up?'

'It's ... it's nothing,' she says firmly, like she's trying to convince herself. 'I'm sorry. I really shouldn't have called. I'm just being stupid, that's all.'

'About what?'

Myla lets out a breathy laugh. 'I'm ... never mind. God, this is really embarrassing. I hadn't even thought that you'd pick up the phone.'

I wait. She'll tell me what's up. I just have to wait. And it's weird, because I do wanna know.

It all comes out in a rush. 'It's just that I'm alone and I thought I saw someone watching the house but now that I'm saying it out loud I realise how paranoid it must sound and that you probably already think I'm nuts and that—'

'I'm going out anyway. Want me to come over?'

Should I have said that? Probably not. She's not gonna want some strange guy in her house, especially if her parents aren't around. What if she thinks I'm hitting on her?

'Would you mind?'

Would I mind? I never get to be *that* guy.

'No. I was just gonna walk Ian.' I glance back at him. He's pawing at the door. 'Can I bring him?'

'Like a guard dog?'

My shoulders drop when I hear the smile in her voice. Didn't realise I was so tense. 'Sure. I mean, he wouldn't be much use. Could probably lick someone to death, but . . .'

Crap, I mentioned death. Stupid! Quick, say something else, backtrack or something!

'I could do with a cuddle.'

OK . . .

'I mean, from Ian,' she says quickly.

I laugh. 'So I'll see you in a bit.'

'Yeah, OK. Thanks, Jamie.'

I hang up. 'Come on, boy,' I say. As soon as the door opens, Ian shoots out, and I follow.

I feel better now. It's good to be outside. Good to have something to do. The whole coming-to-the-rescue thing is cool. *He's* always saying I need to man up.

That wasn't as awkward as before. Maybe we can find some way to get along, me and Myla. As I struggle against Ian's lead, I even start to hum.

The street is quiet, dark. I hear footsteps behind me, catch the smell of cigarette smoke.

Ian looks like he wants to take off. I help him out by walking a bit faster.

The footsteps behind me speed up too.

7

Myla

Can't breathe. Can't breathe, can't breathe, can't breathe.

He's here. I should've done more, tried harder, but I let my sister's killer go free. And now he's come for me. I pace back and forth, back and forth in front of the window, with the curtains tightly closed.

He's here. Outside my house. Oh, God.

Is he? Did I really see someone? Dad thinks it's all in my head. What if he's right and I'm losing it?

Now I've dragged Jamie in, too.

I sit on the sofa, take a couple of deep breaths, a sip of tea. I'll just wait. I'll just wait for Jamie and it'll be fine.

I've already tried to call Mum a couple of times, but the film must've started as her phone is off. I felt so guilty as I dialled her number. Her and Dad haven't had a night out for seven months. The last time they did, I freaked out when I couldn't get hold of them. I ended up calling the police, who clearly thought I was a lunatic when I wouldn't open the door. They had to call my mobile so we could talk.

I watched them from my bedroom window. They hardly bothered to check the street, despite the fact I told them exactly where the figure had been standing – just opposite, beneath a lamp-post. They did point out that it wasn't a crime to stand under a lamp-post.

I didn't make it up, though. I'm *sure* I saw someone, just like I did tonight. At least, I think I'm sure ... When everyone's telling you you're crazy, you start to believe them. And the thing about being crazy is, you're not aware of it. You're the only one who's not aware of it. What must it feel like, to believe that you're the only sane one and that everyone else is mad? Very lonely, I suppose.

I know exactly what lonely feels like.

Sometimes I follow Mum around the house, chatting about random stuff. And sometimes I can't stand being in the same room as her. I hate that she's all I've got.

Eve is always there for me on days like that. She listens, sympathises. She's always been there when I needed her. She never thought I'd lost it when I told her about Si being innocent. She talked to me for hours, sometimes until three in the morning, telling me I had to be kinder to myself, trust my instincts, try not to let Dad get to me.

The day after I'd made the scene in the courtroom, Mum

tried to get me to stay at home, but I was determined to see the trial through to the end.

We were running late. Dad was in the car, engine on, and Mum was scrabbling around for her shoes. When she flew down the front steps, I caught a glimpse of Dad drumming his fingers on the wheel, glancing at the seconds ticking by on his watch.

I placed a foot on the top step outside the door. A man was walking down the opposite side of the street. I didn't recognise him, which was odd. In the summer, Stratten becomes swollen with tourists and there are strangers everywhere, but not in the winter. Who was he? Why was he walking down our street? Could he have been . . .

Suddenly everything inside me crunched up very small and very hard. My throat clamped shut. I didn't know what was happening. I backed away from the step and collapsed in the hallway, staring in horror at my hands, which were tingling with pins and needles. They didn't feel like my hands. It was like I wasn't really there.

Mum called the doctor, who came straight out. After some poking and prodding, and what felt like several hundred questions, she told us it was a panic attack, that it was perfectly understandable, given the circumstances, and that it was hopefully a one-off.

It wasn't. The next time Mum tried to convince me to go out, I ended up in the same position, cowering on the hallway floor. I thought I was going to die. I just couldn't get enough air.

We tried once more, but when it happened again, I think we all knew that enough was enough.

Dad arranged for a counsellor to come to the house. He was old, posh, and clearly thought a lot of himself. He made snide comments about the place smelling of curry and not being able to understand Mum's accent, so we didn't ask him back.

Then there was the hypnotherapist. He definitely succeeded in putting me under. I don't remember anything that he did to me, but whatever it was, it didn't work.

Every time Dad looked at me, all I saw was disappointment. Disappointment that I'd abandoned Asha; that I couldn't remember enough to give a clear statement; that I didn't trust the police to do their jobs; that everyone was talking about the freak who wouldn't leave her own home.

Jamie's going to think I'm a freak now, too. I wish he'd hurry up. I imagine someone prowling through our garden, stalking up to the back door. I gasp and rush through the house to check it's locked. I should turn the TV on, make it seem like there are people around. But then I won't be able to hear if he tries to break in.

Something creaks upstairs. What was that?

I've got to go up, check it out. It's probably nothing. I'm being stupid. Probably nothing. I mouth those words under my breath, again and again, as I creep up the stairs, heart racing, throat squeezing shut. I have to stop, take a moment to fight the panic down.

I tiptoe across the landing like *I'm* the one who's the intruder. I peek around Mum and Dad's bedroom door. Oh my God, what's that? It's OK. Just Mum's dressing gown. Next, the bathroom. I swipe the shower curtain back really fast. It's clear.

I stop outside Asha's room. The door's closed. None of us go in there any more. I steel myself, take a breath, fling the door open and snap on the light as quickly as I can. Nothing. It's so bare, cold. Oh, Asha.

Now my room. I'd left the light on and the door open, but there are still places where someone could hide. I check the usual spots: under the bed, behind the door, in the cupboard. OK. There's no one here. That creak was just the house settling, cooling down for the night.

Then I freeze. My curtains are open. If he's still out there, watching, he's got a perfect view of me. I duck down, crawl on all fours to the base of the window, and pull the curtains closed from the bottom.

Then the doorbell rings. I scream. Jamie. It's just Jamie. At least, I hope it is. Don't be stupid, Myla. A creepy stalker wouldn't ring the bell.

I hadn't thought this far ahead. What am I going to do now? I can't answer the door. Argh, why is this so hard?

I'm still crouched below the window. If I can open it, maybe I can call down. How weird is that going to look? A disembodied voice floating out of the window.

The doorbell rings again, then there's a soft knock. He's going to give up and leave in a minute. Please don't go, Jamie!

Then I realise what I need to do.

I fly downstairs, stopping just behind the door. 'Jamie?' I call out.

'Er, yeah. You all right?'

'Yes. Look, I'm really sorry. I can't ...' God, this is awful! '... I can't open the door. If I unlock it, will you wait a few seconds, then let yourself in?'

'Sure.'

I pull the chain back, turn the key, then rush into the living room. I hear the front door open and close, then the skitter of Ian's paws against the wooden flooring.

Ian noses open the living-room door and trots straight towards me, tail wagging. Jamie follows. Thank you. Thank God! I let all my breath out at once.

'You all right?' Jamie asks again.

'Yeah, thanks.' My heart's fluttering like there's a trapped moth in there. I reach down to pat Ian.

'Sure?'

I try to smile, but somehow it turns into tears. I bury my face in Ian's hair. 'Sorry,' I mumble.

'S'OK.'

I sniff and lift my head, try a proper smile this time.

'So,' Jamie says. 'Where do you think this person was?'

Think. So Jamie doesn't believe me either. But I did tell him I was being paranoid. 'He was on the other side of the road, under the lamp-post.'

Jamie moves towards the window. 'There wasn't anyone

there when I walked past.' When he suddenly pulls back the curtains, I gasp, shrink away.

'No one there.'

Jamie turns back and notices my laptop on the sofa. I inhale sharply. I was working on my 'Free Si' site earlier. I don't really want to get into that with Jamie right now.

He clears his throat and says, 'You want me to check the rest of the house?'

He's enjoying playing the tough guy. I could say that I've already done it, but he seems to want to. 'Yes. If you don't mind.'

Jamie leaves and I reach for my laptop. That comment is still there – the one about me being right about Si's innocence. I should delete it. It'll just be a journalist, fishing for a story, though it's a bit odd that they'd get in touch now, after two years.

What if it isn't, though? What if it's someone who knows something? Someone who can help me find the truth? No. It could be anyone. I'm going to ignore it. Just focus on my first post, making it as convincing as possible, laying down all the reasons why I believe Si is innocent.

I hear Jamie moving about upstairs and I call up to him, 'You want a drink?'

'Just water, please.'

'Really? I hate water. We've got squash, fizzy drinks, tea.'

'Just water, thanks.'

By the time he comes back, I've shut the laptop down

and am curled up at one end of the sofa, a mug nestled in one hand, the other stroking Ian's soft ears. 'Listen, thanks for coming. I feel a bit embarrassed for dragging you out for nothing.'

'S'all right. We were on our way out anyway.'

'How's it going with Ness? What's it been, a week now?'

Jamie leans back, runs his fingers through the fuzz on the top of his head. 'Yeah. It's different, I guess. Ness isn't used to having someone else in the house. She wanders around in her pyjamas without a bra on, stuff like that.' He smiles when he sees the face I'm pulling. 'And she never locks the toilet door. I've walked in on her a couple of times.'

I laugh. 'That's hilarious!'

I think that's the most I've ever heard Jamie say in one go. He must realise it, too, as he quickly looks down at his fingers, picking on a hangnail.

'Ness has always been really . . . open,' I say. 'She cornered me at a party once and spent ten minutes telling me about her urine infection.'

Jamie grimaces and says, 'Gross,' under his breath.

'She's a good person, though,' I add.

Jamie looks guilty. 'Yeah, she is. I just keep . . . messing up, you know?'

I nod. I do know. Sometimes I'm so angry about everything that's happened. I feel like the house is stifling me, and all I want to do is walk right out the front door, escape. When I get like that, there's no one to lash out at, except Mum. I know it's horrible of me, that she's suffering just as much as I am – more, probably – but I can't stop. Then I loathe myself for being so horrible to her, and I wonder what kind of person I've become.

'Ness is really happy you're here,' I tell Jamie. 'She was so excited before you came. Picking out paint colours for the spare room and all that.'

Jamie smiles slightly. 'She must've run out of time 'cos it's pink. Even got this flowery border.'

I almost spit out my tea. 'She's so scatty. I don't know anyone like her. I mean, not that I know many people.'

Ergh. Now he thinks I'm a tragic case – complete loner. Great!

'My friend Lauren still comes round. Not so much recently – she's been really busy. The others I sort of lost touch with. But I chat to people online.'

'Yeah? I do that sometimes. When I'm gaming. You start seeing the same names, get to know people.'

I smile. 'It's fun, isn't it?'

There's a silence. It's mildly awkward, but nothing on the scale of our first meeting.

'So is that who was messaging you, when I came round before? An online friend?'

For some reason, I blush. 'Yes. She's called Eve. I met her through my blog.'

Jamie nods slowly. I can't tell what he's thinking.

'She's one of my closest friends.'

'So have you met up?'

I shake my head, quickly adding, 'She cracks me up. The other day, she was going on about the bloke from M-pathik. She says he looks like a constipated rhino.'

Jamie laughs. I don't think I've seen him laugh in an unselfconscious way before. It's nice. It softens the sadness in his eyes.

We chat for a while about Ian, who we decide deserves a middle name, seeing as he's already got a human first name. Then we decide he should have a rank. By the time we've agreed on 'Major Ian Reginald Featherly-Bean III', I'm starting to think that Mum and Dad will be back soon.

'I should be in bed when my parents get home,' I say, wondering how to ask Jamie to come back without seeming desperate.

He stands, stretches. I get a glimpse of the hollow of his stomach. 'OK, no probs.'

'So that cookie Mum gave you last time. It wasn't one of my best. If you wanted to, you know, come back another time, I could make some decent ones.'

Jamie pales. 'Er, no. I'm good, thanks.'

So he doesn't want to come back. I'm surprised by how crushed I feel. I don't let my shoulders sag, though, and keep a smile pasted on my face.

'I meant no to the cookies, not no to coming back,' he says. 'I mean, if you want me to. It's just that Ness was giving me this whole guilt trip about promising your mum that I'd come, and then I broke her mirror, so I feel pretty bad.'

Oh, OK. He only wants to come for Ness. Not because he wants to see me. Still, it's better than nothing. 'All right. So, Tuesday? I won't force any cookies on you, promise!'

'Cool. I'll see you then.'

Jamie heads towards the front door.

'Um. Wait. Sorry. Can you just . . .'

He pauses and looks back expectantly.

I sigh. 'Can you just wait until I'm back in the living room before you open the door? Sorry, I know it's really weird.'

He shrugs like it's nothing. 'Sure. C'mon, Ian.'

I watch them leave, then fire up the laptop again, returning to my 'Free Si' site.

Eight months ago, Si Ashworth appealed against his sentence. Mum and Dad were devastated. They were constantly on edge, jumping every time the phone rang. If we'd found out he was going to be released, I think it would've broken them.

To their relief, he lost the appeal. The thing is, *I* didn't feel relieved. I just felt like I needed to do something more for him. I was torn. It was a betrayal, what I was planning, but I couldn't just do nothing, even if I knew Mum and Dad would hit the roof when they found out.

Setting up a campaign website seemed an obvious answer. I have a pretty strong following on my food blog and I know how to get people to pay attention online.

I go back to polishing my first post. I'm almost ready to make it live. I flick back to the site under construction, make sure I'm happy with the design of it. Then my fingers freeze over the keys and my blood ices over. There's another message from 'Anonymous':

I'm not going to wait much longer. Need to talk to you NOW. Contact me.

8

Jamie

I'm kinda smiling as I walk down the steps outside Myla's house. I feel different. Less angry. I thought the rage was switched on all the time. Didn't realise there was an off button. For the last couple of hours, it's definitely been off, though, and now it's like the volume has been turned down.

Tuesday. How many days till Tuesday? I'm trying not to, but I keep thinking 'bout those eyes, those killer eyes. The way she tucks her feet beneath her when she sits, all neat and graceful, like a cat. And that thing she does ...

I hear someone behind me. I glance back, check I'm not being followed again, but it's just a couple of joggers.

Weird that. Was sure I was being followed earlier, but when I turned around, nothing. Must be Myla, making me paranoid.

*

Couple of days later, Ness barges into my room first thing, perches on the end of my bed and starts going on about her mate's allotment. I'm huddled under the cover, wearing nothing but my boxers.

'Anyway,' Ness says. 'I told her you might help out. Is that all right?'

Before I can answer, Ness notices the mirror. I catch her expression in the broken glass. Damn! But she says nothing. That's the worst bit. I want her to yell at me, chuck stuff, tell me I'm gonna work to pay it off. But she just takes a deep breath and says, 'You'd better jump in the shower. We're leaving in twenty minutes.'

As I'm crossing the landing towards the bathroom, I hear Ness on the phone. She's talking to Mum. I try not to listen, but when she says *his* name, I can't help it. 'Well, you already know my feelings about Damian . . . I'm not saying I told you so! . . . Are you sure, Angela? . . . Yes, Jamie's fine . . . Do you want me to check? I think he's about to have a shower.'

I rush into the bathroom and turn the shower on, heart racing. What was all that about? Why were they talking about *him*?

We get in the car to drive to the allotment. For a bit, Ness is quiet, until she blurts out, 'How have things been at home since Damian moved in?'

My chest tightens, but I just shrug. 'OK, I s'pose.'

Ness sighs, shakes her head. 'He's a nasty piece of work, isn't he?'

I just gawp at her. Thought I was the only one who knew what a shit he really is.

Ness swerves into a bus stop, then slams on the brakes, throwing us both forward. 'You can tell me, Jamie. You can trust me. Your mum might not see it, but I know your problems started around the time Damian moved in.'

I tug at my T-shirt, pulling it away from my hot neck.

'If something's going on, your mum deserves to know about it.'

I force a laugh. 'He's not hitting me or anything!'

'OK, but you obviously haven't been happy since he started living with you.'

'I don't – um – really wanna talk 'bout it.'

'It's fine if you don't want to talk to me. If you want to talk to someone else, I'll pay.'

I sink down in the seat, hunch my shoulders. 'You mean like a psychologist? I'm not crazy.'

Ness gives me this soft smile. 'I don't think for a second that you are. I just think you could do with some help.'

'Yeah? Well I didn't ask for any.'

Ness gives me a look, crunches the car into gear and flies back out into the road, causing the guy behind to beep.

I sigh. 'I'm sorry.'

Ness makes a small noise at the back of her throat, but doesn't reply.

I turn my face away from her, stare out the window. I can see how sunken my cheeks have got, how my ears look big compared to my narrow face. I should feel disgusted by it – I look like hell – but that's not what I feel. Not at all.

I've always been thin. When I was a kid, Mum used to call me 'Little Stick'. She's slim. Looking at her and Ness, you wouldn't think they were sisters.

A couple of years ago, Kai and the other boys in my class started to bulk up around their shoulders and chests. It didn't happen like that for me, but I wasn't bothered. I was used to being the weird, skinny ginger kid. No one gave me hassle 'cos Kai was popular.

Least, it didn't bother me till *he* showed up. He's into all that macho crap – body building and stuff. Right from the start, he was on at me 'bout my body. He likes that Mum's 'not got much meat on her', but he reckons 'a man should look like a man'. He was careful – never said any of this when Mum was around. At first, I just laughed it off, told him to do one . . . but he never did. He went on and on.

When we bumped into some of his mates in town, he was all over Mum, showing her off to the lads. But he pretended like I wasn't there.

I wanted to stick two fingers up at him, tell him I didn't give a crap what he thought. But I didn't have the guts. So I found another way. While he ponced around the kitchen, whisking up his four-egg omelettes, I just sat there, watching, my stomach growling, my eyes hard. I wouldn't eat anything he cooked for me.

That's how it started. I realised that I liked it. I didn't have a say in anything else. Couldn't tell Mum who to go out with. Couldn't stop him from laying into me, every chance he got. But I could choose what I did with my own damn body. And if it pissed him off even more, that was a bonus.

I'm not crazy. I don't need help. It's all under control. That's the point.

I turn to Ness. 'He's a waste of space,' I spit.

Ness's grip on the steering wheel relaxes and she turns to grin at me. 'Now that is something we *can* agree on.'

Ten minutes later, I'm sitting on a rough wooden bench outside someone's shed, my nose thick with the smell of damp soil and my trainers coated with mud.

'She'll be here soon,' Ness says. 'You'll get on well. Everyone likes Lil.'

'So I'm what . . . gonna help her plant stuff?'

'Something like that.'

We fall into an easy silence, until Ness leaps up. 'I think Lil keeps a biscuit tin somewhere around here.'

'Wait, Lil? I met her.'

'What? When?'

'On the train. On the way here.'

'Why didn't you say?'

I shrug. 'I forgot.'

Ness rolls her eyes, then disappears into the shed, stomps around a bit, drops something on the floor, then comes out, rattling a tin. 'Found it!'

She sits next to me and offers me the tin as she nibbles a biscuit. Her breath smells of sugary ginger.

A hard fist squeezes around my stomach. Feel a bit light-headed. Maybe I should ... No. I turn my head away, allow myself a little smile for being strong.

'You could just ... try,' Ness says. I can hear it in her voice, how badly she wants me to.

'I can't,' I snap, standing so sharply it makes my head spin. Ness tuts, but doesn't say anything else.

'Cooooeeee!' a voice screeches across the allotment. 'Nessa!'

Ness looks up, then breaks into a smile. She stands and starts to wave madly. 'Lil!' She beckons her over.

Lil ploughs towards us with long, confident strides. I'd forgotten how big she is. Built like a brick shithouse, Mum would say.

Lil plonks herself on the bench with a sigh. She's a bit out of breath. 'Hello, my dear old friend,' she says to Ness. 'It's been a while.'

'It's lovely to see you. And I hear you two have already met.'

'Ah, yes,' Lil squawks, thumping my arm so hard it feels like it's gonna bruise. 'We're old friends.'

Just like before, Lil's skin is plastered with make-up, powder gathering in the lines on her face. When she smiles, the wrinkles all crease up together and her eyes shine. 'So, Ness has dragged you down here to help this poor old lady thin out her carrots? What a bore!'

'I thought it might be therapeutic,' Ness says, frowning at her.

'Leave the poor boy alone, Nessa. Always sticking your oar in.'

Ness huffs. Lil catches my eye and winks.

When they start going on about some old codger with a dodgy prostate, I wander off. It's almost midday and my clothes are starting to stick to me. Someone's left an old picnic blanket on the grass outside a shed. Without really thinking, I flop down and lean back against the warm wooden boards. I close my eyes. Man, I'm tired. Should've brought a satsuma or something, just to stop me passing out. Wouldn't be the first time . . .

When I wake up, it takes a couple of moments to work out where the hell I am. I'm *really* thirsty. My skin is hot and my head is pounding. I might be a bit sunburned.

I stagger back to the bench where I left Ness. I'm so desperate to see her, I actually get a lump in my throat when I realise she's gone. Then I hear, 'Cooooeeee!'

Lil's kneeling in her plot, waving me over. I drag myself towards her, convinced I'm about to keel over.

Lil cackles. 'Someone's caught the sun. We couldn't find you. Ness had to run some errands but she said she'd see you at home.'

I nod, barely able to talk, as I sink down next to her.

'You need a drink?' Lil asks. 'There's orange juice in there.'

She points at a carrier bag. Inside, there's a packet of eight value cartons – the kind that kids get in their packed lunches. I grab one, rip the plastic off the straw, stab it through the foil, and down it in one, without taking a breath.

I instantly reach for the next one. I'm losing it. Can feel myself losing it, and I hate it, but I can't stop.

As I go for a third, I'm sweating and shaking. I pierce the foil so hard, some of the juice spills, and I suck it from my hand, making this gross noise that I don't even care about. The grass around me is littered with crushed cartons, every drop of air squeezed from them.

When I look up, Lil is watching me. I wipe my lips, feeling sick and embarrassed, but better – so much better. There's a small tomato in Lil's hand. She doesn't say anything about the juice, just holds out the tomato.

I take it – what the hell, I've ruined everything anyway – and put it in my mouth. I'm afraid to bite down, afraid that it will come back up again, or that I might enjoy it too much, want more.

Lil nods once, then turns back to her gardening. I hold it carefully in my mouth. I could spit it out. She wouldn't see. But I'm dizzy from the sugar and my body is howling for more.

So I do it. I bite. The leeches wriggle inside my stomach, burping out these vile thoughts. I'm weak. I've got no will-power. I'm pathetic.

But the tomato, it's good. Really good. All the sweet juices and the seeds explode into my mouth. I'm filled with guilt, pleasure, disgust, and I swallow it all down, along with the tomato.

The leeches feast, pouncing on my self-loathing. They swell, ballooning up and pressing against the walls of my stomach until there's no room for anything else. I hate them. Hate this feeling.

'Hold this for me, will you?' Lil says.

I jump. Was so locked in my messed-up mind I'd forgotten she was there. 'Thanks,' I say, shuffling closer on my knees. 'For the tomato.'

'You're welcome.'

I hold one of the vines against a thin wooden pole while Lil wraps a tie around it. Never realised what tomatoes really smell like. They're sweet, a bit like weed.

We do another one. And another. It's all right, this. It's repetitive, but not boring. It's kinda soothing, taking my mind off what I just did.

We're quiet, the silence only broken by Lil coughing every now and then. I reckon she's waiting for me to say something. 'So how d'you know Ness? From bingo?'

'Oh, Ness and I have been friends for longer than I care to remember. We used to work together, at the post office. She's a good egg, our Lil.'

'Yeah, she is,' I say, thinking 'bout how I snapped at her earlier.

'I should be going,' I mumble. 'Gotta walk Ian. Sorry I didn't help more.'

Lil grins. 'Every little helps, said the old lady as she tiddled in the sea.'

I smile back. She's a bit bonkers, but I definitely like her.

'You can come again,' Lil says, going back to her plants. 'Any time.'

I get up and brush soil off my jeans. 'Er – thanks. That's cool.'

I dunno why, but I get on well with older people. I never knew Dad's parents – never knew Dad – and Mum's parents died when I was little. That's why I used to like hanging with Kai and Nana Bo. I miss her. I should sort it out, fess up to Kai, just tell him why I've been weird. But even the thought of it makes those leeches start to squirm.

I head back along the High Street, decide to buy some flowers for Ness, try to make up for the mirror.

When I round a corner, can't frigging believe who I see. Fag in mouth, Finn's chatting up a petite blonde, her legs poking out beneath a short skirt like a couple of match-sticks. She's twirling her hair round her finger and shooting him sexy little looks. Man, she's really into him. How the hell does he do it? I skirt past. Finn's too busy to notice me today.

A group of lads spill out of a pub. They're rowdy, red-faced. Most of them are wearing rugby shirts. For a second, I'm caught up in the middle of them – all beer-breath and BO – and I can't breathe. My stomach starts to churn, all the acid from the orange juice bubbling up, the leeches thrashing about.

The lads jostle me a bit. Not because they're dicks; they're just drunk and I'm in the way, bouncing off their massive shoulders as they shout over my head, giving each other lip. I'm trapped amongst all their banter and bullshit and I hate it.

Then they're gone.

My stomach heaves. No. No . . . no . . . NO!

But I can't control it. Can't keep it down.

My shaking legs carry me into an alleyway, where I fall hard onto my knees, puking up three cartons' worth of orange juice and a small tomato.

9

Myla

I stare at the comment until the words start to blur. Who on earth is this? And how have they found my site when I haven't even started promoting it yet? I wonder what they want – what they have to gain from helping me to get Si Ashworth released.

I don't like this. Not at all. Maybe I should back away, let it drop. But that's not fair. I owe it to Asha to make sure her killer is locked up. This is about the only thing I can do, stuck in here. And this anonymous person, they're not taking that away from me.

I really don't like the tone of that last comment. It sounds threatening, sinister. I delete it, quickly followed by the earlier one.

The sound of the key in the lock makes my heart stop. I

jump up, letting out a little shriek. Then I feel like an idiot. A total idiot. Mum and Dad are home. It's OK.

There's no point trying to pretend that I was asleep. I'm still fully clothed. I sit on my bed and wait for Mum to look in, as I know she will. When she does, the worry on her face sends a stab of guilt through me. She can never really relax, knowing that I'm home alone, probably freaking out.

'Are you OK?' she asks.

I drag up a smile. 'Yes thanks. Did you have a good time?'

Mum grins back, but there's something else: a warning, maybe, or a hint of irritation. 'Wonderful. We had some fabulous linguine at Dolce Vita.'

'And the film?'

Mum shrugs. 'It was OK. It didn't really matter, though. It was just nice to be ...'

Nice to be out. I'm not the only one who's a prisoner in this house. Sure, Mum leaves to go to the shops or for medical appointments, but most of the time, she's just here, with me. This is what I've done to her, because I can't even take one stupid step outside. I turn away so she can't see the twist of my mouth, the reddening of my eyes.

I hear Dad's footsteps plodding up the stairs, then straight into my room.

'Everything OK?' he asks.

I nod, not daring myself to turn and look at him.

'Then shouldn't you be asleep?' he asks gently.

I take a deep breath, then face him. 'I ... er ... Sorry. Just wanted to ... make sure you got back all right.'

Lame. Really lame.

He smiles and raises an eyebrow, then plants a kiss on my forehead before he leaves.

The second he's gone, Mum rushes into my room. 'There are paw prints on the living room carpet!' she hisses.

'Oh, crap.'

'What were you thinking, having him round when you were in the house alone? That is *not* OK!'

'I was frightened. I'm sorry.'

Her eyes soften.

'I didn't know who else to call,' I admit.

Mum gives a little sigh. 'Not again. Ever. I won't tell Dad this time, but if you two are in the house alone again ...'

'He's coming on Tuesday.'

A smile, a light touch on my arm. 'That's good. I'll be around then.'

'What about the paw prints?'

'I'll keep Dad out of the living room tomorrow morning, and they'll be gone by the time he's home from work.'

'Thanks, Mum.'

'Night, darling.'

'Night.'

On Tuesday morning, I check my phone for any overnight messages from Eve. I haven't told her yet that Jamie's going to start visiting. She was so strange the first time he came round, I'm not sure how she's going to take it.

Eve51x: How are you this morning? You sleep OK?

Saffy42: Good, thanks.

Eve51x: What are you up to today?

Saffy42: Not much. I might do some work on my blog.

Eve51x: Which blog? You're not still planning on going ahead with that 'Free Si' idea, are you?

My cheeks flame.

Saffy42: I'm still working on the first post, but I'm definitely putting it out there. And before you say anything, I know what you think, but I'm still doing it.

Eve51x: I just don't see what use it is to drag it all up again. And what about your parents?

Saffy42: I'm doing it, Eve. You can't change my mind. Listen, I've got to go.

Eve51x: No, Saffy, wait! Don't go. I'm sorry. I won't mention it again. I made your cheese and chive scones last night. They were delicious. You're so clever.

Despite myself, I smile and blush. She always does that – knows just how to win me round.

Saffy42: I can't believe you made them. You really liked them? I was worried the cheese flavour wasn't coming through enough.

Eve51x: They were perfect. Honest. You've got a real talent. I can just see you with your own cupcake business one day, or doing wedding cakes, or fancy breads.

I nibble on my fingernail.

Saffy42: Yeah, except for that to happen I'd have to actually leave my house.

Eve51x: You could do Internet orders. You'd be great at it.

I hear a floorboard creak on the landing. I hold my breath, listen for a few seconds. Dad's already gone to work so it must be Mum. It sounds like she's standing outside Asha's room. My heart plummets.

Saffy42: Eve, I'm sorry, I've really got to go.

Eve51x: Already ☹

Saffy42: Yes. Sorry. Talk soon x

I open my door quietly. Just as I expected, there she is, just staring at Asha's bedroom. She's holding an emerald top. For a moment I think it's Asha's – the one she was wearing when she was taken – and my throat closes. Then I remember: it's mine.

Gran always used to buy us identical things, like we were twins. Identical sizes too. I remember I was grumpy because Asha looked great in her top. At two years younger, I was swamped in mine.

A couple of weeks ago, I picked it out of my drawer and put it on without thinking. When I wandered into the kitchen, Mum froze. The colour fled from her face and she burst into tears. I didn't have a clue why, until after I'd given her a hug, calmed her down, and caught myself in the mirror. I looked just like Asha. I glared at my reflection, then hauled it off and chucked it straight in the bin.

Mum must've retrieved it, though. I watch her clutch it like she's a frightened child and the top is a teddy bear, a comforter. Just for a moment, the pain she so carefully conceals is exposed, like she's taken off a mask. And I don't just see it, I *feel* it. So different from my pain, which is all mangled with guilt and fear and frustration. Hers is just raw agony. What would it feel like if I was a parent and lost my child? I can't even …

I clamp my teeth into my lip to stop myself from crying out. Mum hasn't seen me. She's lost, engulfed by it. I creep back into my room, shut the door with the quietest click, and sink down against it, blinking to release the heavy weight of my tears.

Her heart is severed. The mum I see every day is the half she reserves for me. But there will always be half for Asha.

Asha's door handle creaks as it's pulled down, then Mum goes in. She can't stifle her unbearable sobs. I want to go to her, but I can't fix it, fix her.

I'm not sure if she feels the same way as Dad, the same way as me – that it's my fault, that I should have fought harder for my sister. And I couldn't even remember enough to help them catch the right man. I failed her, again and again.

I don't deserve to be the one who survived. I sometimes wish I hadn't, wish that we could change places. The guilt is unrelenting: a waterlogged cloak that bears down on my shoulders, sinking its damp, cold misery into my body. I can't shake it off. It weighs me down, drags heavily behind every footstep, and I know I'll carry it forever.

Mum's still sobbing. I open my door, take the two steps across the landing to Asha's room and hesitate. I hate going in there. It's completely stripped of her – Dad made sure of that. Mum and I held each other, tears sliding down our faces as we watched him stuff her things into bin bags. I couldn't believe him. It was like he wanted to get rid of every last trace, like she was never there.

Then, a few months later, Dad sent me up to his room to fetch his watch, and I noticed his bedside drawer was open. Inside was a cuddly toy that Asha had had since she was a baby: a little sausage dog called Bratwurst. He had a torn ear, a missing eye and a blood stain on his nose from when Asha had fallen over and Bratwurst had 'kissed' it better.

There was something else beneath Bratwurst: a photo of Dad and Asha. He was reclined on a sun lounger and she was lying on him, her feet either side of his head, laughing as he tickled her. I smiled sadly, stroked her silly face, and put the photo back where I found it.

I return to my room and lie on my bed. A few minutes later, there's a soft knock on my door. 'Myla? Are you up? Isn't Jamie coming round this afternoon?'

Mum sounds stuffy. Am I supposed to pretend I don't know what she was doing? No. No way. I fling open the door and wrap my arms around her, so tightly she gasps a little. 'What's the matter?' Mum asks, wrapping her hand around the back of my neck.

'I love you,' I mumble into her chest.

Her hand moves to the top of my head. 'I love you too,' she says softly.

'I'm sorry.'

Mum holds me at arm's length and looks closely at me. 'Sorry for what?'

'I'm just sorry.'

She pauses for a moment, gives me a sad, puzzled smile, then says, 'Come on, let's make some tea,' before heading downstairs.

Mum soon gets distracted by the pile of letters on the kitchen table so I switch my laptop on to check my email. A couple of pieces of spam, an online sale at a clothes shop I like. Then my heart stutters when I see the last message.

Since Si's appeal fell through, I've been contacting charities – the kind that fight to free people who were wrongly convicted. Most never reply or send a standard 'we have too many requests and can't get through them all' response. But this time, it's a personal reply. I skim it.

They thank me for getting in touch ... blah blah ... say sorry for my loss ... they've reviewed the information I sent to them ... blah blah ... and unfortunately, in light of my concussion, didn't think the evidence was strong enough. Damn! The head injury. It all comes back to the stupid head injury.

I huff. Slam my mug down on the table. Mum looks up, a question in her eyes, but doesn't say anything.

How can they be so dismissive? How can they just sit back when an innocent man has been convicted? I know that Si Ashworth isn't an angel. In fact, he's a nasty, violent man, but he doesn't deserve to do time for someone else's crime.

It makes me sick to think of Asha's real killer out there

somewhere, enjoying his life, having a takeaway on a Friday night, meeting up with his mates at the pub, having a laugh, getting drunk. Urgh. I can't. Can't even think about it.

I reread the email. That's it, then. Decision made. I'll have to deal with the consequences, but I need to do this. I go back to my 'Free Si' website (thankfully with no new comments) and publish my first ever post.

I take a deep breath. That felt good! What next? I've become quite friendly with some of my blog followers. If I ask them to spread the word, maybe try to get a petition going, it might go viral and I could get enough signatures to make someone listen.

'You're very quiet,' Mum observes. 'What are you working on?'

'Carrot cake!' I blurt out. 'I'm doing a post on carrot cake.'

When Jamie rings the doorbell an hour later, I'm at the kitchen table, dutifully working on my post about carrot cake.

Mum goes to collect Jamie while I carry on typing. I've finished the introduction, about how people made carrot puddings in medieval times, probably because sweeteners were scarce, and then carrot cake really took off in World War Two because of sugar rationing.

When Mum and Jamie come into the kitchen, I'm working on the actual recipe. I say, without looking up, 'What do you think about decorating a cake with mini carrots made from icing? Too fiddly?'

No response. I glance up.

Jamie blanches. 'Er – I dunno. Don't know much about cake.'

'Well, you must eat it.'

He shrugs. 'Not really.'

My mouth drops. 'Everyone eats cake!'

He just stares at me.

'Why don't you go through to the living room?' Mum says in a strange sing-song voice. 'I'll bring some drinks in.'

'What, not even chocolate?' I ask.

Jamie shakes his head, refusing to meet my eyes. He turns away, towards the living room.

'Leave him alone, Myla!' Mum whispers fiercely.

'He'd like *my* chocolate cake. No one's ever not liked my chocolate cake.'

But as I follow Jamie into the living room, I think about the hollow shape of his stomach, the dark circles beneath his eyes, how he always wears those baggy T-shirts.

I sit down next to him, but don't really know what to say.

Jamie seems just as awkward, as if the other night hadn't even happened.

'How's things with Ness?' I ask.

Jamie shrugs. 'OK.'

'Is Ian all right?'

'Yep.'

A pause, then Jamie asks, 'How are you?'

'I'm good, thanks. Well, better than I was the other night. Sorry about that.'

Jamie manages a small smile. 'I didn't mind, honest.'

The phone rings, making us both jump. Mum answers it. 'Hello? . . . Hello? . . . Hello?' A clatter and a sharp sigh as she puts it down.

'So what have you been up to?' I ask Jamie.

'Went to the allotment.'

I wonder if Jamie ate anything that he picked at the allotment. I wonder how much he eats every day. I want to ask, but somehow I just know he'll shut down.

'Met one of Ness's mates, Lil. You know her?'

I roll my eyes. 'Seriously? This is Stratten. Everyone knows everyone.'

'Still find that weird. I don't even know our neighbours' names at home.'

'I can't imagine that. So how's Lil doing?'

'Seems all right. Bit nuts.'

'Nothing new there, then. So what's the allotment like now? I haven't been for years.'

'Not that exciting. Just some plants, a load of dirt and some old people.'

'Is that creepy scarecrow still there? The one with the bow tie? I used to have nightmares about it.'

'I dunno. There was a scarecrow, but it looked pretty normal to me.'

I lean towards him, eager for more. 'Where else do you go in Stratten?'

'Started walking Ian on the cliffs.'

'Did you? Which cliffs? Where?'

'You know where the war memorial is?'

I nod. 'If you turn left there, you get to the playground.'

Jamie snorts. 'If I turn left there, I end up in the sea.'

'Which way are you facing?'

'Towards the lighthouse.'

'Oh, well yeah. Turn right, obviously.'

'Obviously.'

Jamie smiles. I wish he'd do it more often. I like the way his eyes shed all their sadness, how the flecks of green really stand out against his skin.

'Tell me about it,' I plead. 'Tell me what it all looks like.'

Jamie shrugs. 'Well, there's the beach and sea, I guess.'

'Great descriptive powers, there!'

He frowns, shakes his head. 'I'm no good at this.'

'I'm just messing with you!'

But he still looks really down. I want to reach over and squeeze his hand. I didn't mean for him to feel bad.

Then Jamie looks up. 'I could take pictures . . . if you want.'

'Really? Would you?' I almost squeal.

'You're easily pleased.'

'Well, this is my life,' I say sharply, pointing at the four walls. 'I see the outside world through the TV.'

Jamie goes quiet.

I didn't mean to sound that harsh.

He's picking at the throw again.

'Are you trying to completely demolish it?' I ask with a smile.

Jamie drops it like it's a snake. 'Sorry – didn't mean to.'

'Don't worry. I'm only teasing . . . again.'

'D'you wish you could, you know, go outside?'

'Of course.'

Jamie groans, looks away. I think I hear him mutter, 'Stupid question,' under his breath.

Sometimes I feel like the house is shrinking, pressing down on me, and the air clogs, becomes too thick. Everything keeps getting smaller until it all disappears and I'm just trapped in my own head, circling through the same thoughts again and again and again.

I want to ask Jamie how he thinks it feels, how he would feel. I want to tell him that I'm angry, so angry that I can't just throw that door open, step out into the fresh sea air and breathe. I wish I could've dealt with this like a normal person. Maybe something happened to me when I was knocked out. Maybe something broke in my mind.

'That beach is pretty cool,' Jamie says.

'Which beach?'

'Near where I walk Ian.'

I release my bottom lip from my teeth. I wasn't even aware that I was biting it. I make myself smile, try to brush away the bad thoughts like they're nothing more than cobwebs. 'I love that beach. Asha fell asleep there one year and got really sunburned. Mum was furious.'

CONSUMED

I catch the look he throws me. 'Yes, we can burn, thank you very much. You don't have to be as pale as paper to catch the sun!'

'Tell me about her,' he says suddenly.

'What?'

Jamie closes his eyes, tilts his head back and sighs. 'Sorry. That didn't come out right. I just meant that you don't say much about her.'

I try to fight back a shiver. Jamie notices and offers me the throw, but I shake my head.

'Sorry,' he repeats. 'You don't have to. Forget it.'

'Ness told you, right?'

'Right,' he says firmly, as if the matter is closed.

I sigh. He's trying. If I don't offer him something, he'll pull back again. 'She probably didn't tell you about Asha's hair.'

He sits up a little straighter. 'No, but seriously, you don't have—'

'She had beautiful hair. All thick and wavy and so black it shone. When we were little, she used to let me play with it. I'd put it up for her, in a ponytail, or make pigtails, but she'd take it out when I was finished. Asha always wore her hair down. Always.

'When they . . . ' It feels like my throat is closing around the words, swallowing them down again. Jamie says nothing, just waits patiently. 'When they . . . found her on the beach, two days after she'd been taken, she was naked. They said the killer had removed her clothes to get rid of any evidence. She'd been . . . '

There's no moisture left in my mouth. I cough. I can almost feel two hands clamping around my own neck. 'She'd been strangled. They never found her clothes. But the strangest thing was her hair. When Dad went to identify her, he said . . . ' Tears are rolling down my face. I can't even look at Jamie. I just stare straight ahead. ' . . . Asha's hair was in a plait. It wasn't in a plait when I left her. Someone did that to her.'

Jamie nods. Silence, except for my sniffling. I breathe deeply, trying to rein it in. God, Jamie must be so embarrassed. He doesn't need this. I manage to look up. He meets my eyes steadily. 'I'm sorry,' he says.

'You apologise too much,' I reply, giggling through the tears.

Jamie just shrugs, looking like he wants to apologise again.

We're at opposite ends of the sofa but he shuffles slightly closer and extends his arm along the top, as if he wants to touch me, but can't quite bring himself to do it.

We spend another hour chatting about more cheerful things. Jamie tells me that he caught Ian barking at his own reflection the other day, and that if he takes him onto the beach, taps the sand and says 'Get those mice!' Ian will happily spend the next ten minutes digging a hole.

I laugh. 'You're so into Ian!'

'I'm not really a dog person.'

'You really are.'

'Well, about Ian. I've gotta go. He'll be waiting.'

'OK. See you again?'

'Yeah. Course.'

I let Mum see Jamie to the door. When he's gone, the house seems quiet, too empty. I feel different after letting him see me like that. Not just different ... better. But everything feels really close to the surface now.

I message Eve.

Saffy42: Need a hug ☹

She doesn't reply. She must be out. I try to ignore the stab of jealousy, the totally unreasonable feeling that she promised to always be here for me, but now she's not, now she's outside, enjoying herself, while I'm stuck in here with nothing to distract me from my own misery.

Dad is home early for once.

'Thought I'd do dinner tonight,' he says.

Dad likes to think he's a bit of a masterchef, but really the only two recipes he's ever managed to master are spag bol and shepherd's pie. Mum let him try to cook a curry on her birthday once. I don't think she'll let him try again.

Dad starts to undo his tie. 'How does spaghetti bolognaise sound?'

I smile. 'Well, it's no herb-crusted fillet of beef with a red wine reduction and creamed asparagus, but I guess it'll do.'

Dad comes into my room, ruffles my hair. 'Cheeky. You've been watching too many cooking shows.'

'I like them.'

'I don't know why. Those snooty critics looking down their noses at the contestants. The way they egg out all the drama.'

'Ha! "Egg out".'

He smiles. 'Pun not intended.'

'How was work?'

Dad's face darkens. 'It wasn't great. I felt a bit bad leaving when everyone else was staying late, but I wanted to see you both.'

Later, Mum teases Dad about his paunch as he goes for a second helping of the Mauritian rice pudding she's made. He just smiles and slaps it. 'Well, you shouldn't spoil me so much. The pair of you are responsible. Nothing to do with me!'

'I suppose I should stop baking, then,' I say.

'No!' He laughs. 'Never!'

Mum takes another sip of wine and gently pats Dad's tummy. 'I'm only joking.'

'Just because you can eat what you like and not put on a pound,' he grumbles. 'When you hit sixty it's going to catch up with you and you'll balloon overnight.' Dad blows out his cheeks and holds his arms up to make himself look bigger.

Mum giggles. It's nice to see her smiling after this morning. They're both in such a good mood, I almost can't bear to spoil it, but I can't risk them stumbling across the 'Free Si' site.

I clear my throat. 'I need to tell you something.'

They both stop grinning and turn to me, their faces suddenly serious.

'So ... you're not going to like this but ... ' I look away.

Dad leans forward. 'But?'

'I'll show you,' I say, getting up to find my laptop.

As I leave, I hear them whispering, trying to figure out what it might be.

I set the laptop up in front of them and navigate to the page.

Dad reads for a second, then his eyes ice over. 'Take it down,' he snaps.

'Let me just explain.'

'Take it down, Myla. Now!' he bellows, standing so fast the chair flies out behind him. 'We're not having this argument again.'

Mum starts to cry. One look at her and my own eyes begin to prickle.

'I just want to know the truth!' I wail. 'That's all I've ever wanted. For Asha. This isn't right. This isn't fair. He didn't do it.'

'Please don't make us go through this again,' Mum murmurs. 'Please, Myla. Let it rest. Let her rest.'

My heart breaks a little. Let her rest? How can I, when he's still out there, when he might hurt someone else? Asha would understand. She'd want this.

'The evidence against him was strong enough for a

conviction,' Dad says. 'Her hair was in his house. The charm. For God's sake, Myla, how do you think they got there?'

'I don't know! All I know is that he wasn't the man who chased me on the beach.'

'How can you be sure? You don't remember everything that happened.'

'Yes!' I yell, ferociously tapping the side of my head. 'But maybe if I did, we wouldn't be in this position. If I could just find whatever it is that's hidden in here, we could all move on.'

Dad doesn't disagree. He just glares, sweeps past me and says in a cold voice, 'Take it down.'

10

Jamie

'What are you up to today?' Ness asks, leaning over me to grab the milk. I pretend not to notice that her armpit is right in my face.

I shove aside a pile of old newspapers on the table so I can put down my glass.

'I've been looking for that!' Ness says, pouncing on a magazine about glazing techniques. As she picks it up, a piece of old string slides to the floor, and Ian starts to chew it. I smile slightly.

Ness has got brown stuff on her fingers, her shirt has been buttoned up the wrong way, and her hair is all over the place. She looks back at me, waiting for a reply.

'Might go down the allotment. Myla wants me to take some pictures.'

'You could give Lil a hand again.'

'Maybe. She's cool.'

'She is. Just . . . '

'What?'

'She's more vulnerable than she seems.'

'What you on about?'

'She lost someone,' Ness says softly. 'Her daughter. It was cancer.'

Jesus. That's rough.

'She tries to hide it, but . . . '

I nod. That's what it is then, why she seems a bit over the top sometimes. It's like all that make-up she wears – she's trying to cover the cracks.

I grab a satsuma from the fruit bowl and roll it in my hand. I wanna be strong today. I take an apple as well. Ness clocks me, but doesn't comment, just takes another mouthful of cereal.

'Perhaps you could call your mum before you leave.'

I bite back the response I'd like to snap at her. 'Gotta go. Sorry.'

'OK, OK. Let's not talk about that. I picked this up for you.' Ness slides a leaflet across the table towards me. Some therapist in North Walsham.

I almost flip. Almost. It's like a lit match. But then I take a deep breath, damp it down, remind myself how awesome it is that she wants to pay for me. 'Thanks, but I'm good.'

Then I hurry out, before either of us can say anything else.

I eat the satsuma in my room. Slowly. I've got the bin by my feet in case it comes back up. Can't believe I puked the other day. Haven't done that before. I hated it – hated that I couldn't stop.

Still, it got rid of the calories from the orange juice.

Man, I'm so messed up! Maybe I'm getting worse. No. I shouldn't have lost it at the allotment. My stomach couldn't handle it. I just need to know my limits.

I'm gonna eat this satsuma and it's gonna stay down. I'm in charge and I need some energy so I can help Lil and take pictures for Myla. I remember how excited she was when I said I'd do it. I wanna see that look again.

I know she'd never be into me. I shouldn't think about her so much. But I can't help it. The way she always pulls her hair over her left shoulder before she sits down, that little mole just beneath her chin, how she sucks on her little finger just before she speaks, like she's concentrating really hard about what she's gonna say.

Before I realise it, the satsuma is gone. And the apple. Damn. How did that happen? I never eat that much in one go. I lost focus, lost control again. What an idiot. A greedy idiot. The leeches are bloated, pushing my stomach against my jeans. I swallow down the nausea, grab my wallet and phone and head out.

'Hello, my darling!' Lil shrieks when I get to the allotment. 'How are you?'

I shrug. 'All right, I s'pose.'

'Have you come to help me out? It's a struggle sometimes, old biddy like me managing this all on my own.'

There's nothing 'old biddy' about her. Lil's more well-built than some of those rugby blokes I saw the other day.

He always said I should join a sports club, that I'd have more friends if I did, and I'd bulk up a bit, look like more of a man. It's not my scene, though. He never seemed to get that, no matter how many times I told him.

'Well, are you helping or not?' Lil asks.

'Er ... I'm taking some pictures for my friend, but I could come back.'

'Splendid!' Lil grins and her face creases into a thousand wrinkles.

I amble round, feeling a bit awkward as I take shots of people working, close-ups of different fruits and vegetables. Never really thought about how this stuff grows. It's kinda cool, seeing the onion tips sprouting out the ground, the clusters of raspberries drooping beneath the leaves.

'Here,' says Lil, thrusting a plastic bag at me when I get back. 'Why don't you pick some strawberries?'

I kneel next to her. 'Yeah. I could take some for my friend. She'd love them.'

'Myla.'

There's something slightly bitter about the way Lil said her name. I look up, surprised.

Lil catches my eye and grins. 'Try one,' she says. 'Better than those rotten things you get at the supermarket.'

I don't think. I just pick a fat, bright strawberry and put it in my mouth, chewing quickly. But then I slow down. Wow. She's right. So sweet. Can't remember the last time I enjoyed eating a strawberry. Can't remember the last time I enjoyed eating *anything*.

For a while we work in silence, and I get lost in finding the best berries.

Lil wanders off to make herself a tea. Says she's got a kettle in her shed. When she comes back, she's spritzed herself with perfume. It gets right up my nose, makes me wanna sneeze. Bit odd, bothering about perfume when you're mucking around in an allotment.

'Mint?' she says, offering me a Polo.

I shake my head.

'Come and help me weed, will you? Nasty job like that is easier with two.'

I put the bag of strawberries down and Lil shoves a trowel in my hand. I gawp at it. 'What am I s'posed to do with this?'

Lil chuckles. 'Come here and I'll show you.'

I kneel next to her and follow Lil's instructions for how to sort out the weeds growing near her lettuces.

'Don't be afraid of getting your hands dirty,' Lil says. 'Look at me!' She shows me her hands, the creases in her palms lined with soil. 'I couldn't care cornerwise!'

I'm smiling again. It's weird, the way she speaks, but I kinda like it.

I plunge the trowel into the soil, digging deep to find the root of the weed. After a bit, it's not so bad. The earth is warm and sort of comforting, and I don't even mind the red spot on my finger where the trowel has been rubbing. I stand up to look at what I've done. There's a small pile of weeds at my feet.

'There you go. Look at the difference you've made!' Lil says, clumping a hand down on my shoulder.

I have made a difference. Didn't realise it would feel so . . . good. Maybe Ness is right. Maybe I can make a difference with Myla, too.

'Now get those strawberries home straight away. They won't keep long.'

Lil seems to have forgotten that they're for Myla.

We hadn't planned to meet up today. I don't even have her number. Can I just turn up? Is that OK?

'Off you go!' Lil says, waving me away.

I hand the trowel back, mumble a thanks for the strawberries, and head off.

I call Kai on the way to Myla's. I was a dick the last time we spoke. Need to make it right. It's bad enough that I have to go back to *him* at the end of the summer, without going back to school with no mates.

'All right, Jay?' He sounds wary.

'Listen, man. I'm sorry, yeah?'

'What's with you?'

I sigh. 'I'm just messed up at the moment.' I try to make a joke of it. 'You know me: not right in the head.'

He snorts. 'Damn right. But you been like that since we were kids. What's new?'

'I dunno. Stuff's just not been great.'

'Nana Bo's worried about you. We both are.'

I close my eyes. Why'd he have to bring Nana Bo into it? 'So how's Isma?'

'She's good. She's cool, you know.'

'I know, doofus. You're the one who can't make up his mind 'bout her.'

'Most of the time she's cool. Just, sometimes she's all up in my face about stuff. You know what girls are like.'

'Not really.'

I stop outside Myla's house. If she was my girlfriend, she wouldn't be on my case all the time. 'Listen, I gotta go.'

'Later, man.'

There's no answer when I ring the bell. Damn, I knew this was a bad idea. But she must be in, even if Jav isn't. I bang on the door, shout her name.

A window opens upstairs. 'Jamie?'

'Yeah.'

'What are you doing here?'

'I've brought you something.'

'What?'

'Why don't you come down, open the door and see?'

'I can't. You know I can't.'

'When was the last time you tried?'

'The time I had a panic attack and couldn't breathe. Seriously, Jamie, I don't think I should.'

'OK. I'll just take them home. Shame. Bet Ness will enjoy them.'

She hesitates, then says, 'What are they?'

'Come and see.'

Myla laughs. 'You're mean.'

'I'm trying to help. You said you wanted to leave.'

'I do. I'm just . . .'

'I know. But it's the middle of the day. No one's gonna hurt you. I'm . . . I'm here.'

Yeah. I'm here. I'll protect her, keep her safe.

There's a long pause. Wonder if she's on her way down already. Then she calls from upstairs again, 'OK. I'm going to try. But if I freak out, I'm blaming you.'

'OK.'

I wait. Count the seconds under my breath. Then the latch is turned from the inside and the door opens a bit.

'Jamie!' she whispers, her voice high and panicky. 'I don't like it. I don't think I can.'

'You can,' I say, resisting the urge to nudge the door from my side. 'C'mon, Myla. I wanna see you.'

'You do?'

Crap. I blush. 'I wanna see you do this. I know you can.'

The door moves a little more.

'That's it. Come on,' I say, surprised by how much I want that door to open.

Then her breathing starts to get too fast. This was a mistake. What have I done? 'Myla?'

Nothing. But the breathing – she's definitely panicking.

And then Myla does the bravest damn thing I've ever seen anyone do. She flings the door open. Her eyes are wide and she's sweating, her chest moving too fast. No. No, no, no! What do I do? What the hell do I do?

'Jamie,' she squeaks, backing away, her legs dropping under her, leaving her sprawled across the hallway.

'I'm sorry, I'm sorry!' I say, rushing in after her, pulling the door shut behind me. I sit on the floor, facing her, but Myla's not looking at me. She's starting to wheeze and her skin has gone all pale. Not good. Not good!

Wait. I can't help if I'm losing it too. I need to get it together. I take a couple of deep breaths.

'It's OK,' I tell her, even though it's not. It's really not.

Then I reach out, thinking, *this is the first time I'm gonna touch her*. I put my hand on her arm, leave it there until she looks at me. I carry on with the deep breathing. Not for me any more. For her. God, she looks so scared.

Myla's breathing is starting to slow. She puts her hand in mine. I squeeze it, tell her she's gonna be all right.

Then there's the rattle of a key in the lock. Myla shrinks away as Jav opens the door. Jav freezes, drops her handbag and rushes to Myla, who lets go of my hand. 'What happened?' Jav snaps, looking at Myla, then me. 'I only went out for a minute.'

I blush, focus on the floor. 'It was my fault. I just turned up and made her answer the door. I was trying to help.'

'What, you thought we hadn't tried that? Don't you ever put my daughter at risk again, Jamie. Do you understand?'

'Mum,' Myla gasps. 'Leave . . . him . . . '

She can't even finish the sentence.

Jav's right. This is definitely on me. I screwed up. I'm useless. The leeches churn up the fruit in my stomach. It's acid, toxic.

I'm gonna be sick. Can't even open my mouth to apologise. I get to my feet, lurch along the hallway, out the door, down the steps and into the fresh air. I gulp it in, manage to swallow back the vomit.

That's it, then. There's no way Myla's mum is letting me anywhere near her again. I've blown it.

11

Myla

I don't move from the hallway floor for the next ten minutes. Mum sits with me, stroking my hair, murmuring various comforting things. I'm not really listening. I stare at the door, hoping that Jamie will come back. When he touched my arm, I sort of felt calm, like it was going to be OK. I hope I haven't scared him off.

I'm still trembling and nauseous, but I manage to get up and Mum helps me to my room. I don't have the strength to argue with her but I'm pretty peeved about the way she talked to Jamie. He didn't force me to open that door. I wanted to try.

Mum tucks me into bed. As soon as she's gone, I reach for my phone. I need to talk to Eve.

Eve51x: What's up, Saffy?

Saffy42: I had another panic attack. ☹

Eve51x: God, are you OK?

Saffy42: I'm so sick of being trapped. I feel like I'm breathing in all the grief in this house and it's poisoning me. I just want to get out. I just want to be normal. I'm sick of feeling like a freak.

Eve51x: Calm down, Saffy. I'm here.

Saffy42: I know. You are, but you're not. Not physically here.

Eve51x: What prompted the panic attack? Was it something to do with Jamie?

Why would she say that? I don't think I've mentioned Jamie since I told Eve he wasn't coming around again.

Saffy42: He was just trying to help.

Eve51x: Yes, and look what happened. I don't think he's good for you.

It sounds like she's jealous. But is she jealous of my friendship with Jamie, or is it something more than that? I don't know if I want it to be something more. I'm so confused!

I decide to just ask, straight up.

Saffy42: What's your problem with Jamie?

Eve51x: I don't have a problem with him. He's a nice boy. I just think he's putting you in danger and I'm worried about you.

Downstairs, the phone rings. Mum picks it up. 'Hello? . . . Hello? . . . *Hello?*' She slams it down. It's the second time that's happened. Actually, it might be the third. Mum was muttering about someone playing pranks. Maybe it's the man who's watching the house. Is he trying to scare me into silence, stop me from asking questions about Asha's death?

I hear Mum's footsteps on the stairs, so I tell Eve I have to go. We'll have to pick up this Jamie thing later.

Things between Mum and I have been a little cool since we had the fight about the website, but she's more resigned to it than Dad. I heard them talking last night, her telling him that she doesn't like it any more than he does, but that it's good for me to feel like I'm able to do something. In the end, he softened slightly, pointing out that nobody will take any notice of it anyway.

That made me seethe, but I didn't want them to know I'd been eavesdropping so I just crept back into my room, wishing more than anything that I could stomp down the stairs and straight out the front door, slamming it behind me.

There's a soft knock on my bedroom door before Mum pushes it open. 'Just wanted to check if you're asleep.'

'I don't feel like sleeping.'

Mum smiles but I can see all the worry etched across her face. 'Do you want me to bring you something to eat?'

I get out of bed, close my eyes and fight a wave of dizziness. 'I'll come down. No point staying here if I'm not going to sleep.'

I follow Mum into the kitchen. She's made a salad. I watch her dish it up, then I swipe a few extra slices of cucumber from the bowl.

'Leave some for Dad,' Mum scolds.

'It's his own fault for not being here. Is he working late again?'

'No, he's had to go out for drinks with Andy and someone from the American office.'

'Isn't Andy the one he can't stand?'

Mum smiles. 'I don't think he'll be long.'

We sit and start to eat.

'Can I have Ness's mobile number please?' I ask innocently.

Mum pauses, fork midway to her mouth. 'Why?'

'I just need to check something with her.'

'Like what?'

'Seriously, Mum! Why has everything got to be the third-degree? I want Ness's number so I can ask for Jamie's number so I can apologise for you being so rude to him.'

'I was scared, Myla,' Mum says, slamming her fork down. 'You're . . .' Tears appear in her eyes. '. . . You're all I've got.'

I get up straight away, rushing to her, my arms open.

'I'm fine, I'm fine,' she says. 'Honestly. Don't make a fuss.'

We both know she's not fine.

'OK,' Mum says, sliding her phone across the table to me. 'Text Ness and get his number. But I don't want him trying anything like that again.'

'He wants to help me. And I want to try. I can't stay like this forever, can I?'

Mum doesn't reply, just picks up her plate, puts it on the side and fills the kettle. I sigh, find Ness's number and send her a quick message.

When I look up, I notice Jamie's bag of strawberries on the counter. 'Let's have these for dessert,' I say, reaching for a knife and colander.

When Dad comes in ten minutes later, he takes one look at us and asks, 'What's wrong? You both look awful.'

Mum puts her hands on her hips. 'What a charmer! You can see why I fell for him, Myla.'

He gives her a kiss and squeezes her shoulder. Dad's eyes

are puffy and rimmed with black circles. 'Sorry. I'm tired. You know what I mean. Are you all right?'

Mum gives him a tight smile. 'We're fine. Tough day. I'll tell you after you've eaten.'

We've just finished off the last of Jamie's strawberries when my phone buzzes. Ness has replied with Jamie's number.

'We've talked about this website of yours, Myla,' Dad says.

I put my mobile down and sit up straighter.

'I'm angry that you didn't discuss it with us first. It felt like you'd gone behind our backs.'

'I know. I'm sorry. But I believe in this.'

'I would still like you to take it down.'

'And if I won't?'

Dad meets my eyes, his expression hard, then slowly repeats himself. 'I would still like you to take it down.'

'We can't tell you what to think or say, Myla, but will you at least consider it?' Mum asks. 'For the sake of our family.'

'Of course,' I say softly. 'I'll think about it.'

Mum gives Dad a look that says 'that's the best we're going to get for now'. He nods slightly, but he's not happy. He's *really* not happy.

'How were the drinks?' Mum asks.

Dad shrugs. 'I got away as quickly as I could. Turns out, Andy's nephew goes to Myla's old school. What's his name? Chris?'

I nod. 'Chris Whitely? He was in the year above. Had a bit of a reputation as a ladies' man ...'

'Well I hope you didn't know him too well, then,' Dad says.

I roll my eyes. 'Dad, please. The last time I was at school, I was fourteen.'

His lips tighten.

I scrape my chair back. 'I'm going to read in bed.'

Upstairs, I text Jamie.

Thanks for the strawberries.

Myla? I forgot about the strawberries. I'm sorry. I messed up.

You didn't force me to open the door.

It was my fault.

It's OK. The strawberries were lush.

Yeah, Lil grew them. How did you get my number?

Ness.

OK. Glad you did.

Me too.

Two days later, Mum sticks her head around my bedroom door before Dad leaves for work. 'We need to decide what to do about the opera tickets,' she says. 'The show's tonight. I'm sure if we let them know now, they can be resold.'

I don't want them to go, not at all, but I can't ask them to stay in for the next however-many-years, just to babysit me. Besides, I can ask Jamie over. I just won't tell Mum.

'No, go. I'll be fine.'

Dad chips in, calling from their bedroom. 'See? I told you.'

Mum frowns, glances over her shoulder, then whispers, 'But last time . . . '

'Last time was a mistake. I got freaked out over nothing.'

Mum comes further into my room. 'I'm not talking about that. Jamie's not coming over when you're home alone, Myla. Understand? If you get scared, call my mobile. I'll put it on vibrate and leave my bag on my lap.'

I smile sadly. She shouldn't have to do that. But it'll be fine. I won't get scared because Jamie will be here.

The second Mum leaves, I text him.

Are you up for coming over tonight? M and D going out.

Can't, sorry. Lil's coming over. Her and Ness are gonna teach me poker. Will you be OK?

I'll have to be. I try to ignore the nausea swimming around my stomach.

Later, I cheerfully wave Mum and Dad off. As soon as they're gone, I rush around the house, checking all the locks. I'm going to make brownies. Nothing can possibly go wrong while I'm standing over a bowl of molten chocolate.

I've been working on a chilli version of my classic brownie recipe but I keep getting the quantities wrong. It should be a subtle flavour. So far all I've managed is one batch that made my eyes water, and one that just tasted like normal brownies. Still, it's making for quite an amusing post.

I crank up the volume on the radio and start to sing along. When the brownies are in the oven, and the kitchen fills with their smooth, rich scent, I dance, sashaying around like a finalist on *Strictly*. I'm OK. Happy. Relaxed. OK.

Just after I've taken the brownies out, the phone rings. I stop dead. I don't usually answer it. Nobody rings me on the home phone – it's always for Mum or Dad. Maybe it's one of them, ringing to say they forgot something. I check my mobile for missed calls. Nothing.

'Hello?' I say, trying not to sound as scared as I feel.

'Hello, Myla?' It's a man.

I grip the phone with clammy hands. 'Y-yes. What is it, please?'

His words come out in one great rush. 'I need to talk to you. It's about your sister and Si Ashworth.'

It's him! The person leaving the comments on my blog. How did he get my phone number?

'What do you want?' I squeak in a voice that doesn't sound like me, a voice that's teetering on the brink of tears.

'Just let me in and I'll explain.'

My heart stops. 'Let you in?'

'Listen, I'm not going to hurt you, but I'm standing outside your back door.'

Oh my God. Oh my God, oh my God, oh my God!

The phone slips through my fingers and clatters to the floor. My throat closes. My toes start to tingle and I feel woozy. Don't have a panic attack. Don't have a panic attack!

The security light out the back is on, and I can see his silhouette through the glass door. He's really there. He's actually really there, standing just feet away from me.

'Myla!' he shouts.

'I'm phoning the police,' I scream, diving for the phone.

The door handle rattles. 'I just want to talk. I won't hurt you, I swear. Don't you want to know the truth, too?'

I pause, my finger hovering over the last press of the '9'. 'Leave me alone!' I shriek, pushing the key down.

The latch on the window moves up. It's not locked! The window isn't locked! A hand stretches through, scrabbles around, getting closer to the key in the door. I left the key in the lock. Idiot! Should I try to take it out? No, he'll grab me. I'm going to die. This psycho is going to kill me.

I look over my shoulder, towards the front door. I'll have

to run. I'll have to leave the house. All this time I've been cowering in my own home, thinking it's safe, but nowhere's safe. I can't hide anywhere!

I back away, down the corridor. The phone is ringing through to the emergency number. Come *on*! My eyes are still trained on that hand. He's found the key. He's turning it. Please, somebody answer. The lock is clicking. Come on, pick up! He's in the house!

'Hello. Which service do you require?'

'P . . . ' And then he's on top of me, bowling me to the floor, wrenching the phone from me. I squirm around so I'm facing him, and I scream, kick, struggle. A hand presses down on my mouth. I try to bite it.

'Calm down, Myla,' he grunts.

Calm down? Calm down! I raise my knee, going straight for his balls.

He puts both hands around my head, forcing it to be still. 'Look at me. Stop it. Look at me. You know me.'

I don't stop writhing or bucking, but I do fix my eyes on him, force myself to see him.

Oh.

My.

What?

I do know him.

It's Si Ashworth's nephew. It's Finn.

I was wrong. I was wrong the whole time. It *was* Si. And now he's sent Finn to finish what he started.

'Get off me!' I shriek, trying to strike him with my fists.

'Just wait. Listen. The guy who killed Asha, we both know he's still out there. I need your help to find him.'

The phone rings. We stop, stare at it. Finn must've hung up when he pulled it away from me.

'That's the cops,' Finn says. 'I'm going to tell them we rang by mistake. And you're not going to say anything.'

'You broke into my house, you arsehole!' I yell.

He shakes his head. 'Didn't have a choice, did I? You've locked yourself away so no one can get to you. I tried. I tried leaving you those comments so you'd email me; even tried going through that tosser, Jamie.'

'You did what?'

'I tried calling, too, but you never bloody answer. It's always your mum or dad.'

The phone is still ringing.

'We're on the same side. I didn't want it to be like this, but I'm running out of options.'

Finn lifts himself off me and grabs the phone. Then he takes a deep breath and says, 'Hello?'

I open my mouth, ready to scream. But it dies in my throat. What if he's telling the truth? He's the only other person – apart from Eve – who believes that Asha's killer is still out there.

'I'm sorry,' Finn says smoothly. 'My girlfriend panicked when she thought she saw a burglar, but it was just me. She's had a bit to drink.'

I scowl at him.

'Yes, of course you can talk to her.' He hands the phone over.

'H-hello?'

'Hello there. Can I just check that everything's all right?'

I look at Finn. He meets my eyes steadily. I don't like him. I don't trust him. But he might be my best chance of figuring this all out. I sigh. 'Yes. Everything's fine. I just had a bit of a fright.'

A pause. 'If you're being forced to say that, just say "yes" now. I can send someone over to you straight away.'

I make myself smile. 'No, honestly. It's a bit embarrassing. I'm really sorry to waste your time.'

I hang up.

Finn shuts the back door. 'Sorry for – you know. Coming in all heavy like that.'

'Coming in? *Breaking* in, I think you'll find.'

Finn's eyes drop. He's quite good-looking, but it's obvious that he knows it, which instantly gets my back up. Is he the one who's been watching the house?

'How did you know I was alone?'

'I saw your parents in town. I didn't know if Jamie would be round, but thought I'd risk it.'

I don't know whether to believe him or not.

'I *need* to talk to you. I'm desperate! You know what it's like, living with it, obsessing over it.'

'What do you want from me?'

'I want to know everything you know.'

'I told the police everything I know.'

He snorts. 'The police!'

I fold my arms. 'I'm not telling you a thing until you tell me what *you* know.'

'I know why that charm was in Si's house.'

My breath freezes in my chest.

I wait.

Everything rests on the pause between his words.

And then, reluctantly, Finn continues. 'My garden backs on to Si's place. He was out most nights, down the pub, stalking his ex, whatever. I used to hop over the fence, get his spare key from under a rock and let myself in.'

I just stare at him. I have no idea where this is going, what it has to do with Asha.

'We had to keep it secret, because of your dad. She was so paranoid. No texts or anything. She wouldn't come round to mine. So we met up at Si's once or twice.'

'Don't you dare!' I lunge forwards, my hand raised to slap him. I only just stop myself. 'Don't you dare try to tell me that Asha was going out with *you*. I know what you're like. All those girls. She wasn't one of your girls. She wouldn't.'

'She wasn't just any girl!' Finn spits, angry tears in his eyes. 'She was . . . '

I'm shaking my head, failing to hold back my own tears. 'No,' I say. 'No.'

But then I think back to the perfume she'd started to wear,

how she'd been staying out late 'with friends', and I know, as sure as anything, that Finn's telling the truth. He's even the type of guy she would've fallen for.

'Why are you only saying this now? Why didn't you come forward at the time?'

Finn sighs. 'I legged it. Thought they might find out about us, try to pin it on me. I slept rough for a bit, then found myself a place, a job in London. But when I heard about the appeal falling through, I came back.'

'You let your own uncle go down for murder?'

'I was sixteen! I was bricking it!' Finn bellows, smashing his fist against the wall. 'I don't need you to tell me what a shitty thing I did!'

I flinch, step away from him.

'I've lived with it for two years. I thought he'd get off. Look, I'll come clean. But I want to make sure they get it right this time. I really liked Asha. A lot. I want to see the filth who did this behind bars. So are you in? Are you going to help me?'

A trail of goosebumps winds up my arm. This is it. This is what I've been waiting for. The first chink of evidence that Si Ashworth didn't kill my sister, that her real murderer is still walking free.

12

Jamie

I lie on my bed, plucking the fat around my stomach. I've put on weight. Deffo. This isn't good. I'm losing my grip on my own damn body. I need to sort myself out, get control again. But if I don't eat, how can I help Myla?

Jesus.

Since she got my number, Myla's started texting. Just little things about what she's up to or what she's thinking about. She seems to like having me around. How can she stand to look at me when I'm like this, though? This flab. It's weak. Pathetic. Inside, I feel the leeches stir.

I need to get out, clear my head, but I hardly ate yesterday so I need to today. Couple of cream crackers. That's all. I can deal with that. I get off my bed, head spinning a bit, and start down the stairs.

Lil came over for dinner and poker last night. Ness cooked a roast, made me sit with them while they ate it. She gave me a plate of food. It was like a kid's portion. I chopped it all into tiny pieces, mixed it up, then separated it out again. It felt good, being around all that food, my stomach hollow and grumbling, but not eating. It's powerful, that kind of willpower; addictive. I put a chunk of beef in my mouth to try to keep Ness happy, but spat it into my hand when she wasn't looking and fed it to Ian under the table.

Ness and Lil giggled like kids as they told me what they used to get up to when they were younger. They had both drunk too much and Lil got a bit rowdy and starting telling dirty stories. She didn't get to finish the last one as she was laughing so hard she had a coughing fit.

Downstairs, I root around the cupboards for the cream crackers. I eat them quickly, so I don't have time to think about it, grab Ian's lead, give Alonzo a quick squeak, and wait for him to come running.

I'm going up on the cliffs today. Thought I could take some pictures for Myla. Even if her mum won't let me in the house, I can still text and email her stuff. Maybe if Jav sees that it's cheering Myla up, she'll let me back in.

On top of the cliff, I have to keep Ian on the lead. Feel bad for the little guy, but it's so windy I'm worried he might get blown over the edge. It's not a great day – the clouds make the waves look dark and moody. I try to catch some stuff on my phone, but it looks crap. I want to make it good, for her.

I'm trying to take a photo of this dog charging across the beach when my phone rings. I smile when I see it's Myla.

'Hi. All right?'

'Can you come round?'

'What's the matter?'

'I need to see you.'

'I've got Ian.'

'That doesn't matter. Can you just come round, please?'

'Yeah, I'm coming now.'

Twenty minutes later, I'm outside Myla's, heart thudding. I walked here too fast. But she sounded really upset.

Jav must know we're coming because she's holding an old towel when she answers the door. I take a step back while she cleans Ian up. I clear my throat, watch a snail inching across the path, pick at a bit of moss on the wall. 'I'm sorry, about before,' I manage.

'I know you meant well.' Jav's voice is clipped. 'And I suppose I shouldn't have snapped at you like that.' She sighs, drops the towel and gives me a long, hard look. 'Were you here last night?'

I shake my head. 'Ness had Lil over for dinner so I stayed in.'

'You didn't sneak out, come and see Myla?'

'I was with Ness and Lil the whole time, I swear.'

Jav's eyes soften. 'Myla's been acting strangely since last

night. I don't know what's the matter with her. She won't leave her room, won't eat. Will you try to talk to her?'

'Sure. Should I go ...' I point up the stairs. Jav nods and moves to the side of the door, but stops me before I go past. 'Just ...' She looks away, two spots of colour in her cheeks. 'Just leave the door open,' she says quietly.

I try to run up the stairs, ignoring the head rush. I just need to know that she's OK.

I knock on Myla's bedroom door, then suck in some deep breaths, try to fight back the dizziness.

Myla opens it straight away, hurtling forwards and wrapping her arms around me. OK ... I dunno what to do with my hands.

Myla pulls away and I follow her inside. She starts to close the door.

'Er – your mum said to keep it open.'

Myla nods once, but nervously looks at the open door. She moves a small stack of washing to the end of her bed so I can sit down. Her eyes are bloodshot, ringed with black shadows. There's something hidden under her duvet cover. I pull it out. A rolling pin. 'What the hell is this?'

'For protection,' she says hesitantly, like she knows how ridiculous it sounds.

'What happened last night? Why didn't you call me?'

Myla sighs and her mouth twists, like she's trying not to cry. 'I thought I was safe here. The one place in the world I thought I was safe, and he just ... broke in. Easy as that.'

I blink a couple of times. 'Someone broke in? Who?'

When Myla doesn't answer, I grab her shoulders. 'Myla, who?'

'Finn.'

I fly up, my fingers scrunching into fists. 'That bastard! Who the hell does he think he is? You called the police, right?'

Myla shakes her head, biting her lip.

'Why not? Why didn't you tell your parents?' My stomach spasms into this hard, hot ball of rage. 'Wait. Did he hurt you? If he touched you ...' I peer at her face, her arms, looking for any trace of a mark. 'Call the cops. If you don't, I will. And I'll tell your mum.'

I start to get up, but she grabs my hand. 'Listen. Just listen. We're not telling my parents. They don't believe me about Asha's killer still being on the loose, but Finn does.'

'Why?'

'So you know that Finn is Si Ashworth's nephew?'

Si Ashworth? I recognise that name.

Myla reads my expression. 'The man who was convicted for Asha's murder.'

I close my eyes, try to stop the room from spiralling. What is she saying?

'Jamie? Are you all right? You look pale ... well, paler. Do you want some water?'

'Yeah. Please.'

Myla gives me the glass from her bedside table. 'You don't look so good. Did you eat this morning?'

A memory. Mum, asking me the same question. *Him*, telling her I just needed to get over it, stop being such a girl.

'Don't fuss,' I snap, drinking the water in four gulps. 'So let me get this right. Finn's the nephew of the bloke who killed Asha?'

'The nephew of the man who was *convicted*,' she corrects.

'So what's he want from you?'

'He wants to find out what really happened to Asha, just like I do.'

I'm already shaking my head. 'I don't trust him, Myla. He's dangerous.'

'I know. I don't trust him either.'

'He only wants to get his uncle out.'

'It's not just that. He was seeing Asha in secret. He was using his uncle's place to meet up with her. That's why they found her phone charm there, and the fingerprints. It proves that Si Ashworth is innocent.'

I take a moment, think it through. 'It doesn't prove anything. How do you know Finn's telling the truth?'

Myla's eyes flash. 'I know my sister, and there *was* something different about her. She was keeping something from me. It all adds up.'

'Everything all right up there?' Jav calls up the stairs.

'Yes,' Myla shouts back. 'We've still got all our clothes on and the door's wide open, if you want to come and check.'

'Jesus,' I mutter, blushing.

Myla turns on me. 'Why are you so determined not to believe me? You're just like everyone else!'

'You say you want to get better. Well, maybe you need to work out some way to let this go. Don't listen to Finn, stirring up old stuff. He doesn't care about you.'

Not like I do.

'He cared about Asha.'

I snort. 'Myla, I've seen him around. He's a player.'

'He cared about her. I could tell. It doesn't matter what he's like now. She meant something to him.'

'So what does Finn want from you?'

'He thinks it might help if I . . .' Myla looks away, shudders. When she turns back, her eyes are too wide and her lip is trembling. She swallows heavily, opens her mouth, closes it, then tries again. 'If I . . . go back to Heartleas.' She lets out a sob. 'To the beach where it happened.'

I can't even think about the pain that's gonna cause her.

But Myla sweeps the tears away, takes a big breath and looks right at me. She's made up her mind. 'Finn says if I go back, I might remember enough to identify the killer. And I think he's right. This is serious, Jamie. Someone's been watching my house. They're probably thinking the same as Finn – that if I can leave, it might jog my memory. They're trying to scare me into staying inside.'

I bet it was Finn watching the house. I'm about to say so when I remember the rolling pin. Finn's already spooked

Myla enough. She doesn't need to get wound up about him hanging around all the time.

'There is no one watching the house,' I say gently. 'You said so yourself: you were being paranoid.'

Myla gasps. 'You think I'm crazy, don't you?'

I try to think of the right thing to say, but from the look on her face, there isn't one.

Myla doesn't give me a chance. 'Eve believes me. Why can't you?'

Argh! Bloody Eve! 'Because I'm trying to make you see there's nothing to be afraid of. I'm trying to help you get your life back. What does Eve do? Nothing. She can't even be arsed to come and see you!'

Myla pulls her head back, her eyes screwed up like she can't decide whether to be angry or upset. 'Makes me wonder why *you* bother coming to see me, when you so clearly think I'm deranged!'

'I don't think you're crazy, Myla. I think you're great.'

Crap.

Did I really just say that?

'You think I'm ... what?'

'You're all right, I s'pose. For a girl.'

Silence. Then her shoulder gently nudges mine. 'You're all right, too. For a boy.'

For a moment – just a moment – I think about kissing her. But then Myla sighs. 'I've got to get out of this house, Jamie.'

'Well, the first step would be getting out of this room.'

Myla laughs. 'You mean I can't barricade myself in here with a rolling pin for the rest of my life?'

I hold out my hand. 'C'mon. Think your mum's doing her nut while we're up here. I'll show you some pictures downstairs.'

Myla doesn't move. 'I'm scared,' she admits. 'If Finn can break in that easily, the murderer can too.'

'Not in the middle of the day, while me and your mum are here.'

As I get off the bed, I knock some of the washing over. I hesitate, not knowing whether to pick it up. But it doesn't look like there's any underwear so I bend down and grab some stuff. There's a green top with butterflies on it. 'Haven't seen you wear this one before,' I say, trying to hide the fact that I'm blushing.

Myla winces. 'Asha had one just the same. She was wearing it when she … when it happened. But they never found it. I accidentally wore it the other day and Mum freaked out. She won't let me throw it away, though.'

Myla takes my hand and lets me lead her down the stairs. I can hear the gaspy way she's breathing, feel how much she's trembling. Man, this sucks! She shouldn't feel like this in her own frigging home.

I don't want to, but I let go of her before her mum sees us.

'Ah, you've emerged,' Jav says, trying to look casual as she waits for us in the kitchen. 'Well done, Jamie.'

Myla heads straight for a cake box on the side. 'I'm starving,' she says, picking out a brownie.

I'm holding my breath, but Myla doesn't offer me one. She must be getting it by now. I watch as she makes herself a cup of tea, pours me a glass of water without asking, and heads into the living room.

I follow. I'm feeling slightly out of it, so I kinda drop down on the sofa next to her, much closer than I'd normally sit. I can smell Myla's shampoo. Some of her hair is resting on my shoulder.

Myla studies me. She looks worried. 'I really think you should eat something.'

Then, without warning, she shoves the brownie in my face, right up against my lips. I turn my head away, knock her hand back. Hard. Too hard. It makes this nasty slapping sound. Myla moves to the other end of the sofa.

'Sorry,' I say quickly.

'No, it was me. I don't know why I did that.'

I lick my lips, pick up a crumb. I haven't eaten chocolate in . . . I can't even remember. Maybe I could just have a tiny bit, off the corner. I dunno how much longer I can cope with that expression on her face.

'All right,' I say, picking up the brownie, breaking a bit off, nibbling it. It's . . . wow. My stomach flips. I dunno if it's with pleasure or pain.

'It's incredible,' I say, honestly.

Myla scoots closer, her eyes shining. 'Really?'

'Yep.'

She beams at me.

'Should've just waved that brownie under your nose. That would've got you outta your room.'

Myla laughs, then she turns all serious. 'So,' she murmurs. 'Step one: leave bedroom. Step two: whole wide world.'

'I'll help. We can do it slowly.'

'Thank you. I'm so glad you're here.'

I wanna help. Wanna be here for her. But we've only got a month before I leave.

When Myla goes to the loo, I pick up her phone from the armrest. I don't wanna do this, but I can't let it drop. It's been rotting in my stomach since Myla told me what Finn did.

I didn't protect her. I knew he was trying to get to her. Should've stopped him, told someone. Those leeches, they're loving it, how much it's eating away at me. I gotta do something.

Part of me is hoping I won't find anything, that she didn't swap numbers with him. He'll just hassle her more. She doesn't need that.

When I see him in her contacts, I swear. Then I feel this instant twinge of jealousy. I tell myself not to be an idiot – there's no way he's her type. But if Myla's right to believe him, Finn was her sister's type . . .

I copy his number onto my phone, put Myla's mobile back and get up just as she comes in. 'I've gotta go,' I say. 'Gotta get Ian home.'

Dunno why I said that, what I might have to get him home for, but Myla doesn't question it. She just pouts. It's cute. Really cute.

I promise to text her later.

I'm dialling Finn's number the second I'm out of Myla's front gate. Takes him a while to answer.

'Finn, it's Jamie.'

'Who?'

'Myla's friend.'

'Yeah?'

'I wanna know what the hell you think you're playing at, breaking into her place, scaring the crap outta her.'

He laughs. 'What are you going to do about it, you lanky streak of piss?'

Just before he hangs up, I hear something in the background: a musical beeping. Arcade. He's near the arcade on the pier.

I grit my teeth, take heavy breaths through my nose. I can't leave it. I need to talk to him, make him see that I'm gonna help Myla get out the house because it's what she wants, not because he's scared her into it.

And maybe if she goes to Heartleas Cove, and if she remembers, she'll realise that it was Si Ashworth after all, and she can let all this go.

Fifteen minutes later, Ian and I are on the pier, dodging kids with balloons and grannies with greasy bags of chips. Finn's near the end, chatting to the girl with matchstick legs.

She's leaning against the railing, looking at him like he's some shiny prize that's just dropped out of a slot machine.

When he sees me coming, Finn growls, 'Come 'ere,' wraps his hand round the girl's waist and pulls her towards him. I slow down, hesitate. How does he do it? So confident, cool.

But I shake my head, keep walking straight at them, ignore the fact that they're necking, and tap him on the shoulder.

They break apart and the girl rolls her eyes at me. 'Freak,' she mutters, before tottering off down the pier, her heels clicking along the boards.

Finn sniggers, watches her arse as she leaves, then glances down at Ian. I suddenly wish Ian was a Rottweiler or something but all he does is wag his tail and try to lick Finn's hand.

Finn lights a fag, takes a drag. 'All right. Say what you came to say, then you can sod off.' His eyes bore into mine – so cold, so intense.

'You know she's really messed up, right? You know she's terrified of being in her own house now? She doesn't think anywhere's safe. She should've called the cops. I still might.'

Finn blows smoke in my face, smirking when I cough. 'I'm helping her. We both want the same thing.'

'Is it true, 'bout you and Asha?'

In a second, the bravado drops and I see the truth all over his face – the grief, the regret, the guilt.

Finn moves suddenly, jerking his fist up like he's gonna

slam it into my face. I feel like I hear the crack of my nose breaking before he even touches me, so I flinch.

'You don't say her name. We're not talking about her. We're talking about Myla.'

'I just want you to leave Myla alone.'

'And I just want answers. She's got them. Locked in her head.'

I take a step closer. Finn might be ripped, but I'm taller than him, tall enough to look down on him. 'You need to stay away from her. I'll get your answers. My way. And only because she wants it too.'

Finn squares up to me. 'You need to back off,' he says in a low, menacing voice.

I don't move. I should, but I don't.

'I'm warning you. Get out of my face.'

'Will you stay away from Myla?'

'What are you going to do about it?' he says, shoving me. 'Pussy.'

I stumble back a couple of steps. I'm so fucking sick of people pushing me around!

I bellow, then charge at him, digging my shoulder into his. Finn resists, leaning all his weight against me. He punches me just below the ribs. Jesus! My body is firing with shock, adrenalin, fear.

Then we're locked together, pummelling each other. I taste sweat and blood, smell his smoky clothes as his arm is rammed into my ear. I kick out at his leg and he drops. We grapple across the pier, our limbs tangled as we roll danger-ously close to the edge.

Finn's much stronger than me. I'm getting weaker by the second. He's gonna kick the crap outta me. But as soon as I think this, I start punching even harder. No one gets to walk all over me. Not Finn, or *him*.

Then Finn's lifted clear off me, kicking and swearing and struggling. Some red-faced guy is pinning him to his chest. 'That's enough!' he bawls, right in Finn's ear.

I catch the look in the man's eyes. Can tell he wants nothing more than to start beating the hell outta both of us. I glance round, realise we've got an audience of shocked pensioners and bloodthirsty teenagers. I blush and look away.

The man chucks Finn onto the pier, more roughly than he needed to, then takes a breath, glaring at me. 'You're a bloody disgrace, the pair of you. Either of you say a single word and I'll arrest you.'

Arrest us? Ah, crap. I hold my hands up in defeat. Then I realise how much pain I'm in. My ribs are bruised, my lip's split and I can see my mangled knee through a hole in my jeans.

'Get up!' the copper spits, looking from one of us to the other.

'You,' he points to Finn. 'Go home.'

Finn gets up, still glaring at me, then slouches off into the arcade.

'And you,' the bloke points to me. 'I'll take you home.'

Course, he would know exactly where I live.

'Er, no. It's fine,' I say as I get up, pretending that I'm not shaking. 'I can walk myself back.'

'Come on,' he says, grabbing the top of my arm and marching me down the pier.

I sneak a glance at him. The cop looks strait-laced and stern, his face clean-shaven to within an inch of its life. Even his hair is all neat and nicely combed.

He doesn't say much as we walk. Fine with me. I could do with some time to figure out what the hell just happened. I mean, I stood up to Finn! True, I would've got my arse handed to me if the copper hadn't stepped in, but that's not the point. I never would've done that before.

Then the cop says, 'I don't know much about you, Jamie, but I know that boy comes from a very disturbed family, so I'll give you the benefit of the doubt this time. Otherwise we'd be having words about you helping my mother in her allotment.'

Wait . . . no way! Lil's his mum?

'Thanks,' I say. 'And thanks for – y'know – breaking it up.'

'Don't step out of line again,' he warns.

When we get home, I dunno whether to let myself in or ring the bell. But the cop steps up and raps on the door.

Ness gasps when she sees me. 'Jamie!'

'Don't worry, Ness,' the copper says. 'He won't be doing it again.'

'Oh, William, I'm so sorry. Thank you for bringing him back. Do you want to come in for a tea or something?'

'I'm fine, thank you. My shift starts at six.'

They say goodbye, Ness making him promise to stop in for tea one day to make it up to him.

As soon as the door shuts, she turns on me. 'Jamie, I can't believe you! How could you do something like this? Who were you fighting with? Why?'

I clear my throat, rub my hand across the back of my neck. There are bits of grit clinging to my skin. 'I'm gonna clean up,' I say, heading out the kitchen, ignoring Ness as she calls after me.

I stand under the shower for ages, but the water can't wash away the thought that I haven't helped at all, that all I've done is make Finn more impatient to dig that information out of Myla's mind. And I'm scared about how far he'll go to get it.

13

Myla

A floorboard creaks outside my room. I jump up from my bed, body braced to run, charge at whoever is lurking outside the door.

Mum. It's just Mum, dropping off some washing. She smiles at me, gives me a slightly puzzled look.

'Just waiting for Jamie to video call,' I say, pointing at my laptop, as if that explains why I'm poised to bust some serious karate moves on her.

The laptop starts to beep. I sit back down, answer the call, and speak into the microphone. 'Hello? Can you hear me?'

'Yeah, but I can't see you.'

I can hear seagulls screeching in the background. Jamie's on the beach. My heart lifts.

'Turn the webcam on,' he says.

'OK, just a minute.' As I'm trying to figure out how to

make it work, Jamie's face pops up on my screen and I gasp. His eye is half-closed and bruised, his lip swollen and cut. 'What happened? Oh, Jamie. You didn't go after Finn?'

He doesn't answer.

'Are you all right?' It looks so painful. I wish I could lean into the screen and touch him.

He shrugs, smiles his awkward, shy smile. 'I'll live.'

'You shouldn't have gone after him.'

I can't believe he did that for me.

'Do you want to see the beach or not?'

'Yes.'

He starts to sweep the camera around.

'Wait, stop! Pan out a bit, to the left. That's where Frank Mok kissed me. And Lauren was making out with Rob Dawson behind that rock.'

Jamie laughs. I can't see his face, but I know he's embarrassed. That's just the stupid sort of thing he gets embarrassed about.

'Myla, I still can't see you.'

'You don't need to see me. I'm just in my room. It's boring.'

'Yeah, but it's weird that you can see me but I can't see you.'

'OK, just a minute.' I finally work out how to turn the stupid thing on, then I grin and wave. Jamie waves back. Then his face goes red, like he's just remembered he's in public.

'What do you wanna see?' he asks.

'Anything, everything!'

Sometimes, when the wind blows from the right direction, I can smell the sea from my house. I open the window and let the salty breeze waft in, gulping down great breaths of it. Or if Dad brings fish and chips home on a Friday, I close my eyes and imagine I'm dangling my legs over the pier, sharing a chip bag with Lauren, stuffing my face with oily, soft mouthfuls, smothered with salt and vinegar.

Jamie's camera focuses on his trainers crunching over the pebbles.

'Bring me back a stone, or a shell,' I plead.

Jamie puts the phone down, face-up, so my screen is filled with the bright blue sky. I hear the rattle of him sorting through the stones, then he's back in shot, proudly waving a small, perfectly round, white pebble.

I shake my head. 'You'll have to do better than that.'

He snorts. 'Picky!'

Jamie puts the phone down again. There are a few cotton-wool clouds in the sky. I watch them break into little tufts that are swiftly swept away. I wonder where they go. Do they keep getting smaller, until they disappear, or are they blown far, far away? I wonder if any of them ever end up in Mauritius. I wonder if I'll ever make it back.

I've been once before, a few years ago, but I want to return, meet my extended family, see the places where Mum grew up. I want to walk along a beach again, feel sand squishing between my toes.

'Jamie, I want to see the sea.'

'OK. Just a minute.'

The camera jolts around as he picks it up. I get a pretty detailed view of the inside of Jamie's nose before he realises what he's doing, then quickly points it towards the ocean.

My breath hitches. My chest swells. My mouth goes dry. There it is. God, I miss the sea. The waves tumble and curl over each other, their endless song comforting and sooth- ing. *Shush-shush-shush*. I can almost hear the sound of our shusher, coming from a CD player in our bedroom, Asha's deep breaths matching its rhythm.

I drink in the infinite, steel-blue water, flecked with white foam, stretching out, out, out, until it licks the horizon.

'Jamie?'

'Yeah.'

'I want to go outside.'

'All right.'

'I want to go outside now. Today.'

Twenty minutes later, Jamie's standing in my living room, discussing how we're going to do this without Mum finding out. In my hand is a beautiful, pearly shell that he brought me. I stroke the creamy inside, trailing my fingers across the strands of pink and silver as they catch the light.

'I could think of some errand to get her out of the house?' I suggest.

Jamie bites a fingernail. 'You sure about this? I dunno about going behind her back.'

'Jamie, there's no way she's going to let me try again. And I really want to.'

He sighs, shakes his head. 'You're so stubborn,' he mutters.

'You'd better get used to it,' I reply, leaping off the sofa and rushing up the stairs. I nip into the bathroom, grab a packet of paracetamol from the cabinet, take out the pills, stuff them in my pocket and head into Mum's room.

Before I can open my mouth, she says, 'What on earth happened to Jamie? He looks terrible.'

'He just got caught up in something with a local boy,' I say carefully. 'Nothing serious.'

Mum gives me a long, hard look, then finally notices the pained expression on my face. 'What's the matter?'

I groan. 'I've got a massive headache and we're out of paracetamol.'

Mum glares at the empty box in my hand. 'Who's taken the last one and put the box back in the cabinet?'

'I don't know, but will you go and get some more, please? It's really sore.'

She puts her book down straight away. 'Of course I will. Wait a minute, I might have some in my bag.'

Mum reaches for her handbag and starts to rummage through several weeks' worth of receipts, crumpled tissues and shopping lists.

'This one is really bad. I think I need the super-strength pills.'

Mum places her hand on my forehead. 'Poor thing. I'll

go now.' Then she frowns. 'You and Jamie ... You'll be OK?'

'I think we can manage to spend ten minutes together without jumping into bed!'

As soon as I say this, I feel a little tingle.

'Myla!'

I follow Mum down the stairs and into the living room, dragging my feet and grimacing, just in case she turns around.

'I'll be as quick as I can,' Mum says, brushing the top of my head with a kiss.

The second we hear the door close, I stand up straight and fix Jamie with a look. 'Right, let's do this!'

'What do I do?' Jamie looks so helpless, it's actually quite sweet.

I smile, despite the fact that my stomach is churning, my heart palpitating. 'I don't know. You were great last time. Just keep telling me that it's going to be OK.'

He nods. 'I can do that.' Then he grins. 'You can do this!'

'We'd better hurry up. Mum will be back soon ... Wait a minute.' I grab my phone, fire off a quick text asking her to stop at the grocer and get me some bananas. 'That'll delay her for a bit longer.'

We go to the front door together. Just walking down the corridor makes my legs start to tremble. I swallow the fist-sized lump in my throat.

'Jamie.' It comes out as more of a squeak than an actual word.

'You'll be all right,' he says firmly.

We get to the door and Jamie faces me. He takes a deep breath, then his neck goes red and he grabs both of my hands. A thrill runs up my spine. I let out a nervous laugh.

Jamie unclasps one hand and, without taking his eyes from mine, reaches behind and unlocks the door. I gasp, but Jamie quickly says, 'You've done it once. You can do it again.'

I'm sweating. Jamie must be able to feel it in my hands. 'Just look at me,' he insists. 'You're safe, I promise.'

My legs have taken root in the carpet. I can't move them. Jamie's leaning back slightly, into the open air, but he's not pulling me.

'No one's gonna hurt you. It's just paranoia. You said so yourself. It's all in your head.'

Just paranoia? A wave of anger sweeps through me, dampening my fear. I take a step outside, almost pushing Jamie back. 'I'm – not – nuts,' I pant, as my chest starts to squeeze and my breathing becomes laboured.

A quick flash of a smile. 'OK, OK. Sorry. You're doing good. Really good. Another step?'

My eyes scoot around him, trying to see if there's anyone on the street.

'Don't look,' Jamie says. 'Just focus on me.'

'What? Look – at – your – ugly – mug?' I wheeze.

'Yep. Right here,' he urges. 'You're outside. You've been outside for about twenty seconds, and nothing bad's happened.'

He moves away from me, so he's on the second of the

three steps. There's too much space between us. I close the gap. I can smell his deodorant now. Sweet and slightly spicy. Not overpowering. It's nice.

Jamie grins. 'You're awesome, you know that?'

'Now – is not – the time – to be – flirting – with me.'

He blushes, but laughs. 'I'm not.'

'What's the matter? You don't like brown girls? Racist!'

Jamie properly laughs this time. He's so different from that surly boy who walked into my kitchen a couple of weeks ago. I wonder if this is the Ness-effect. Part of me hopes that some of it might be the Myla-effect.

'Why don't you try to guess my type?' he asks, a teasing smile on his lips.

'Busty brunettes?'

'Nope.'

'Please don't tell me it's blonde bimbos. I may have to banish you from my house.'

He shrugs.

'Well, who then?'

'Hey,' Jamie says quietly.

'What?'

'Look where we are.'

I lift my eyes from his face. Oh my … He was distracting me! I didn't realise what I've done. What *we've* done.

I'm standing at the gate. I've walked all the way down the steps, along the path and I've reached the actual gate. The pavement is about two feet away. Oh, God. I can't. I snap my eyes shut, breathe deeply through my nose. I feel the first flutter of panic in my chest. Then my stomach. Oh, no. No, no, no!

Jamie starts to pull one of his hands from mine. My eyes fly open and I grip the other hand harder. My fingers are stiff. Just how tightly have I been clutching on to him?

He reaches back towards the gate as he starts to say, 'Do you want to—'

A woman rears into view, yabbering on her phone. She's so close! I unlatch my fingers from Jamie's and bolt up the steps, almost tripping in my haste, my *need* to get back inside.

Jamie's quick to follow me. I hear the slam of the door behind him as I sink onto the sofa, my breaths steaming in and out. In. Out. In. Out. Fast. Too fast. I can't. I'm losing it.

'Myla?' he says. 'Don't panic. Please don't have another panic attack. Your mum will kill me!'

Despite the fact that I'm starting to get tunnel vision, a laugh burbles up. The panic recedes a little.

'Fight it, Myla,' Jamie says. 'Please.'

But it's clawing up my throat, drawing it closed, squeezing the air from my windpipe.

'You're inside now. You're safe.'

I'm inside. I'm safe.

I clear my throat, swallow. I can do this. It doesn't control me. This is *my* body.

I make myself breathe fully, stretching my lungs to their

capacity. When I let my breath out, it judders, but I'm getting there, reining it in.

A few seconds later, Jamie sighs. 'Thought you were gonna lose it.'

There's a comfortable silence while I get my breath back. I was outside. I really did that! I can't believe it! I spin round to face Jamie and squeal, 'I did it!'

He smiles and holds up his palm for a high-five. I slam my hand into his, grinning and giggling, breathless and euphoric.

That afternoon, I push the sofa to the edge of the living room and move the coffee table so I can do one of my exercise DVDs. I need to burn off some adrenalin. I'm still buzzing, long after Jamie's left.

Mum comes in when I'm doing lunges. 'Headache gone, then?' she says, arching an eyebrow.

'Yes thanks,' I gasp. 'Those pills were great.'

I wish I could tell Mum, wish there was someone else I could share this with. I miss Lauren. I hate that we've drifted apart. She was the last of my old friends.

I abandon the lunges and grab my phone.

Hi Lauren. Did you get my texts? Hope you haven't changed your no. Wondered if you fancied popping round? Would be ace to see you. Mx

I spend a while reading up on criminal cases where convictions have been overturned. I find and follow a few organisations on Twitter who seem interested in getting justice for innocent people, then send out a Tweet with the link to my site.

Then I log into Messenger. Eve's going to be so proud of me!

Eve51x: How are you doing, Saffy? I missed you today.

Saffy42: Sorry I wasn't online this morning. Been busy.

Eve51x: Busy doing what?

Saffy42: You'll never guess what happened.

Eve51x: What?

Saffy42: I went outside!

Eve51x: When? How?

Saffy42: Jamie helped me.

Eve51x: Why does Jamie think it's safe for you to leave? Does he not believe that Asha's killer is still out there? Does he think you're crazy, like everyone else?

Saffy42: He's just trying to help.

Eve51x: Is he? Or is he putting you in danger?

Saffy42: You know what? I'm getting really sick of people telling me what to think and how to feel.

Eve51x: I care about you.

Saffy42: Do you? Then why won't you come and see me? You know what my life's like, trapped in this house twenty-four-seven. You know how much it would mean to me, but you still won't come.

Eve51x: I don't want to fight. I DO care about you. Things are just . . . complicated.

Complicated? Perfect. Because my life is completely straightforward.

I log out, lie back on my bed.

My thoughts are all tangled and I don't even know how to start unravelling them.

I want so much to leave this house – this suffocating, air-less house, which seems to get smaller every day – but I'm afraid to.

I want to find those missing memories. I can almost feel

Finn breathing down my neck, trying to make me remember. But I'm afraid of that too.

I want to keep everyone happy, but I'm being pulled in way too many directions and I just don't know who to trust.

14

Jamie

'Myla's gonna try going out in the garden tomorrow,' I say.

Ness's eyebrows fly up. 'Really? That's fantastic. See, I knew you'd be good for her.'

'Not really 'cos of me.'

'Don't be so quick to put yourself down, Jamie. It *is* because of you.'

Do I put myself down too much? Thought *he* was the expert at that.

Ness smiles. 'I'm so pleased you two are getting on.' Then, annoyingly, she winks.

There's a bowl of dried fruit and nuts on the kitchen table. I know Ness has left it out for me. I see her pretending not to watch as I pick out a raisin, squeezing it between my fingers. Not much to a raisin. No fat. Probably mostly water. I eat it.

'So have you thought more about that therapist?' Ness asks.

'Nothing to think about. I already see this bloke at school.'

'All right. Well if you ever want to chat to me about anything.'

'Thanks,' I say quickly. 'So how was work?'

Ness talks about this old lady who comes into the post office once a week. Even though she doesn't drive, she always asks for a driving licence application. They all know she's just lonely and only comes in for a chat. Bit sad, really.

Ness gets up. 'I'm going to put dinner on. Do you want anything?'

She always asks. I always say no. It's my cue to leave, though. As I scrape my chair back, I glance down at the bowl of fruit and nuts and my stomach flips. Crap. I've eaten most of it. How did that happen? I've even eaten some of the nuts. Ah, man. That's disgusting. *I'm* disgusting. Inside my stomach, the leeches stir.

'Jamie, you all right, love? You look a bit peaky.'

I nod and head upstairs, leaving Ness chopping onions. As I pass the bathroom, I stop. Should I? I could undo everything I just did, get rid of all the guilt. Never stuck my fingers down my throat before. The leeches start to gurgle and belch.

I shouldn't go there. I've got enough crap to deal with. But I wonder what it feels like, how bad it is.

I stay there for a long time, just staring at the door. Then my phone buzzes. Myla? I pull it out of my pocket, my face cracking into a smile as I read a list of evidence she's gathered about her mum having a crush on Andy Murray.

I head back into my room as I write a reply.

Next day, I head down the allotment before I go to Myla's.

Lil puts me to work straight away. I'm soon up to my arms in soil. Lil's telling me this weird story about a chicken with a bag on its head. She's laughing so much, she can hardly get the words out. I can't really follow what she's saying, but I'm kinda laughing with her. 'Oooh!' she shrieks. 'I think a bit of wee just came out!' Then she just sits there, cackling. 'You'll get old one day,' she says, prodding me in the arm.

We're quiet for a bit. It's all right, weeding. Easy to get lost in, forget about other stuff.

I sigh as I pick out another cigarette butt, throw it in the pile with the others. 'Who's been chucking their old fags here?'

Lil mutters, 'Bloody kids.' Then she gives me a cheeky look. 'See those carrots? Before he died, my husband always got cross if I picked them too early, but baby carrots are delicious – so sweet. Shall we be devils and pick a couple?'

I shrug.

Lil looks up to the sky and calls, 'Sorry Henry!' Then she digs her trowel in and grabs a bunch of carrot tops. She leans back, putting all her weight into it. I almost ask if she needs a hand, but I forget how strong she is. When the ground suddenly releases them, Lil staggers back a bit, then shakes the soil off the roots. 'Will you go to the tap, give them a rinse?'

When I get back, Lil grabs a carrot and bites into it, closing her eyes. 'A baby carrot, straight from the ground. What more could you want?'

She grins, then turns back to her tomatoes, leaving me standing there with a bundle of dripping carrots. I plonk them on top of a plastic bag, pick one up and nibble a bit off the end. She's right. Tastes amazing! Myla would kill to get her hands on some of these. Wasn't she on about a carrot cake?

I ask if I can take some for Myla. Lil nods, then frowns as she plunges her trowel into the soil. 'Terrible business, what that family's been through. Hard not to lose yourself when you go through something like that.' Lil doesn't look at me, just glares at the ground as she turns it over with quick flicks of her wrist. 'No parent should have to bury their child. It's unnatural.'

Her daughter. She's talking about her daughter. Crap. What do I say?

'Yeah,' is all I manage. Think of something else, idiot! Say something comforting.

But Lil suddenly gets up. 'Just going to get the . . . '

She doesn't even finish the sentence, just wanders off.

I dunno what to do. Go after her? Never seen her like that before.

A few minutes later, she comes back, biscuit tin in hand,

and she's all smiles and laughs again, telling me this story about a bloke she met on a bench who had a bucket of fish-heads.

'You're sure about this?' Jav says later, biting her bottom lip. I can see how badly Myla wants to roll her eyes. 'Mum, honestly. I told you I want to try. We'll only be in the garden. If I freak out, I can be inside again in seconds.'

'I just don't know, Myla. It's been so long.'

'Exactly. Do you have any idea how long it's been since I've properly felt the sun on my face? If I carry on like this I'll be as pale as Jamie!'

I cough, trying to hide the fact that I'm laughing.

I look outside. It's well hot out there. I'm blatantly gonna burn.

Jav sighs.

'We're doing this, Mum,' Myla insists.

She's got her hair up today. I like it. Nice to see her face. She's got this little bit of toothpaste in the corner of her lips – looks really sweet. I wanna . . .

'Jamie?' Jav says. I jump. Jesus, if she knew what I was just thinking about her daughter . . . 'You'll keep an eye on her, won't you? You've seen her having a panic attack before, so you know the signs.'

'Yeah,' I say. 'Course.'

'Stop worrying, Mum. I thought you were going to sort out the food.'

Food? There's food?

Jav glances at me. 'Um – OK. Sure.'

She goes to the fridge and starts pulling out mini quiches, potato salad, strawberries, coleslaw. I look away, my stomach rolling.

I know what *he* would say. 'You're going to eat that. She's paid for it and you'll look like an ungrateful little turd if you don't eat it.'

I shake my head, focus back on Myla. She's staring out at the garden, chewing on her lip, just like her mum was doing earlier.

'S'all right,' I murmur.

Myla takes a sharp breath and looks at me like she'd forgotten I was there. 'Thanks,' she whispers, giving me this small, scared smile. 'OK.'

'Now?'

'While Mum's busy. I don't want her fussing. She'll make me more nervous.'

We walk to the back door. Jav's crouched on the floor, rooting around one of the cupboards and muttering something about paper plates.

'Like before,' Myla mouths. I nod, then switch places so I have my back to the door. She takes one of my hands and I reach behind with the other to open it. I don't take my eyes off hers. Those eyes ...

The second the latch clicks, Jav freezes. She pulls her head out of the cupboard slowly, then watches us.

I take a deep breath. Myla takes a deep breath. Jav is holding her breath.

The door opens behind me. Myla gasps. I squeeze her hand. I hate what this is doing to her. 'Just think about your tan,' I say.

She smiles. Takes a step.

'Er – and think about my tan.'

Myla snorts. 'What tan, freckle-face?'

Another step. I can feel her shaking, can see way too much of the whites of her eyes. I wanna tell her to stop, not to put herself through this, but she wants it. She *really* wants it.

'Think about . . .' I swallow heavily. ' . . . the food. Can't eat it inside. It's picnic food.'

We're outside on the step now.

'This is going to sound weird,' Myla says, 'but I haven't walked on grass for . . . years.' She bends down, runs her hand across it. Then we move outta the shadow of the house and the sun's blasting down on us and Myla tips her head back and the look . . . the look on her face is like nothing I've ever seen. I clutch her hands tightly 'cos all I wanna do is touch her, run my hand across the bottom of her jaw, down her neck.

I hear a loud sniff. Jav is standing in the doorway, watching us, smiling as she cries. 'Thank you,' she says quietly. I nod.

Myla's looking around now. I guess she's seeing bits of the garden she can't see from the house. 'What happened to Grumpy?' she says, letting go of one of my hands to step towards a gnome.

'He's getting old,' Jav replies.

'All his paint is chipping off.' Myla picks him up and runs her fingers over his cracked face.

We walk round the edge of the garden. It's weird, how new this is to Myla. She wants to touch everything, trailing her fingers along the fence, stroking leaves and flowers, picking up a rusty watering can. We stay away from the side of the garden that faces the road. The trees are tall enough to shelter us, but we can still hear the traffic.

Jav brings a picnic blanket out, laying food on top of it. I kinda think I should help, but there's no way Myla is letting go of my hand, and I don't want her to anyway.

'How you feeling?' I ask.

She gives me a weak smile. 'Petrified.'

I pull her over to the picnic blanket. Try not to think about all the food. I know Myla, though. If anything will make her feel better, it's food.

She drops my hand when we sit down, but makes sure she's close enough for our legs to touch. 'This may shock you,' Myla says, 'but I'm not massively hungry. My stomach's all churny.'

I nod. I know exactly what she means.

Myla picks up a strawberry, plucks the stem off and twirls it between her fingers. 'You eat, though.'

'I'm – er – still full from breakfast.'

Myla pauses, thinks. Then she says, 'You're never hungry, Jamie.'

She looks straight at me, waiting.

I shake my head. I've got nothing.

Myla sighs. I've disappointed her. But she brushes it off, smiles, and says, 'Ness is a bit of a feeder, isn't she? There was this one time when she was babysitting us and she let Asha eat three pieces of cake before bed. When Mum got home, Asha was bouncing off the walls. Mum was not happy.'

I smile. We're quiet for a minute, until Myla says, 'Hey, do you have any brothers or sisters? I never even asked you.'

I shake my head. 'Nope. Just me.'

'I can't imagine growing up without a sister.'

Myla's eyes darken. I search for something to say. 'Bet you were a right little madam when you were a kid.'

She laughs and lightly slaps my knee. 'Shut up. I wasn't. OK, well, maybe a little.'

The sun vanishes behind a cloud. Myla looks up and shudders. 'I feel strange. Like there's . . . too much space. It's odd because I'm used to feeling like there's never enough. But this . . . '

She takes a nervous breath in, then starts to bite the tip of her thumb. Her breathing's changing, speeding up.

'Wait,' I say, getting to my feet. 'I've got an idea.'

'Don't go!' she cries, grabbing my hand.

'I'm not. It's OK. Help me move this food.'

Myla stands awkwardly, like her legs are weak, but she helps me shift the food onto the grass. I tell her to sit back down, then I sit with her, dragging the blanket over both of us. It's dark underneath, and frigging hot, and it smells like damp grass and Myla's shampoo.

She gives me a faint smile. 'A den.'

'Yeah. I made one like this with my mate, Kai. We drank a litre of Lucozade each and burped the alphabet.'

'Jamie, don't be gross!' says Myla, pushing my shoulder. She's laughing, though, and her breathing's calmed down.

'This is great. You're so clever.' Myla leans in and pecks me on the cheek.

Oh . . . wow. God. She kissed me! That was . . . wow.

'Jamie?'

'Yeah?'

'You've gone bright red!'

'Shut up,' I say, poking her in the ribs. Myla squeals and squirms away, giggling, then she comes back at me, going for my waist. I twist out of her way, laughing.

Then the blanket is whipped off. What the . . .

Someone's looming over us.

I blink away the bright spots of light.

Shit.

It's Myla's dad.

15

Myla

Oh. My. God.

Dad? Dad's here. What's he doing here? Why isn't he at work?

His gaze flicks from Jamie to me. From me to Jamie. He doesn't say anything. He doesn't need to.

'Dad ... I ... '

Mum comes out, working a tea-towel in her hands like it's a stress ball. 'Ryan, what are you are doing home so early?'

He doesn't answer.

My stomach is clenching, my heart beating a quick, staccato rhythm.

'Jamie, why don't you head on home?' Mum suggests.

'OK. I'm – sorry,' he says to Dad. 'Nothing was happening, I swear.'

'Mmm,' Dad replies.

I turn to Jamie, an apology in my eyes. He doesn't look at me, just stumbles to his feet, then leaves without saying goodbye.

'Let's go inside,' Dad says.

I stand on trembling legs, start to follow him. 'Aren't you pleased?' I ask in a small voice, feeling the hot sting of tears and trying to hold them back. 'Aren't you pleased to see me outside?'

'Of course I am, Myla,' he says tightly, as he heads for the back door. 'I just wasn't expecting to come home and find you . . . like that.'

Inside, Dad puts his briefcase on the kitchen table, removes a box of Lemsip and fills the kettle. So that's why he's home early. He's not feeling well. This just gets better and better.

Mum hovers behind him, the tea-towel still gripped in her hands.

Tiny bubbles start to appear in the kettle. Dad stares at the mug. Mum and I stare at each other. The water starts to spit. This is excruciating! I wish he'd just let me have it. The scorching water climbs up the kettle walls. The hiss of the machine intensifies as the bubbles erupt and steam billows from the top.

Then it clicks.

Dad swings around to face Mum. 'I let you convince me of this on the understanding that you'd supervise them. Now I come home and they're doing God-knows-what under that blanket.'

I know he's not talking to me, but I can't help it. I have to wade in. 'It's not like that. He's just a friend.'

Mum adds, 'Myla needs a friend. Can't you see what it's doing to her, being stuck in this house?' She gives me a quick look, then lowers her voice, as if I won't be able to hear her. 'Most of her other friends have stopped visiting.'

I gasp and clutch my stomach, as if the pain is physical. She's right. I have no friends.

'That doesn't mean we should just let *anyone* into her life!' Dad bellows. 'He's obviously been getting into trouble. Did you see the state of his face?'

Mum raises her voice too. 'It was just a scrap. And Jamie's not just anyone – he's Ness's nephew.'

Jamie and Eve, they're all I've got. I'm a loner. A loser.

'I don't care if he's first in line to the throne – he treats my daughter with respect.'

'Oh come on, Ryan. They weren't doing anything. You need to put a little more faith in your daughter.'

My parents stop yelling at each other and look at me. For a second, I wonder why, then I realise I'm sobbing. Not quiet, ladylike crying. Big, gut-wrenching, noisy sobs.

Mum's at my side in an instant, pulling me close, stroking my hair. Dad's shoulders drop and he sighs. He puts one hand round Mum, gives her a hug, and rubs my back with the other, just like he did when I was a child. 'I can't have it,

Myla,' he says softly. 'Can't have him sniffing around you, in my own house.'

'Jamie's just a friend,' I wail. 'Please don't take him away from me!'

I turn back and look at him. Dad's eyes are red. 'You're my baby girl, Myla,' he says, his voice cracking. Oh God, no. Please. I can't bear to see him break down. 'You're my only baby girl.'

Dad clears his throat and turns away, tearing the top off the Lemsip packet and tipping the powder into his mug. 'I'm sorry, but he's not coming round again.'

Mum and I share a look. That's it, then. Matter closed.

I storm up to my room. I can't believe him! What right does he have to say who I can and can't see?

But he has every right. Of course he does. This is his house, his rules. And there's nothing I can do about it. There's no other way I can see Jamie.

I pick up a textbook and hurl it across the room, straight at the wall.

I hate this! I hate this house, this prison. But most of all, I hate the fact that I'm my own jailor. I hate that I'm doing this to myself. My life is difficult enough. Why do I have to make it harder?

And it's not just my life. It's Mum's too. She used to have a job, meet up with friends to play badminton, go out for drinks. It's not just me who's chained to this house.

I wish I could just remember. The answer is in here

somewhere, buried in my brain. I just can't reach it. If I could, it would unlock everything. I'd be able to leave this stupid house, get on with my life.

I call Jamie. 'I'm sorry,' I say as soon as he answers. 'I'm really sorry.'

'What happened after I left?'

'Big family fight.'

Jamie doesn't reply.

I sigh. 'Dad's always been overprotective. This is why Asha kept Finn a secret. But since she died, he's been worse.'

'What's this mean, then?'

I take a deep breath, feel my throat closing around the words. 'It means he doesn't want you to come around any more.'

Silence.

'Jamie?'

'We'll figure something out.'

My voice goes all high and squeaky. 'Really? How?'

'I dunno. I just . . . I dunno, Myla.'

He sounds so defeated, so sad, I can't hold back the tears any longer. I don't want to spend the next five minutes weeping down the phone so I say I've got to go, hang up, then let it all out.

I'm really not in the mood to talk to Finn when he calls later, but I answer, just in case he has some news.

He doesn't even ask how I am before he starts questioning me. 'Have you been to the beach yet, like we said?'

'What did you do to Jamie?'

'Don't start on me about that. He came after me. And he gave as good as he got. He's not the only one with a black eye.'

Really? Good.

'So – the beach,' he prompts.

'Two weeks ago I couldn't even answer my front door without having a panic attack. I'm not really up for a stroll along the beach just yet.'

'Well you need to try harder then,' he growls.

'Try harder? Are you actually serious? Do you have any idea what my life is like? Any idea at all? You've got a nerve, putting pressure on me when you're the one who's been sitting on your arse for two years.'

I hang up before he can reply. Who does he think he is?

When Finn calls back, I don't answer, then I ignore the ping of my phone that says I have a voicemail. He's not pushing me around. No way. If Finn had the guts to come forward in the first place, I wouldn't be in this mess, Si wouldn't be locked up and the murderer wouldn't still be out there, laughing about how easily he got off. Honestly, I don't know what Asha saw in Finn, apart from his stupid good looks.

One hour and several pieces of chocolate later, I listen to the voicemail.

'I'm sorry, yeah?' Finn says roughly. 'I just want to get

the bastard who did this. That's all I want. I never stopped thinking about it, thinking about her. It's been eating me up, you know?' He pauses, sighs, then says softly, 'You do know. You're the only one who knows.'

I close my eyes, feel my stomach flip. Finn's right. Whether I like it or not, we're in this together.

I cross the sand, towards the sea. I shed my shoes at the shoreline and wade into the cold water. I glance back, but can't see Asha. She's snug and sheltered in the hollow of the sand dune.

My breathing is deep and slow and regular. The sea breeze plays gently with my hair. My lips taste of salt.

I drift along the coast a little, watching the light seep from the sky. Seagulls swoop above me. I pick up a shell, examine it, then throw it back into the sea. I squidge some seaweed between my toes.

Then I hear something. Something that doesn't belong. I stop, heart hammering.

Asha is screaming.

I'm out of bed before I've even fully woken, stumbling towards the door, towards her room. But I remember, just before I pull down the handle. I remember and I sink to the floor, shuddering with stifled sobs.

I'm so sorry. Sorry I can't remember. Sorry I failed you. Asha, please forgive me.

Why, *why* can't I remember? It's like I'm standing on

one side of a chasm. I can see the start of the bridge – the memory of lying in the warm sand, content and peaceful with my sister, before leaving her to go paddling. I can see the end of the bridge – waking up alone, cold, frightened; that sickening dash across the beach to escape her attacker. I just don't know what happened in between. If only I could find the pieces, I could rebuild that bridge, reach the other side. I could end this.

I drag myself back into bed and reread my post on the 'Free Si' site. I tweak a couple of phrases, go over the facts, make sure everything's accurate. It hasn't had as many hits as I'd like. Maybe I should Tweet about it again? I'll think about that in the morning.

There's no way I'll sleep again tonight. I turn to my cookery blog, respond to a couple of comments, start to think about my next post.

But then I wake a few hours later, my laptop balanced on my chest. It's 7 a.m. and I can hear the scrape of cutlery as Mum and Dad eat breakfast.

I approach Dad with caution. His nose is all red, his eyes puffy.

'How are you?' I ask, hoping he'll admit that he over-reacted yesterday, that Jamie can come round, providing we're properly supervised.

He gives me a weak smile. 'Not so great. I'm going to go in, though – can't let the project fall behind.'

'If you're not well, you should be resting,' Mum scolds.

Dad ignores her and asks how I am.

I shrug. I'm not making this easy for him.

'I see. You're still sore with me about yesterday.'

I nod.

'I've lost one daughter,' he says, as if that explains everything, as if I don't already know.

I give him an icy look. 'If I was a normal teenager, I'd be out all the time, and you wouldn't have any say about who I could or couldn't see. Just because I'm stuck in here doesn't mean you can control me.'

'It's only because he loves you,' Mum says. 'You can't begrudge him that.'

Dad coughs. 'I want you to understand, Myla, to see this from my point of view.'

'Then please explain how stopping me from seeing one of my only friends makes this better for anyone.'

'I'm just trying to protect you.'

I sigh, fold my arms.

Dad looks away, his eyes misting over. 'I should've protected her.'

My heart judders. 'What?' I ask in a wavering voice. 'You couldn't have done any more to protect her.'

'She was my responsibility,' he says in a voice thick with tears. 'Just as you are.'

I reach for his hand. 'Dad, you have no reason to feel guilty. If anyone should, it's me.'

Mum puts her cup down so fast it almost smashes on the work surface. Dad just stares at me, his skin pale and pinched.

Tears trail down my cheeks as I struggle to choke out everything I want to say, everything that's been swilling inside me for so long. 'I'm sorry that I didn't fight for her, that I ran and hid. I'm sorry that I'm the one who's left, and not her.'

Dad's on his feet in seconds, moving around the table towards me. Mum follows.

'You listen to me,' Dad says, taking my face in both hands and gently pulling it round to look at him. 'Don't you ever – *ever* be sorry for any of that. Do you hear me?'

I can't nod. I just look at him, wide-eyed.

'If you had tried to fight, we might have lost both daughters.'

Behind me, Mum lets out this huge, gaspy sob.

'And that could not have happened. Because it would have killed us, Myla.'

Mum's hand is on the back of my neck. 'You have nothing to feel guilty about, *either* of you. That man. He's the one who did this to us.'

'I miss her so much,' I cry, my shoulders shaking. 'Why does it still hurt like this?'

Mum crouches down beside me. 'Sometimes I still can't believe that she's gone.'

'She is,' Dad murmurs. 'She's really gone.'

As soon as he says it, something inside me rips, then again, and again, until I'm all shredded, until there's nothing left of me. I can't find myself among all the pain.

'We love you, Myla,' Mum says, cradling the side of my head with her hand.

'Don't you forget it,' Dad adds.

Mum steers my head towards her chest. Dad shuffles closer and puts his hand around her shoulders, completing a circle around me.

16

Jamie

The back door is wrenched open, caught by the wind. Drops of rain hit the doormat and a gale roars through the house like some demented animal. Loads of Ness's old letters and bills fly off the table and land all over the kitchen.

Ness stands on the top step, fighting with an inside-out umbrella. I get up to help her, but she fixes it herself, stumbling into the kitchen. I put my hands on her back to stop her from falling into me.

'God, Jamie. The weather! You'd think it was January, not the middle of the summer.'

Ness peels off her bright yellow raincoat, then goes straight for the kettle. As she fills it, I notice her hands are shaking. 'All right?' I ask, leaning round so I can see her face. No, she's not all right. Her cheeks are flushed, her lips pulled tight. 'What's the matter? Did something happen?'

Ness won't say anything until the tea is brewed, until she's sitting across from me. 'I bumped into Albie, one of the local characters, tonight. He's homeless, bit of a drunk. Mostly OK, but tonight he was misbehaving, shouting at some girls as they walked past. I was going to ignore it, but he started following them down the street and I think they got a bit frightened. So I stepped in.'

'Did he hurt you?' I ask, my fingers twitching.

'No, but he gave me a good mouthful. Shook me up a bit.'

'You should tell the cops. Call William.'

Ness nods, then heads over to the phone, looks up a number in her address book, dials and waits a few seconds. 'William, it's Ness. I was wondering if you'd like to pop over for that cuppa. Yes, I'm fine. No, it's nothing to do with Jamie. I just want a quick chat.'

Fifteen minutes later, William's standing in the kitchen, water rolling off his coat and dripping onto the tiles. He's staring at the puddle gathering beneath him.

'Oh, don't worry about that!' Ness says. 'Let me take your coat. Just milk in the tea, isn't it?'

William sits opposite me. Even though his hair is wet, it still looks proper smart. His pale eyes drift over the clutter like he's desperate to tidy it up. Ness plonks a mug on the table. William's lips twitch and he reaches for a pottery magazine to use as a coaster.

'How are you doing, young man?' William asks me. 'Managing to stay out of trouble?'

I shrug. 'Yeah, I s'pose.'

'Glad to hear it. As I said, that lad is a bad sort. You're best to stay clear.'

William and Ness chat for a bit about the weather, then he cuts to the chase. 'So what can I do for you, Ness?'

Ness tells William what happened. He nods and listens carefully, then asks if she wants to file a report.

Ness shakes her head. 'Call me soft, but I feel sorry for the poor man. He wasn't harming the girls. He frightened them, that's all. I just thought I'd let you know.'

'Well, I appreciate that. It's good to know what's going on. Thank you for the tea. You take care, Ness.' He gives her a brief smile and Ness sees William to the door.

It's rubbish not being able to see Myla. Apart from walking Ian or going down the allotment, there's nothing else to do.

'You're really missing her, aren't you?' Ness says the next day.

I nod.

'I'm sure once Ryan realises how upsetting this is, he'll come around.'

'She was doing really well. I was helping her, like you said. She was getting better.'

'I know, darling,' Ness says softly. 'You both were.'

We sit in silence for a bit, then Ness gets up. 'Will you take Ian out for me today? I've got a few errands to run after work so might not be back until late.'

'Yep, sure.'

As soon as Ian hears me pick up his lead, he gets so excited he starts to shake, sitting patiently in front of me while I put it on. I smile, pat his head, call him a dumb dog. I leave him by the door and head to the kitchen.

Myla told me about this mega walk. You go along a board-walk that cuts through a marsh. Keep going for an hour, she said. Then you hit this incredible beach: white sand, almost deserted, beautiful.

I wanna try it. I know Ian would be up for it. Poor dude doesn't get out much. But there's no way I can make it on three grapes and a low-fat yoghurt. There's a couple of apples in the fruit bowl. An orange. Some bananas. I haven't eaten a banana for over six months. But if I made it to the beach, I could video-call Myla. She'd be so happy to see the sea again.

I pick up the fruit. As I start to peel it, I think 'bout her smile. Ian patters through and starts nudging my knee. 'All right!' I say, pushing him off. 'Just let me eat this.'

I finish the banana quickly. It's ripe so it's pretty sweet. Nice.

Ian's not gonna let me hang around much longer, so we head out. Ness said it's cool to take Ian on the bus, so we catch one to this small fishing village ten minutes down the coast. He's dead excited. Can't stop his tail from wagging. Everyone on the bus makes a fuss of him. I blush and stare out the window. At least one of us likes being the centre of attention.

When we get off, the village is just like Myla said: a tiny harbour, a couple of art galleries and an ice-cream van. The boardwalk runs along this huge spit of land, with the marsh either side. I can see these massive sand dunes in the distance.

I keep Ian on the lead to stop him pelting into the boggy water, but he's still loving it. Makes me feel good, seeing how happy he is. Apart from Myla, I haven't seemed to make anyone happy recently.

The sky is so big here. I draw in a massive lungful of the air, all fresh and slightly salty, and it's awesome.

We go about twenty minutes before my legs start to ache. I ignore it, push on until my head begins to pound. Another five minutes and I'm feeling faint.

I glance back at the ice-cream van. Idiot! I could've bought something from there, a lemonade or something, in case I needed it.

'Sorry, mate,' I say to Ian, sinking down on a bench. 'We're not gonna make it today. Another time.'

He gives me this look, and it's like he's telling me I brought this on myself, that it's my own frigging fault I can't even do simple things like taking a dog for a walk.

Jesus. What am I on about? Am I really so down on myself that I think the dog hates me, along with the rest of the world?

For the first time in ages, I wanna talk to someone. Kai texted me a couple of days ago, asked how I was. I could call him. I reach for my phone, start scrolling to his number. My finger hovers over it. Should I? Me and Kai, we don't do this. We don't spill our guts. But he did say he was worried 'bout me.

I ring him.

'Jay, my man! How's it going?'

'Not bad.' I sound surly. He's gonna wonder why I bothered ringing. But he doesn't say anything, just waits.

'So there's this girl . . . '

I pause, wait for him to make some blokey comment, but there's nothing.

'And it was cool, hanging with her, you know? But her dad is strict and kinda freaked out the last time I was over, and now I can't see her any more.'

'Dude, that's rough.'

'And I just tried to take the dog for a walk, but I can't make it to the end, and I feel bad, like . . . I dunno . . . I keep letting people down.'

'Man, what you saying? You think the dog gives a crap about how far you can walk?' He puts on a stupid voice, pretending to be the dog. 'I don't give a shit about anything, Jamie, so long as I can eat, drink and hump.'

I snigger. 'Fool.'

He laughs back at me.

'So what's up with you?' I ask.

I hear him take a slurp of drink, then he starts talking.

I snort and roll my eyes when Kai tells me how Isma was

on a night out and handed in some keys that she found on the bar floor, only to get home and find out they were *her* keys. Then I crack up when he says he got such bad wind after one of Nana Bo's bean stews he thought he was gonna shatter a window.

By the time I hang up, that walk back to the bus stop doesn't seem so far.

I video-call Myla that night. 'Hey, you,' she says, her voice slow and heavy.

'What's up? Is it your dad?'

She looks away, then back at me. 'It's a long story. I'm OK, though.'

She doesn't look OK. God, I wanna be there.

'Dad's being so stubborn!' Myla cries. 'He can see how unhappy I am without you.'

'We can chat like this.'

'It's not the same. You and Eve, you're all I've got. Now I don't get to see anyone face-to-face.'

Eve. Something slithers through my stomach. Jealousy? Am I jealous of Eve?

'So Finn got in touch today. He mentioned that Ness had got caught up in something with a local homeless man called Albie.' Myla sees the look on my face. 'Yes, word spreads fast here. Is Ness OK?'

'She was pretty shaken up.'

'Apparently there have been a couple of complaints about

his behaviour, especially around girls. Finn's going to try to get me a picture, see if it will jog my memory.'

Just how much has Finn been texting her?

'Is he hassling you? If he's being too heavy, you gotta tell your parents.'

'But he's the only one helping me to find the truth. He's the only one who wants to know as badly as I do.'

She thinks he's on her side. But I'm on her side, too. Does she trust him more than she trusts me? The coil of jealousy wraps round me like a snake, tightening across my chest.

'Finn *really* wants me to come up with an answer.' Myla sighs, then tries to smile, changing the subject. 'What did you do today?'

I tell her about taking Ian on the bus. She laughs when I call him a traitor for switching seats because some old lady was making a fuss of him.

'There are some beautiful places to walk around here. I wish I could come with you.'

'Yeah. Me too.'

Myla smiles shyly. Then she pauses, listens to something. 'I think Dad's home. I should go.'

'OK. See ya.'

'Bye.'

I lie on my bed for a bit, thinking about that sexy smile.

My phone rings. I grin and pick it up. 'So it wasn't your dad, then?'

'Jamie?'

Shit.

I close my eyes and take the phone away from my ear, a finger hovering over the button to hang up.

'Jamie?'

God, she sounds so hopeful. I sigh. Put the phone back to my ear. 'Mum.'

She laughs. 'It's so good to hear your voice. I miss you. How are you?'

'OK. You?'

'I'm ... Yes, I'm all right.'

'Sure?'

She sighs. 'Well, Damian has been a bit stressed recently, but it's fine. All fine.'

'What d'you mean, stressed?'

'Can we talk about something else? Something nice. What have you been up to with Ness?'

'Not much. Walking the dog. Giving her mate a hand down the allotment.'

'Ness said there's a girl.'

'There's no girl,' I say quickly.

'OK. So have you been to the beach or the arcade?'

'A couple of times.'

'Why are you making this so hard, Jamie? I just want to talk to you. That's all I've been trying to do these past few weeks. I don't understand why you're so angry with me.'

'You know why!' I spit. 'You sent me away. Didn't want me around. You wanted it to just be you and *him*.'

She gasps. 'How can you say that? Is that what you really think?'

'It's the truth.'

'Jamie, sweetie. You've got to be honest with yourself.'

'Stop it. Stop talking!'

'You know it wasn't my idea for you to go to Ness's. And it wasn't Damian's.'

'Shut up!'

'It was your idea.'

I hang up. Then I chuck my phone at the wall. I wrench my T-shirt away from my neck. Hot. So hot! My hands are shaking, my breathing all heavy and weird. I retch. No warning. It just comes up. I leg it to the toilet, just about make it before I puke.

The leeches are having a field day, spewing up all their foul thoughts, all this crap that's been festering in them for so long. I'm selfish, a liar, a pussy.

I storm back to my room, pace the floor. I stop, glare at myself in the mirror. There's this skinny, red-faced ginger kid, so full of anger he looks like he's gonna explode.

I sink down on the bed, tears glinting in my eyes like shards of broken glass.

I blink.

And I see.

I see who I'm really angry with.

It's the coward staring back at me in the mirror.

17

Myla

I pop downstairs to say hi to Dad. I'm still glowing from the chat with Jamie, my heart thudding just a bit too fast. Is that normal? It wouldn't feel like this if I'd just got off the phone to Lauren. I sigh. I'm not even sure if Lauren is a friend any more; she's been completely ignoring my texts.

Things between Dad and me have been a little easier since we talked properly about Asha's death. I never realised there was someone else carrying around so much guilt. That damp cloak is resting a little lighter on my shoulders now.

I'm still cross with Dad about the whole Jamie thing so I only stay downstairs for a few minutes – enough time for him to moan about at least three people from work – before I slink back to my room.

I sign in to Messenger, then smile. Eve's logged in. I love that she's waiting for me.

Eve51x: How's my sweet Saffy?

I stiffen. 'Her' sweet Saffy? What does that mean? Do I want to be 'her' sweet Saffy? The more I speak to her, the more confused I feel.

Saffy42: I'm OK.

Eve51x: Only OK? What's up?

For the hundredth time, I wonder what it would be like if Eve could come over. Dad definitely wouldn't have a problem with that. I maximise her profile photo. There's a gap between Eve's two front teeth, a strand of straw-coloured hair dropping into one of her eyes. Her eyes shine as she smiles, perfectly reflecting her sweet, open personality. I imagine what it would be like to hear her voice.

Saffy42: Can we chat on the phone, Eve?

Eve51x: Soon. Promise.

Saffy42: I don't get why we can't now. I could call you tonight. We could be talking in less than thirty seconds.

Eve51x: I told you. I don't have a phone, Saffy. Mum took it away after I got that massive bill.

Saffy42: I'm just . . . I don't know . . .

Eve51x: Lonely?

Saffy42: Yes.

Eve51x: Don't be sad. I'm here. Always. You can tell me anything.

I lean back, close my eyes before a tear can sneak out.

Saffy42: Dad said that Jamie can't visit any more.

There's a pause before she replies.

Eve51x: I'm sorry that you're sad, Saffy, but maybe it's better this way.

Saffy42: Don't start, Eve.

Eve51x: OK, OK. I don't want to argue. I don't want you getting any more upset. I wish I could be there, give you a big hug.

Saffy42: I wish you could, too.

Eve51x: You'll have to imagine it. Picture I'm there,
wrapping my arms around you. I could stroke your hair.

The hair. It's always about the hair with Eve. I feel a shiver
at the base of my neck, like I can actually feel her hands there.

'Myla,' Mum calls up the stairs. 'Can you give me a hand
with dinner?'

'Coming,' I yell back.

Saffy42: I've got to go ☹

Eve51x: So soon? But we've only just started talking. I
want to make sure you're OK.

Saffy42: You're so sweet.

Eve51x: ☺ x

I'm just about to head downstairs when Finn calls. He
doesn't even bother to say hello. 'You're running out of time,'
he snarls.

'What's that supposed to mean?'

'It means I'm losing patience.'

'Don't you think I want to know as much as you do?'

'I'll do anything to find out who killed her. Anything. And

if that means I have to break into your house again, chuck you in my car and drive you to the beach myself, I'll do it.'

'Don't you dare threaten me!' I yell. He's already hung up, though.

I grit my teeth against a scream of ... I don't even know what. Fear, frustration, anger. God, what if he does break in again? What if he climbs up the drainpipe, creeps into my room? I stare at the window, my mouth dry. Nowhere is safe for me any more.

Should I just end it now, call the police and say he's hassling me? But if Mum and Dad find out I've been talking to Si Ashworth's nephew, they'll go mental. They'll ban me from using the phone, the Internet. I'll be even more trapped than I am now.

Should I trust Finn? He wants the same thing as me – to find out the truth. Asha trusted him. And I trust her.

The next morning, I lie in bed, staring at nothing. There isn't much point changing out of my PJs if Jamie's not coming over. I don't know what I'm going to do today. I'd become so used to my strange, solitary life, but now ... what? Am I supposed to go back to where I was?

I pad down to the kitchen.

Mum's at the table, nursing a cup of tea. 'Morning.'

I reply in a monotone, then pull a packet of pancakes out of the cupboard.

Mum raises an eyebrow. Pancakes are usually a weekend treat.

'Do you want one?' I offer.

She shakes her head.

I heat the pancake in a frying pan, slap it on a plate and slather it with golden syrup.

'OK?' asks Mum.

I nod, my mouth full. 'Mm-hmm.'

By ten o'clock I'm sprawled on the sofa, watching a chat show and munching a chocolate digestive.

I sense Mum loitering in the doorway. I crane my head over the back of the sofa and she says, 'Fancy making *mithai* today?'

I shrug. Years ago, the prospect of making sweets would've been enough to send Asha and me racing for the kitchen, fighting over who got to measure out the ingredients. 'Not today.'

Mum sighs. 'Well, you might consider getting dressed, Myla.'

'Why?'

'Because it's not good for you, spending so much time in your pyjamas. You need to do something, keep your mind active. What about the next post on your blog?'

I reach for another biscuit. 'I don't feel like it today. Why do I need to "keep my mind active"?'

'Don't pick a fight with me. I'm not the one who ...' She stops, lowers her eyes. 'I'm working on your father, I promise.'

I turn back to the TV. I know it's not her fault. But there's no one else to take it out on.

Mum heads upstairs and starts to potter. That's what she

does when she's anxious. She can't sit still, has to be constantly moving.

My eyes close. I'm feeling queasy from all the sugar, but sleepy. So sleepy.

Mum wakes me up by plonking herself on the sofa next to me. 'I've got an idea.'

'Whaaaaa?' I mumble. 'I don't want to get dressed. Leave me alone.'

'Myla,' she snaps. 'Listen to me.'

I heave myself up. 'Mmmm?'

'What if there was another way to see Jamie?'

'What?' I say, instantly alert.

'What if you met him somewhere else? A café, perhaps?'

My stomach tumbles and heat floods my face. 'Go outside properly?' I shake my head. 'Mum, I can't.'

She fixes me with a long look. 'How much do you want to see Jamie?'

'What about Dad?'

'Dad's not here every day to see how this is affecting you. He doesn't understand.'

'Dad's never here,' I say bitterly.

Mum gives me a sad smile. She knows that. She must miss him as much as I do.

'I thought you were scared about me having more panic attacks.'

'I am. But I'm worried about you, Myla. I can't watch you get depressed.'

I snort. 'I'm not getting depressed.'

'Really?' Mum eyes the empty biscuit packet on the floor, the crumbs littering the sofa.

'Mum, going into the garden is one thing. Getting in a car and driving to a place that'll be full of strangers, that's totally different.'

Mum rests her hand on mine. 'Jamie's had a big impact on you. I don't want you to lose that. I can pull the car right up to the kerb outside the house. You'd only have to walk down the steps and straight into the car. I'd be with you the whole time.' She taps my leg as she leaves. 'Think about it.'

I don't sleep that night. I'm hot and headachy, wriggling around the bed, flipping over the duvet, the pillows, trying to find a cool spot. Does Mum really think I could do it? I might have a panic attack in the café, and it's a long way to make it home if I do.

But Jamie. I could do it for him, couldn't I?

What does that even mean? I feel like he's different from any of the friends I used to have before. Special. Or is he just different because he's the only friend I have right now . . . the only one I can actually see, touch?

If I'd bumped into this awkward ginger kid at school, I'm not sure I'd have been drawn to him. I definitely wasn't at first. I didn't even like him. Do I judge people too quickly? God, I wish I could just sleep!

I need some water. I head for the door. As soon as I open it, I catch the sound of Mum and Dad talking downstairs. I check the clock. It's past midnight. They're not usually up this late.

Mum's voice is high-pitched, like she's trying to stop herself from getting angry. 'You're not seeing it from her point of view, Ryan. She's been so different since Jamie started visiting.'

'She's too young to have a boyfriend.'

I can hear Mum's sigh, even from here. 'How many times do I have to tell you? Nothing's happened. I would know.'

'I've made my decision, Jav. I'm sorry it's hurting her, but she'll live.'

'Sometimes I think you want her to stay inside for the rest of her life!' Mum snaps. 'So you'll always know exactly where she is, what she's doing. You can't protect her forever.'

'No, but I can try.'

Her voice softens. 'You couldn't have saved Asha. You weren't even there.'

'Exactly.'

Just that one word, all the resignation, the guilt, the grief, makes my heart shatter. Oh, Dad. Tears crawl down my cheeks, one after another after another.

'What kind of future do you see for her, Ryan?'

I close my eyes, breathe deeply. Mum's crying. Dad doesn't answer.

'Will she live here, with us, for the rest of her life? No

chance to go to university, fall in love, start a family. Asha wouldn't have wanted that. And I don't think you do either.'

Asha. She's right. Asha wouldn't have wanted this for me. I imagine her standing before me, that mocking smile playing around her lips as she puts one hand on her hip. 'Chicken,' she says. 'Stop hiding. Get out there.'

'OK, Asha,' I whisper. 'I'll do it.'

I turn and go back to bed.

Mum looks awful the next morning. She's drinking coffee. She *never* drinks coffee. Each time she takes a sip, she winces.

I pour some cereal in a bowl, add milk, and sit opposite her. 'I've decided,' I say. 'I'll try.'

She looks up, her eyes brightening. 'You'll try going to the café?'

'Yes.'

'When?'

'Today. Before I change my mind.'

Mum sits up straighter, puts down her coffee mug and grins. 'Are you going to call Jamie, set it up?'

I abandon my cereal and head straight for my room.

I have to wait ages before he picks up.

'Jamie?'

A pause. A muffled groan. 'Hi.'

'Did I wake you up, lazy bones?'

'Er – yeah. What's up?'

'I want to see you.'

A sigh. 'I know, Myla. I'm still trying to figure something out.'

'Well don't worry because me and Mum have a plan.'

'Oh yeah?'

'What about meeting in a café?'

'A café?'

There's a long pause.

'Jamie, are you still there?'

'How are you going to get to a café?'

'I'll work it out. I'm going crazy here. I want to see you.'

I take a couple of minutes to tell Jamie how we're going to make it work and which café we're going to, then I hang up and rush off to get ready.

I stop halfway through putting on my mascara. This feels like a date. I've never been on a date before. This is . . . this is massive! No, don't be stupid. It's not a date. Mum's going to be there. Definitely not a date.

But if it's not a date, why am I using my Bourjois lipstick instead of the Rimmel one?

I stand at the top of the stairs, take a deep breath. 'I can do this,' I murmur, setting a foot on the first step. 'I'm not hiding any more.'

Another step. My heartbeat quickens.

Another. My legs start to tremble.

I close my eyes, imagine Jamie sitting in the café, waiting

for me; that shy smile, the flushed face. I open them and charge down the rest of the stairs.

Mum's waiting for me in the hallway. She looks almost as nervous as me. 'I've brought the car round so we just need to make it down the path.'

I nod, swallow heavily. How am I going to manage this without Jamie?

'OK,' Mum says. Then, more positively, 'OK! Let's get a move on – don't want to keep Jamie waiting.'

She smiles tightly, grabs my hands, and backs towards the door. The second it opens and the warm air hits my face, I feel an answering flicker of panic. 'I don't like it!' I say in a voice that doesn't sound like mine.

'I know you don't. Look, the car's right there. Just a few steps away. Nothing can hurt you once you're in there.'

We inch along the garden path, my breaths growing more shallow with every step.

Mum frowns. 'We can . . . '

'Don't!' I say at once. 'Don't suggest that we go back. Don't give me the option. We're doing this.'

'I'm proud of you. You're doing so well. So brave.'

We reach the gate.

'Just a few more steps,' Mum says.

It's so much more than a few steps to me. If I go beyond the gate, it'll be the furthest I've been from the house in two years.

I glance up and down the street. There are a couple of kids

blasting out rap music from a phone. We wait for them to pass. Mum gives me a tense nod. 'It's empty. We can go now.'

'Go now,' I repeat, mostly because I can't get any more words out.

'Jamie's going to be so thrilled to see you.' Mum reaches behind her, clicks up the latch, and pushes the gate open.

We step forward. The car seems so far away. I feel sick, hot, faint. My legs buckle and Mum practically drags me to the car door, flings it open, and pushes me in.

Mum rushes around the car, then seconds later, she's at my side. 'Myla? Myla?' she asks, her voice high and anxious.

I can hear the noises I'm making, the scary way my breaths are steaming out, way too fast. I close my eyes, lean my head back and say, 'I'm OK. Just drive.'

18

Jamie

A café? Jesus. Myla will wanna eat something, will expect me to as well. She already suspects, but now she'll know what a freak I really am.

I stare into the shattered mirror. What if she sees everything? What if she sees what a wuss I am? She thinks I'm this brave guy who looks after her, makes her feel safe, but I'm not. I'm the guy who does a runner when things get tough. I'm the guy who can't man up and just tell his mum's crappy boyfriend where to go. I'm the guy who's so messed up, he can't even admit to himself that he chose to leave, rather than being kicked out.

What would she think if she knew it all? Doubt she'd still be so desperate to see me.

I wanna see her. I *really* wanna see her. But my stomach's

cramping, tighter and tighter. The leeches are twisting them-selves into knots.

Mum's sent another text:

Pls don't ignore me again. Speak soon? X

I hate this! Can't text to say sorry, ask if she's all right. *He* reads her texts. Caught him doing it once. He just smiled, put the phone down and said he was looking for someone's number. He's smooth. So bloody smooth. Mum doesn't see it, what he's really like. He's got one face for her, another for me.

If you saw him down the pub you'd think he's a nice enough bloke: bit of a lad, likes a laugh. That's what I thought at first.

He'd been living with us for a couple of months when it started. Just a little joke, mate, about your skinny arms or your red hair. Hilarious. Tried to play along, for Mum's sake. And she was giggling. So I thought, OK he's actually a bit of a dick, but Mum's into him. I can deal.

But then he ramped it up a gear. He's a clever bastard. Never did it when Mum could hear. He'd hiss 'weed' at me as I passed him on the way to the loo, or he'd wait until Mum's back was turned, grab the top of my arm and mutter 'pathetic'.

Mum said he's been stressed recently. What's that mean? Far as I know, he's always treated her really nice, but ...

No. He wouldn't. He loves her. Whatever he thinks about me, he loves her.

But what if he has started putting her down? What if,

now I'm not there, he's started on her? It would be my fault. Because I left. I left her with *that*.

I'm disgusting. I feel it in my stomach: the leeches spitting out great gobs of poison. I could puke it all out – the fear, guilt, shame, anger. I feel the acid rising, but I swallow it down. No! I'm not going there.

I pelt to the bathroom, slam the door behind me, splash cold water on my face. I've got this. This is my damn body and I don't want this. I don't wanna start puking.

A minute later, someone knocks. Ness? It's not Ness. It's *him*, pummelling the door. 'For Christ's sake, come on! What are you doing? Three hours in there won't change the fact that you're an ugly little runt.'

I lost it that time, flung open the door and went for him, arms flailing, scratching at his arms, his chest, his stupidly chiselled face. But he swatted me away, laughing. Like I was nothing.

I look at my pasty reflection in the mirror. 'I'm not nothing,' I murmur. 'Not to Myla.'

Ness is pacing the floor when I come out. 'Are you all right? You weren't sick, were you?'

'Almost,' I admit.

She nods slowly. 'You're a strong person, Jamie. You have a lot of willpower. If you decided that you wanted to, I know you'd have the strength to get better.'

I just stare at her. I thought I was OK, thought I had it all under control.

'I'm – er – gonna meet Myla in a café today.'

'A café! That's . . . Well, that's brilliant! Do you think she'll make it?'

'Hope so. I wanna see her.'

Ness winks. 'I bet you do!'

I blush, rub my hand across the back of my neck.

'And how are you feeling about it? Being around all that food?'

'She doesn't know.' The words just fall out my mouth. I take a surprised step back. 'Least, she has an idea, but I haven't told her.'

'Why?'

'I dunno.' I look away, think for a moment, then catch Ness's eye. 'I guess I don't want her to know I'm weak.'

'You're not weak, Jamie.'

I snort. I am. That's why I left.

'You have a problem, but that's not all of you, as a person. You're lots of other things. Lots of other good things. She sees it.'

I look down.

'I see it. *You* just need to see it.'

Ness moves in for a hug. I tense, but let her. 'Thank you for opening up to me,' she says.

I don't reply.

Ness pulls away. 'Right, I need to get to work. Text me. Let me know how it goes.'

*

Myla's not there when I get to the café. I look through the steamy windows but there's just a couple of old folk eating cake. It's a small, local place. None of the tables or chairs match.

I can't go in on my own. All those pastries, muffins, sandwiches. My stomach squeezes.

Will Myla wanna sit by the door, so she can escape, or in a corner, so she feels sheltered? Wonder how she's feeling now, where she is, whether she even made it out the door. Wish I could've been there to help.

I wait for a few minutes before a car pulls up. There she is! That's ... that's just epic. She's such a legend.

I grin, wave. Don't even think I blush. Myla waves back, but she looks scared. After a moment of standing there, feeling useless, I rush over to open the door for her.

The second I do, Myla throws her arms around my neck, pulling me tight. So tight I can feel the fast beat of her heart against my chest.

Jav gets out of the driver's side and stands behind me on the pavement.

'I did it,' Myla breathes into my neck.

'You're awesome,' I whisper.

We're so close. If I just leaned back ... No. What the hell? Her mum's standing right there, watching us, for God's sake.

Seems like Myla doesn't want to let go, though. She's pretty strong, for someone so small.

'You know you have to get out of the car, right?'

Myla doesn't respond.

I pull her hands away, take a step back. 'You coming?' I say, nodding at the door.

Myla chews her bottom lip. 'Can't we stay in the car?'

I shake my head. Take another step away from her.

Some bloke saunters down the pavement, walking between me and Myla. In the second I can't see her, I hear her gasp, then the car door slams.

Jav and I look at each other, then I go to the car and open the door again. 'C'mon. You've got this far.'

Myla crosses her hands tightly over her chest. 'I can't, Jamie. It's too much, all at once. I mean, even this . . . ' She points at the car. ' . . . is a big deal.'

'I know. But I don't wanna speak to you in the car. It's hot. C'mon.' I step away. 'Me and your mum are going in.'

Myla looks past me, to the café. 'Wait!' she says, reaching out. 'Don't go without me.'

I turn back to Jav. 'Do you wanna . . . '

She shakes her head, smiles sadly and says, 'You do it. I'll get a table inside. Sit where you like. I don't want to be a third wheel.'

I take Myla's hand and gently pull her outside. She flinches when a couple of girls walk past, giggling and shrieking. I just squeeze her hand and say, 'I'll look after you.'

Myla's pale, her skin damp. She gives me a half-smile. 'This better be the best damn cake ever!'

I try not to grimace.

We take tiny steps across the pavement. I turn away from Myla to open the door. She tightens her grip on my hand, but says nothing.

The door swings open and we step inside.

We're inside!

Myla's eyes are shining, her mouth slightly open, like she can't believe we're here, that this is happening. 'We did it!' she says.

'We did,' I reply, grinning.

We just stand there and stare at each other. Feels like every second since I met her has been steering us here, like this is the reason I came to Stratten.

Then someone opens the door behind Myla, nudging us out the way.

Myla grabs a chair close to the door. 'Let's sit down.'

Jav's sitting in a corner, smiling. Pretty sure she's crying too.

Myla glances at the counter. 'Oh my God, I'm so excited. Cake!'

My stomach flips. I clutch it.

Myla notices, frowns slightly, but just forces a smile and says, 'I love it here. It's such a cool place.'

I look around. The walls are bowed and cracked. They're covered with cheap prints of local beaches, sunsets, cliffs. There are proper old-school tablecloths and menus printed on flowery folded cards. It's pretty quirky. I get why she likes it. 'I can see you running a place like this one day.'

Myla beams.

When the waitress comes over, Myla orders iced coffee and chocolate cake.

'Just water please,' I say.

'Two spoons for the cake?'

'No!' I fire back.

The waitress gives me a look, then leaves.

Myla leans back in her chair. She's relaxing a bit, but I can tell she's still on edge. 'So this is weird, seeing you somewhere other than my house.'

'I know. But good weird.'

There's a shell on the table with packets of sugar in it. Myla picks one up and starts to twist it through her fingers. 'What have you been up to?'

I smile. 'Since I spoke to you an hour and a half ago? Well, I had a shower, got dressed . . . '

She rolls her eyes, smiles. 'Sarcastic Jamie. Not sure I like him so much.'

The packet tears and sugar spills onto the table.

'Oh, really? So how much do you like non-sarcastic Jamie?'

She glances down, then gives me this smoking-hot look up through her eyelashes. 'Enough.'

We say nothing for a couple of seconds. Then the waitress comes and plonks the plate in front of Myla. 'Drinks are on the way.'

Myla sneaks a look in Jav's direction, then shuffles her

chair closer so our knees are touching beneath the table. She focuses on the sugar, gathering it into a little mound, then pushing her finger into the top of it. 'How's Ian?'

'He's cool. Gonna take him out this afternoon. Have another crack at that walk you told me about, across the boardwalks.'

'Wish I could come.'

'Me too. Though that might be pushing it.'

She smiles, nudges my knee. 'You think?'

'Hmmm, not so sure I like sarcastic Myla.'

'Come on! You like any kind of Myla.'

'Really? Pretty sure of yourself, aren't you?'

Myla raises an eyebrow and takes a bite of her cake. I watch her as she sizes it up. 'Good?'

'OK. Bit dry. Maybe too much sugar. It stops the chocolate flavour coming through.'

The door opens. A pretty blonde walks in, holding hands with an Asian guy. They head to the counter and order. Myla puts down her fork and her eyes follow them.

They grab drinks in takeaway cups, then come back towards the door. The boy has clocked Myla and is staring at her. The girl hasn't noticed, though.

'Lauren?' Myla says.

The blonde stops, does a double-take. 'M-Myla?'

The boy recovers first. He smiles. 'Hi, Myla.'

'No way,' Lauren breathes.

'How are you doing, Frank?' Myla asks.

Frank. Hasn't she mentioned him before? Frank Mok. The guy Myla was kissing on the beach. My eyes narrow.

'I'm good. I mean, we're both good.' He looks at his hand, clasped with Lauren's.

Myla doesn't say anything for a second. Then she looks back at me. 'Sorry. This is Jamie. He's Ness's nephew.'

'Er – hi.' Lauren's got this long necklace thing on, and she's wrapping it around her fingers, tighter and tighter. 'Listen, Myla, I . . . '

'Have you changed your number?' Myla asks, nicely enough.

Lauren's cheeks darken. 'No. I'm sorry. Listen, can I text you later? We're catching a bus into town. Got to go, or we'll miss it.'

'Sure,' Myla replies, with a small smile. 'Have fun!'

'It's really good to see you out, Myla,' Frank says.

The second the door shuts behind them, the smile drops from Myla's face and she lets out this massive sigh.

I wait until she wants to speak.

'I didn't even know they were seeing each other,' she murmurs. 'I've missed so much.'

'Not jealous, are you?' I tease.

Myla giggles, then sweeps her sugar pile off the table. 'Hardly. I always thought she liked Frank, though she used to go out with this guy called Rob Dawson.'

Myla goes quiet for a bit, poking the ice cubes in her coffee and watching them bob up to the surface again. I hate how much she's hurting. I think of something to ask her, anything to keep her chatting. We start talking about books we've studied at school.

The bloke behind me orders a full English breakfast. When it comes, I turn my head away, trying not to breathe too deep. It's like he's chomping right next to my ear, though, making all these grim noises, and his breath reeks of meat, oily eggs, sugary beans.

Don't be sick. Don't let her see you like this. You're the strong one, remember.

I close my eyes. Myla's talking about some bread recipe she wants to try with sun-dried tomatoes, but I can't focus on what she's saying. My stomach feels restless, the leeches all shifting around. I start to sweat. Man, I can't even be around food any more. This is crazy. This is wrong.

The waitress walks past with a jacket potato. The cheese on top oozes with grease.

Shit.

I make a dash for the door, fumbling with the handle, mouth clamped shut.

Don't be sick. No. Don't!

But then I'm out on the street, doubled over, spitting out a stream of clear stuff.

Some woman steers her dog away from me, making a disgusted noise. I wipe my mouth with the back of my hand. I can't turn around, can't see Myla's face.

Why did I have to ruin things? We were having such a

good time. Stupid, Jamie! Thought I was in control, but I'm not. Not at all. I can't go on like this.

My face is flaming and I'm shaking. I force myself to look back.

Myla's hovering in the doorway, a napkin in her hand. She looks worried. Not grossed-out. God, she's sweet. 'You OK?' she mouths.

I shake my head slowly, move towards the door. As I open it, someone walks behind me, smoking. A trail of smoke follows me into the café.

Myla freezes. Her eyes go all blank. 'Oh my God,' she murmurs.

I grab her shoulders, try to make her see me. 'Myla, what?'

'Oh my God, Oh my God, Oh my God.' She's starting to hyperventilate, her breaths coming out far too fast, tears flying down her cheeks. She's backing away, further into the café, her legs folding underneath her as she collapses.

'Myla?' Jav asks, running over. 'What is it?'

But she doesn't answer either of us. Myla tucks her body into the smallest ball she can manage. Her nostrils are flared, mouth open as she gasps for air.

'Get her up,' Jav snaps. 'We've got to get her home.'

I just stare at her.

'Now, Jamie!'

I reach under Myla's arms, try to pull her up. I can't do it. Can't lift her. I'm still weak from being sick. I hear *his* voice: Weed. Nothing.

Jav barges me out the way, hoists Myla up and practically carries her through the café. I manage to dodge around them to open the door, but that's about all I can do.

Jav shoves Myla in the car, then races around to take the wheel. Feel like I should apologise for being so useless, for leaving her alone, for everything.

Myla's still staring into space. Her body is rigid. She's terrified. Paralysed. Her face is – it's like it's not even her face.

What the hell have I done?

19

Myla

I'm flying across the sand, my feet moving so fast they barely touch it. Heart racing, breaths heaving. Asha! What's happening? Please let her be OK. She has to be OK.

She screams again. My name. She's screaming my name. I'm coming, Asha. I'm coming!

I hurtle up the sand dune, the setting sun so bright in my eyes, I can't see. I can't see anything! I blink. Dazzling spots of light float out of my vision. There. Asha writhing and twisting, him struggling to control her. He's got a fistful of her hair – her beautiful hair – in his hand, and is using it to pull her whole head back.

No! I try to move, but my feet are prisoners of the sand, my legs locked. Move, Myla, move! But I'm frozen, cold tears streaking down my face. I want to look away. I can't watch this happen, but I can't wrench my eyes off them.

Then Asha sees me. 'Myla!' she screams.

Her voice sends a shot of adrenalin through my veins, releasing my feet. In an instant, I'm running towards them. 'Get off my sister!' I bellow.

I get close. Close enough to grab Asha's arm, to feel the last precious touch of her skin; close enough to smell his reeking, smoky breath.

Something thuds against my head. I careen sideways, almost collapse. The ground ripples beneath me; the horizon sways.

Asha is screaming, but she's so far away. I can't get to her. I'm losing her. Asha! My Asha. Stay. I need to stay for her. Stay for ... I need ... need to stay.

Can't breathe. My eyes are clamped shut. Open them. Open them now. He's here. No! God, no! I can smell him. He's in the car. His stink is all around me. Get out. I have to get out!

A screech of brakes. I jolt forwards, the seatbelt cutting into me. 'Myla, what are you doing?'

I look. The car door is open.

'He's here. I can smell him. He hurt Asha. He's going to hurt me.'

Someone grabs me. I fight them off, screaming, pushing, kicking. 'Asha? What have you done with Asha? Get off me, you bastard!'

My eyelids are stuck together. So heavy. I try to open them, letting in a tiny crack of light, then let them drop again. I like the darkness. The light is too painful. Everything is too painful. I need the nothingness again. I want the nothingness.

What's that? Voices. They try to pull me from the nothingness. Don't listen. Go back. Ignore them.

They won't be ignored.

'I'm not leaving!'

'How dare you? This is my house. I'll throw you out if I have to.'

'Leave him alone, Ryan. You can't blame him.'

'Can't I?'

'It was my idea. I couldn't watch Myla go back to how she was. Don't you see how much she needs him? She wouldn't have been forced to leave if you hadn't stopped Jamie from coming over.'

'Are you saying this is *my* fault, Jav?'

'For God's sake! What does it matter whose fault it is? What does any of it matter?'

'Shut up,' I try to say. Did any noise come out? I didn't hear anything. My mouth is dry. So thirsty.

I fumble for the glass of water that's usually on my bedside table. My hand collides with something. It crashes to the floor.

Suddenly they're all in my room, crowding around me, saying my name.

'Shut up,' I repeat.

One of them laughs softly. Jamie.

'Let me sleep.'

I roll over. Sink blissfully back into the nothingness.

*

A cool hand on my forehead. Smells like almond moisturiser. 'Mum?'

'Yes, I'm here.'

I open my eyes. It's dark. 'What time is it?'

'Early. Three in the morning.'

'What happened?'

'You went to the café with Jamie, remember?'

'Is he still here?'

'No, he stayed for a few hours, then left. Your dad promised to text him with any news. He was really worried.'

'Worried? He probably thinks I'm a freak.'

'He was worried,' she says firmly.

'He was sick. Is he OK?'

'He's fine. Try focusing on yourself instead of him.'

I struggle into a sitting position, my head thudding persistently. I try to focus on the door handle of my wardrobe, but it won't stay still.

Mum looks at me, her eyes full of questions she doesn't dare to answer.

'What happened after we left the café?' I ask.

She shakes her head. 'It was like you were hallucinating. You barely knew where you were.'

I gasp. I remembered! That's the first time I've ever remembered what happened after I heard Asha screaming. This is one more piece of the bridge. One step closer to crossing the chasm.

Mum is frowning at me. I can't tell her. Not yet. Not until I have something more concrete.

'Did I open the car door?'

Mum nods.

'While it was still moving?'

She nods again. 'I had to slam the brakes on, try to stop you, but you were confused. You didn't know who I was.'

'What happened then?'

'I drove you to the doctors', dragged you in, kicking and screaming, and they sedated you. I called your dad and we brought you home.'

'I'm sorry I'm such a pain,' I say in a small voice.

Mum smiles, runs her hand through my hair. 'You're not. What you did yesterday was incredible. Just because you went too far, it doesn't mean you can't try again.'

Dad appears in the doorway, wrapped in a dressing gown, his eyes bleary. He looks old and tired.

'You're awake,' he says, quickly coming to my side. 'How are you feeling?'

'Probably as bad as I look.'

He smiles and brushes my forehead with a kiss.

'I heard you,' I say sternly. 'Fighting with Jamie.'

Dad holds up his hands. 'I apologised afterwards. I was just scared.'

Mum gives him a look.

Dad sighs. 'OK. We're doing this now?'

I look up sharply. Too sharply. Pain shoots through my head. 'What?'

Dad says, 'Jamie obviously cares about you a lot. And he seems to make you happy.'

'And? So?'

'So he can come round again.'

'That's brilliant!'

Mum smiles. 'And I can give you a bit more space. You won't have to be supervised all the time.'

Dad's eyes redden. 'Since when did my little girl start growing up?'

I reach forward and pull him into a hug.

Mum gets up. 'Why don't you try to get a bit more sleep? If you're feeling up to it later, Jamie can visit.'

I yawn and snuggle back into the bed. 'OK. Night.'

'Night.'

The second they're gone, I reach for my phone. It rings for ages before he picks up, his voice muffled by sleep. 'H-hello?'

'Finn?'

'Who's this?'

'It's Myla.'

A sharp intake of breath. I plough on before he can speak. 'I remembered something. I went out today. I smelled cigarette smoke and it – it triggered a memory. The man who took Asha, I could smell cigarettes on his breath, on his clothes. It was really strong, like he was a heavy smoker.'

'You said before that he coughed.'

'Yes, it was . . .' I shudder. ' . . . this horrible noise. And his breathing was all rough and grating.'

Finn grunts.

'I thought you'd be pleased. I remembered something. It's got to help, right?'

'Right, so he's a smoker. That *really* narrows it down. You've got to try harder if we're going to find this guy. There must be more. Something more concrete. Something that proves Si didn't do it.'

'I don't have any proof. I've never had any. All I have is what I remember.'

But that's not enough for Finn. He wants the whole story – and he knows it's in my head. I just wish I could find it. I wish – more than anything – that I could find it.

'What if you did see his face, the killer, but you've blocked it out or something?'

'I didn't, Finn. The sun was in my eyes. And when I was up close, I was just trying to free Asha. He was tall, sort of looming over me.'

Finn doesn't answer.

I sigh. 'So you said you were going to find out more about Albie.'

'I'm trying to track him down, but he's a slippery bastard. He's disappeared. Did you hear what happened to that girl?'

'What? No. What happened?'

'He tried to grab her when she was just outside her house. Her dad heard her screaming, turned on the outside light, and chased him away.'

'And they think it's Albie?'

'Maybe. Guess that's why I can't find him. He's laying low or something.'

'This is all related. It has to be. What if he kills someone next? I can't take this!'

'You can. You will,' he growls. 'It all rests on you. You owe her this.'

'Don't. Just ... don't.'

'I need answers, Myla. We all do. You, me, your parents, Si.'

'No pressure then!'

'We need to find this guy. Fast.' He pauses, then says, 'I'm coming over. We're leaving now. Going back to the beach.'

'Are you crazy? It's the middle of the night.'

'I'm sick of waiting!' Finn yells.

Then he hangs up, leaving me staring hopelessly at my phone, heart sprinting, head reeling.

Is Finn really going to come? No. He wouldn't. Surely he wouldn't.

But if he's desperate enough to break in ...

I can just see Finn, grappling with Dad, pushing him away so he can drag me out of the house, bundle me into his car. Oh, God! He'd kidnap me. He'd actually kidnap me to get what he wants.

The police. I should call the police.

But if I did that, would Finn still confess to taking Asha to Si's house? No. He wouldn't trust the police to find the right man. We have to do this his way. Finn's my best chance of solving this.

I text Jamie. Are you awake? I stare at my screen for a few minutes, willing it to light up, but it doesn't.

I lie in bed, my eyes wide open in the darkness, clutching the duvet cover as I wait for Finn to start pounding the door, or for the sound of breaking glass as he smashes a window.

An hour later, I'm still in the same position, but there's been nothing. I take a deep, shaky breath. If he was going to come, he would be here by now.

He's not going to wait much longer, though. If Finn doesn't get answers, he's going to do something stupid.

I suppose I should try to sleep. I close my eyes, imagine I'm somewhere else, away from all this.

We went to Mauritius three years ago to visit some of Mum's family. There was this beach. Miles away from the touristy bit. It was just like the pictures: coconut trees, the turquoise sea so clear you could see straight down to the pearly sand. I'd wandered off, away from my family, and had sat on the shoreline so the sea was just tickling my feet. I'd leaned back on my elbows, tilted my face to the sky, and just breathed.

I can feel it now. The hot prickle of the sun on my skin, the soft scratch of wet sand against my thighs, the sea lapping at the soles of my feet, soothing me with its endless rush and fall, rush and fall.

Burning. I smell burning. Smoke. Cigarette smoke. He's here! He's in my room!

I sit straight up, whimpering as I scramble for the bedside

light. Come on. Find it! Come on! My fingers flounder, then find the switch. Light streams through my room, cutting away the darkness. Not here. He's not here. Of course he's not.

I don't want to try to sleep again. I check my mobile to see if Jamie's replied. Nothing. Guess he's not *that* worried about me, then. Should I call? Seems a bit mean to wake him.

Eve. I'll see if Eve is up. I know she doesn't sleep that well. She often chats to me into the early hours of the morning, then tells me to go to sleep, get some rest.

Saffy42: Eve?

Eve51x: What are you doing up at this time?

Saffy42: Couldn't sleep.

Eve51x: Bad dreams?

Saffy42: Yes ☹ Wish you were here.

Eve51x: Me too. Sending you a hug.

Saffy42: I want a real hug.

Eve51x: I know, Saffy. And, believe me, I wish I could be

there to give you one. So what was the bad dream about?
Want to talk about it?

I sigh. She's going to be cross, blame this all on Jamie.

Saffy42: Something happened today.

Eve51x: What? You OK? Are you hurt?

Saffy42: I freaked out a bit.

Eve51x: How so?

Saffy42: I had to be sedated.

Eve51x: God, Saffy.

Saffy42: I know. It's OK. I'm OK now. Just tired.

Eve51x: But you can't sleep.

Saffy42: Exactly.

Eve51x: What brought that on?

Saffy42: Don't be mad.

Eve51x: Hmmmm. What might I be mad about?

Saffy42: I went out again.

Eve51x: What? Where?

Saffy42: To a café. I went out to meet Jamie.

There's the longest pause. I catch my lower lip in my teeth and nibble on it. Come on, Eve. Let me have it. Just say something . . . anything!

Eve51x: I really don't think you should've gone out. You had to be sedated, for God's sake. Isn't it just safer to stay inside?

Saffy42: Why would you say that? Why do you want me to stay trapped in this house? I need to go out. I need to know the truth.

Eve51x: And you're willing to risk your own safety to find it?

Saffy42: I'm the only one who can do it, Eve. I'm the only one who has the key to this whole thing. It has to be me. I have to go back to Heartleas Cove, try to remember.

Eve51x: I can't believe you'd do anything so dangerous! Why would you listen to Jamie over me? You and I, we've been friends for longer. Are you really saying you trust him more than me?

I swallow heavily, tears shimmering across my eyes.

Saffy42: I've never even met you, Eve. I don't know who to trust!

Eve51x: If I were you, I'd be very careful about trusting him. This person is still out there, Saffy. I'm just trying to protect you.

Saffy42: Well you can't. And you can't control me, either. I can do what I like.

Eve51x: You can, but I don't have to stick around to watch you lose everything.

Saffy42: You don't have to 'watch me' do anything, Eve. You're hundreds of miles away.

Eve51x: I see more than you realise, Saffy.

My fingers freeze. A chill works up my spine, then tingles along my arms, leaving a trail of goosebumps in its wake.

20

Jamie

I lie awake, staring at the ceiling. That damp patch looks like it's growing. How long before the whole lot comes down, crushes me in my sleep? I'm being paranoid.

It's definitely growing, though . . .

Wish I had my frigging mobile. Must've left it at the café. What if Myla's trying to call? She might need me. What if something happened, and her dad texted, like he promised?

Wonder if I'll get my phone back. Bet some arsehole has nicked it. Hang on a minute . . . there's that app, the one that lets you track where your mobile is. Why didn't I think of that earlier? Idiot!

I jump out of bed, find my tablet. Minutes later, I'm logged in and looking at a map with a glowing red dot on it. I zoom in. It's at the café still. Nice. Someone must've handed it in.

Keep forgetting that this isn't London, that people actually give a crap here.

I check the video-calling app that Myla and I use, see if she's logged in. She's not. I send her an email, telling her I've lost my phone but I'll get it back tomorrow, and that I hope she's OK.

I lie back on the pillow. God, it's hot. I'm used to feeling cold all the time, but it's really hot tonight. I get up again, push the window open more. Lie back down. My throat's all dry. Forget it. Just forget it. Go to sleep. No. I can't forget it. I head to the bathroom, scoop some water in my hands, chuck it in my mouth.

What *was* that, today? It was like Myla was having a flashback, like she was reliving it all. That was worse, far worse, than the panic attack I saw. Thought she was gonna stop breathing.

I shouldn't have agreed to it, should've known it would be too much for her. For me, too. Didn't want her to see me like that. What a loser. Didn't realise I'd got that bad, that I can't even be in the same room as food without bottling it. What's she gonna think of me? Maybe she's forgotten, after everything that went down yesterday. She's got enough of her own stuff to deal with.

There's no way her mum will let her out the house again, no way her dad will have me back. Am I not gonna see her again? I can't even think about that.

OK, sleep now. Time to sleep. Can't keep going over it. Can't keep seeing that look on her face. Can't keep imagining what she went through, wishing I could've done something to make it better.

Stop it. Stop it! Just go to sleep.

The home phone is ringing. What time is it? I reach for my mobile. Damn, I don't have my mobile. Where's Ness? Why isn't she answering the phone? Ian starts to bark. Ah, man. Ness must've gone to work already. That means it's late. I meant to get up early, get to the café as soon as it opened.

I roll out of bed and stumble down the stairs. The second I'm in the kitchen, Ian's all over me. He's well excited, jumping up and trying to lick me, breathing his meaty breath right in my face. I push him off, stroke his head, tell him to stay down.

I'm too late for the phone. Ness's answer machine kicks in. 'Ness? Jamie? Is anyone there?'

I pick up the handset. 'Lil, it's Jamie.'

'Jamie, my love. Thank God! The smoke alarm keeps beeping. I think the batteries have gone. I've tried calling William but no luck. And I'm not supposed to climb ladders.' She sighs. 'Old age never comes alone. Think you could pop round, sort it out for me?'

'Yeah, sure. Be there in a bit. I just woke up.'

She shrieks with laughter. 'Oh, to be young again! I was up at five!'

She gives me directions – it's just round the corner. I hang up, find Jav's number in Ness's address book, and dial. Hope Ryan's left for work already . . . unless he's taken the day off.

Huh. Didn't think of that. I'm just about to end the call when Jav answers. I let my breath out slowly. 'Er – hi. It's Jamie.'

'Hello, Jamie. Are you phoning to find out how the patient is?' She doesn't wait for me to answer. 'Do you want a word?'

'Yeah. Please.'

Jav calls up the stairs, then Myla picks up another extension. 'Hi,' she says in a small, shy voice.

'Hi. You all right?' What kind of question is that? Course she's not! 'I mean, how you feeling?'

'Tired. Still woozy from the drugs, I think. I woke up early this morning and couldn't get back to sleep. They should've given me something stronger.'

Silence.

'Sorry,' we both say at the same time.

There's a pause. Then Myla says, 'I'm sorry you had to see that,' at the same time I say, 'I'm sorry that it happened.'

We both stop again. Laugh a bit.

'Why is this awkward?' Myla asks.

'I dunno.'

Myla lets out this shaky sigh. 'So I remembered something,' she whispers. 'When I smelled the cigarette smoke, I remembered something.'

'Yeah, I thought that was probably what happened.'

'The man on the beach reeked of cigarettes. All over his breath and his clothes. So I phoned Finn.'

'You did what?' I snap.

'I phoned Finn.'

'Myla, honestly. He's proper mental.'

'Tell me something I don't know. But he's the only one helping me find out the truth. Let's talk about something else. It's obvious that Finn and I are on our own with this.'

'No, I—'

'Are you coming round today? Dad says you can.'

'Really?'

'He's changed his mind. I suppose he wants to avoid a repeat of yesterday.'

Something lifts inside me. I think I'm grinning like an idiot. 'That's great!'

'So are you coming over?'

'I can't now. Gotta go over to Lil's. Sort her smoke alarm out. Then I've gotta go to the café, pick my mobile up.'

'You left your mobile?'

'Yeah, I reckon so. Didn't you see my email?'

'No. OK. So I'll see you later, then?'

'Yeah. See you.'

Lil's in her garden when I get there, kneeling by a flowerbed. 'How now, brown cow!' she calls.

I frown, shake my head. Haven't got a clue what she's on about.

She uses her trowel to point to the house. 'Please turn that bloody racket off – I can't stand the noise.'

'That's the point. So it wakes you up.'

She tuts and holds out a hand for me to help her up. I lean

back to try to take most of her weight, but Lil almost pulls me over. I always forget how solid she is. Strong, too. She's got this really tight grip.

'Come on, then. Come and sort me out,' she says, leading me towards the house. 'I don't know. You'll get old one day.'

Lil's chewing gum. Funny thing for someone her age to do, but she's not like other people her age. When I ask if she's got any more, Lil pulls a face. 'Believe me, you don't want this rotten stuff. It tastes like a mangy horse!'

I smile, shrug, decide not to ask why she's chewing it then.

'What's happening with Myla?' Lil says suddenly. Her voice sounds odd, strained. She catches the weird look I'm giving her and makes an effort to smile. 'I just feel out of the loop. Haven't seen Jav in ages.'

'She's doing well. I mean, she freaked when she went out yesterday but she's pretty stubborn so I reckon she'll keep pushing to leave the house.'

Lil doesn't answer, just opens her front door and lets me in.

It's nice inside. Beneath the smell of her perfume, there's something else – slightly stuffy – but I don't stop to think about it 'cos I'm so shocked by how clean everything is. I must've got used to the chaos at Ness's because it doesn't feel right. What if I drop something on the carpet or mess something up?

Lil sees me looking. 'William keeps it ship-shape for me. He's a bit of a neat-freak.'

'Does he live here?'

'God, no! But he's only around the corner.'

She opens a cupboard under the stairs, shows me where the ladder is, and gives me a new pack of batteries.

After a few minutes of struggling to get the case off, I manage to open the smoke alarm and ram the new batteries in.

We wait to see if it will beep again, then Lil sighs and closes her eyes. 'That's better. Now what can I get you to drink?'

'Thanks, but I've gotta go. Left my mobile somewhere and I have to pick it up.'

Lil ignores me, brews two mugs of tea, thrusts one in my hand and heads into the living room. I have no choice but to follow.

'Thank you,' she says, sinking onto a flowery sofa. 'It was driving me nuts. Well, nutt*ier*!'

I sit on a beige armchair opposite her.

Lil takes a sip and smiles. Her eyes almost disappear in all the wrinkles. 'So what do your parents do in London?'

'Dad's ... not around. Mum works in a school. Teaching assistant.'

'Lovely. She must enjoy spending so much time with children.' Then her voice tails off slightly and she murmurs, 'I know I would.'

Lil's looking at this picture on a bookshelf. Her daughter. Gotta be. She's a couple of years younger than me, with curly brown hair and a big, toothy grin. Man, it sucks. It really sucks.

'What wouldn't I give to have you back, my darling Beth,'

Lil whispers to the photo. 'What fun we'd have. I'd do your hair for you, just as you like it.'

Feels like I'm intruding. I clear my throat, try to remind her I'm still here, but Lil carries on. 'And I'd let you use my posh lipstick, just like I said you could when you were old enough.'

My hairs are standing on end. I gotta say something. Can't just sit here while she talks to the photo like I'm not here.

'I'm sorry about Beth,' I say.

Lil's eyes snap back to me. 'What do you know about it?' she snarls. 'Nothing!'

Then she gets up and rushes into the kitchen, where she starts to sob.

I follow. I dunno what I'm s'posed to do so I just stand there like a lemon while her shoulders heave. 'Oh, Jamie, I'm sorry.'

'S'OK.' I rest my hand on her back, then take it off again, blushing.

I wait till she stops crying, then Lil takes a deep breath and a giant gulp of tea. 'Well, it's a bit depressing in here. Blow that for a pack of cards. Nobody likes a coffee-pot face, do they? Let's have a tea-pot face instead.'

I laugh quietly through my nose. Not sure if I'm s'posed to laugh. 'What's a tea-pot face?'

'Like this.' And Lil shows me a weak smile. Then she starts telling me how she met her husband and that – the first time she saw him – she was sitting on a wall mending a hole in a pair of knickers.

After she finishes that story, Lil seems OK. I'm about to

get up and say I've gotta go when there's the sound of a key in the lock.

'Well,' Lil shouts in the direction of the door. 'Here he is! I had to drag poor Jamie round to sort me out.'

William steps into the room. 'I was on duty.'

I stand up. 'Er – well. I should go.'

'Are you still staying out of trouble, Jamie?' William asks, picking a hair off his uniform.

'Course he is. What kind of trouble do you think he's going to get up to with me?' Lil says, with a cheeky wink.

William rolls his eyes. 'I dread to think.' He stares long and hard at Lil's face, which is still a bit puffy and red. 'Everything all right?'

Lil nods. They share a look and his eyes swim with sadness, like he knows exactly what she's upset about.

His sister. He lost his sister. Just like Myla.

'I've really gotta go,' I say, almost tripping over the chair as I leave.

'Well, thanks for coming over, my love,' Lil says.

'Yes, thank you,' William adds. 'That was good of you.'

I say goodbye, step outside and drag in a massive lungful of air.

I check my phone the second I leave the café. A text from Myla's dad (short, sweet and to the point: She's sleeping), and a text from Myla at 3.20 in the morning, asking if I was awake. Damn! I probably was.

There's also a message from Kai.

Dude, what's happening with you and the girl? Isma's on about setting you up with one of her mates, but I think it's the one who sounds like a dolphin when she laughs.

I smirk and switch over to my call log. Five missed calls. All from Mum. Crap. What's the matter? I slip into an alleyway next to the café to call her. She picks up after only two rings. 'Jamie?'

My stomach scrunches up. Her voice is all gaspy, sort of desperate.

'Mum? What's up?'

'Why have you been ignoring me again? I've been trying to get through for ages.'

'Sorry. Lost my phone.' Even *I* know how lame that sounds.

'I just wanted to hear your voice. I miss you. Things have . . . not been great.'

'What do you mean?'

Silence.

'Mum?'

A shaky sigh. 'It's Damian. He's . . . different.'

No. NO! I was right. He's turned on her. My breath's coming out in angry snorts. 'Different how?'

'He's just been . . . I don't know . . . I must've done something to make him angry.'

'No, Mum. It's not you. It's him. What's he been saying?'

'He's just been putting me down a bit.'

I pace along the alley. My skin burns. I should go home now, sort this. But what about Myla? 'You should kick him out, Mum.'

'It's not all the time. And when he's nice, he's wonderful. So caring. I do love him.'

'He's no good for you. Tell him to leave.'

'You know it's not that easy.' A pause. 'Jamie?'

'Yeah?'

'When am I going to see you again?'

'In a few weeks.'

'OK.'

I close my eyes, lean my head against the fence. How does she manage to squeeze so much pain into one tiny word? How can I do the right thing for Myla, for Mum, for me? Any way I look at it, someone's gonna be let down.

'Listen, Mum. If you want me to come home early, help sort this out . . .'

'No. I'm fine. We're fine. Damian's just a bit stressed at work, that's all. It'll pass.'

'Mum, you should come here. Come to Ness's. Just tell him you wanna see me. You, me and Ness, we'll sort this.'

'Jamie, I can't. We don't need to involve Ness. Don't mention any of this to her. It's not worth worrying her.'

'Why?'

'Jamie, *promise* me you won't tell Ness.'

236

'Not until you tell me why.'

'She's never liked him. She's been trying to tell me for ages, but I wouldn't listen.'

There's a noise in the background. 'He's just got home. I'd better go.'

'Wait – Mum!'

A muffled voice – he's asking her something. She replies, 'Jamie.'

Now he's closer, so I can hear exactly what he's saying. 'How's the squirt? Has his voice broken yet?'

So he's not even trying to hide it from Mum now. Cocky bastard.

Mum laughs. She's faking.

I clench my teeth, feel my jaw lock.

'He still in Norfolk, or have they run him out yet? Didn't know they let gingers across the border. They've got enough to deal with – all those webbed feet.'

'I'd better go, Jamie,' Mum says.

'OK, bye.'

'Bye, runt,' he shouts. And then he kisses my mum loudly, right down the phone.

I hang up.

'Shit!' I yell, hurling my mobile against the fence. Then I lob my fist against it too.

21

Myla

Dad's got something to say. I can tell by the way he's staring into his cereal bowl, poking his cornflakes around. He keeps opening his mouth, then closing it. Come on, just spit it out!

Finally, as Mum takes a seat next to me, he says, 'I was wondering if we could chat about Myla's website again.'

I bite my lip.

'Someone from work came across it, Myla. If he can find it, it won't be long before a journalist does.'

I just about stop myself from saying 'good'.

'Can you imagine the headlines? How they'll rake over everything.'

Mum pales. 'Please, Myla. Take it down. I can't go through it again. All of them swarming over the lawn like locusts.'

My heart falters. I don't want that either. I haven't had

that many hits on the site. Perhaps it is all a waste of time. And – if I really can make it back to Heartleas, help myself remember – maybe it's not so important any more.

'OK,' I agree. 'I'll take it down.'

Dad lets out a massive breath and his shoulders drop. 'Thank you,' he says, getting up and moving round the table so he can give me a hug. 'I know I haven't been very present recently. If I'm honest, I've been throwing myself into work so I didn't have to think about everything else. And I'm sorry. I'm sorry I haven't been around enough. But I want that to change.'

'We've missed you,' Mum says.

'Just promise you won't start trying to cook dinner,' I add. 'Leave that to Mum.'

Dad looks at Mum. 'What's wrong with my cooking? You said you liked that curry I made on your birthday.'

Mum just smiles, kisses him, and hands him a cup of tea.

After Dad's gone, I pace up and down the corridor, my mind circling around Eve, the last thing she said. I know I'm driving Mum mad, but I can't help it. I need to clear my head, stop dwelling on how creepy it was. God, I'd give anything to just throw open the front door and go for a massive run. It feels like all my blood cells are vibrating.

'Why don't you do your exercise video?' Mum asks.

I shake my head. 'I've got a better idea. I'm going to make a cake.'

In the kitchen, I smack an egg against the side of the bowl.

It shatters and pieces of shell go everywhere. For God's sake! I *have* to stop thinking about Eve . . . but I can't.

I add some flour. It comes out too quickly, in one massive flump, and poofs out, peppering my top. I sigh as I brush it off. What did Eve mean about seeing more than I realise? Has she been lying to me this whole time? Or was she just trying to freak me out, punish me for listening to Jamie instead of her?

I stare at the mix in the bowl. I don't even know what I'm making. At the moment, it looks like a plain Victoria sponge. Boring. I know, I'll turn it into a green tea and lemon cake.

Maybe Eve has some way of watching me. Maybe it was her, standing outside my house that night. No. That can't be possible. It was a man. I could tell by his body shape.

I pluck a teabag out of the box. I wrote a blog about green tea when I first made this recipe. It's amazing to think that it started life as a plant in Japan, that someone picked the leaves by hand. I wonder what they were thinking, whether they were happy or sad, worried about money, in love, cross with someone. I wonder if they spared a thought for me, standing in a kitchen thousands of miles away, thinking about them. I tear it open and add the powder to my mix.

I trusted Eve. If I found out she was deceiving me, I don't know if I could handle it.

Jamie's always been suspicious of her. At least he'll still be here for me, even if she isn't. But that's getting complicated now. I was flirting with him in the café, and I'm pretty sure he was flirting back. It can't go anywhere, though. He's leaving in a couple of weeks.

I don't notice that Mum's standing behind me until she clears her throat. 'What are you looking for in that bowl of cake mix?'

'Answers,' I mutter. 'I just want answers.'

'Answers to what?'

'Everything.'

A pause.

I keep my eyes down. 'Jamie's got a problem with food, hasn't he?'

Mum sighs. 'It's not for me to tell you.'

'But you know. And I don't. How is that fair? I'm the one who's close to him.'

'Have you asked him?'

'I tried to. He just clammed up.'

I should've figured it out sooner. I'm too wrapped up in myself.

I look over my shoulder. 'I feel like an idiot. I've been trying to ram food down his throat since he got here. I'm surprised he came back.'

'He likes you,' Mum says with a soppy smile.

I find myself smiling back.

I return to the cake mix, picking up the zester and a lemon.

Mum comes up behind me, circles her hands across my chest, and pulls me close. 'Can I ask you something?' she murmurs into my hair.

'Mm-hmm.'

'What went on at the café? What did you see?'

I stiffen. I want to draw away, but her arms feel tight, like she's trapping me. 'What makes you think I saw anything? It was just a panic attack.'

'You were somewhere else. And you were talking about ...' She rushes over the next words like they're hot coals beneath her feet. 'You were talking about Asha.'

I swallow heavily. I can't lie to her, but if I tell the truth, it's going to lead to an argument. 'I smelled cigarette smoke and it ... took me back to that day. He stank of smoke, the person who took her.'

'Well I suppose Si Ashworth is – or was – a smoker.'

I break her hands away, turn around. 'Except that it wasn't Si Ashworth.'

Mum sighs. God, she looks so tired. This weird mix of guilt and pity rushes through me, dampening down my irritation.

'You just agreed to take the website down. I thought you were ready to move on.'

And then the anger's back. Hot and fiery and fast. 'I won't move on until the psycho who did this is behind bars.'

Mum shakes her head and I know exactly what she's about to say: head injury, blah, blah ... traumatic experience, blah, blah ... understandably confused. I stalk out of the kitchen before she can open her mouth.

'Shall I put this cake in the oven?' Mum shouts after me.

'Do what you want!'

Upstairs, I throw myself on the bed. I'm so sick of everyone doubting me. I feel so alone, like I'm stranded in this vast, dark ocean, and I can see everyone I care about on the shore, and I'm shouting at them, but they don't listen. They refuse to cross the murky, cold darkness to reach me – and it feels like I'm going to drown if I try to get to them.

Why does no one trust me? They think I'm crazy.

What if they're right?

No. I know what I saw, what I remember. I *hate* that they're making me doubt myself. I wish they had more faith in me.

Eve's the only one who's ever had my back, and I haven't got a clue how to deal with her now. Why did she have to go all weird on me?

I've never searched for Eve online. Never thought I needed to. I wonder why it hasn't occurred to me before. Maybe I was worried about what I'd find out.

Heart thumping, I grab my computer. My fingers are resting lightly on the keys, and are actually trembling. This is ridiculous! I just need to type her name.

I do it, then take a deep breath and skim through the results. The top one is her profile page, the one she initially used to contact me. Most of her friends are boys. I flick through their pictures, trying to ignore each twinge of jealousy.

A couple have written on her wall, telling her how fit she is. She hasn't replied to any. Why are there no photos of her with friends, no family shots, nothing apart from that one profile picture?

I go back to the search page, click on a few more links. It's not her, though, just some people with the same name. Is that good or bad? I'm not sure. I don't know what to think.

My phone pings. Eve? Please let it be Eve. Maybe she's realised how unreasonable she's being. Maybe she wants to take it all back, apologise.

It's from Lauren. I stare at the screen for a few moments before I open the message.

Can I come round?

I don't see why not. I'd quite like to know why she's been giving me the cold shoulder recently. Sure I reply.

Mum must've put the cake in the oven because the house is starting to smell of it when the bell goes.

'I'll get it,' I say as I run down the stairs.

I hover behind the door, heart thudding. Come on, I can do this. I went outside, for God's sake. I can open the stupid door. I struggle with the latch, my sweaty fingers sliding off it.

I paste a smile on my face and open the door with the chain on, just to check that it's her.

Oh my God. Finn!

I try to slam the door shut but he props it open with his foot, glaring at me through the gap.

'It's time,' he snarls. 'We're going now.'

Could he break that chain if he kicked hard enough?

Probably. From the look in his eyes, nothing will stop him. I feel sick when I think of what he would do to Mum if she got in the way. My chest squeezes and I blink spots from my eyes. Don't have a panic attack. Don't have a panic attack!

I try to keep the tremor from my voice. 'I'm not going with you. When I do it, it's on my terms, not yours. Now get off my doorstep before I call my mum.'

'Myla, *please,*' he says, taking a step closer. 'You've got to help me. I'm just trying to make this right. For my uncle. For Asha.'

And then – just for a moment – I see what Asha must've seen in him. I see a flash of the vulnerability he keeps so well hidden. I see how much he cares, how much she meant to him. I see his guilt, how heavily it weighs on him. And I understand.

I blink back tears, glance over my shoulder to check that Mum's not around and whisper, 'I will go back. But not like this. Just a few more days. I know you're desperate, but you're scaring me. Do you think Asha would've wanted that?'

Finn's face drops. My heart breaks for him. Me, Mum and Dad, we're not the only ones dealing with this, not the only ones trying to put their lives back together. He says nothing, just shakes his head and backs away.

'Who was it?' Mum asks as I close the door.

'Er – someone collecting for charity. I thought it might be Lauren. She said she's coming over.'

Mum's eyebrows shoot up. 'Oh, right.'

Ten minutes later, the bell goes again. I make sure I peep through the spyhole first, check it's really her.

Lauren seems surprised when I answer, but she recovers quickly and says, 'Is that cake? It smells awesome.'

I step back to let her in, turning my face away from the noise of the road, trying to stop my breaths from hitching.

'It's a green tea and lemon cake.' I think I sound normal, just about.

Lauren smiles sweetly. She's pretty. *Really* pretty. She has these big babydoll eyes, the smallest nose and an elfin face with a delicate pointed chin. She's clever, too, though she often tries to hide it. She says that boys find it intimidating.

We head into the kitchen. I half-expect Mum to be waiting to pounce on Lauren, make a fuss about her being back, but she's made herself scarce.

'So, you and Frank!' I say as I make her a cup of tea.

Lauren twirls a strand of hair around her finger. She always does that when she's nervous. 'Um, yeah. It just sort of happened. I hope it's . . . OK.'

I snort. 'We weren't exactly an item. I kissed him once.'

She gives me a look.

'OK. More than once. But it was years ago. We were kids. I think we only did it because we were the odd ones out in our oh-so-very-white school. Seriously, I'm happy for you. I haven't seen him in ages. He's hot now.'

Lauren gives me a quick smile. 'He's always been hot.'

I carry our drinks into the living room. Lauren perches on

the edge of the sofa, her back straight, hands folded neatly in her lap.

I roll my eyes. 'Relax. I'm not going to give you the third degree.'

She glances at me, then looks away again.

'It's OK, Lauren. I get it.'

I shouldn't let her off so lightly. She ditched me because my little world is no competition for everything else out there. I can keep up with fashion news by reading blogs, but I can't see the outrageous outfit Helen Burnett was wearing to the cinema last Thursday. I can see who's friends with who on social networks, but I can't chat about how sexy the new boy's accent is, or what Graham called Mr Scott in assembly in front of everyone.

'It was great to see you out the other day,' Lauren says.

Is that why she's here? She thinks I might be cured, that she might have a 'normal' friend again.

'It wasn't just me. Jamie helped.'

'So, you and Jamie?'

My cheeks redden. 'No. Not at all.'

Lauren raises a perfectly plucked eyebrow. 'Really? I saw how he was looking at you.'

'There was no looking!'

Lauren lets me squirm for a few moments, until I burst out with, 'OK, so I really like him!'

She laughs. I laugh back. And for a second, it almost feels comfortable again. Until the silence settles.

Lauren's staring at the carpet. I ask her what's new. She looks up and her eyes widen. That's why she's here. She's got some juicy piece of gossip. Seriously, I couldn't care less if Caitlin has got a new piercing or if Jonas got Gemma pregnant.

Lauren takes a deep breath, lets the moment stretch out a little longer. Then she says, 'Some creepy guy chased me the other night.'

And, just like that, she has all my attention. 'What? Who?'

'I don't know. Me and Flo were walking back from the bus stop on Friday night and we cut through the park. Stupid, really.'

'So what happened?'

'He just came at us, charging down the path, shouting. Proper mental.'

'Did you see his face?'

'No. I was too busy running. He actually grabbed Flo's arm, but she managed to push him away. He was really scary, Myla.'

'I bet.'

'We made it to the road, then he gave up.'

'Any idea who it was?'

Lauren shrugs. 'Everyone thinks it's Albie. A few people went after him.'

My skin goes cold. 'To do what?'

Lauren picks at some chipped nail polish. 'I don't know. Get him to confess?'

Now I'm the one who's sitting on the edge of the sofa. 'And?'

'And, they couldn't find him.'

'So what you're saying is, there's some weirdo out there stalking girls?'

Lauren gives me a small, scared smile. 'I'm not allowed out on my own at night. Not even if Frank is with me.'

'So what are the police doing? Do they think it's connected to Asha's death?'

Lauren gives me a strange look. 'No. Why would it be?'

I shake my head. I'm not going over this again. 'Never mind. So what's happening? What are they doing about it?'

'They're looking for Albie, obviously, and there's more of them patrolling the streets. You see them all the time, even in daylight.' Lauren leans forward. 'You know William? He was the one who got there first when we called the police. He was so brave, checking out the park, making sure we were safe. He's not bad – you know – for an older guy.'

But I'm barely listening.

This is him. It has to be. I don't know if it's Albie or not, but this must be the guy who killed Asha. The same one who's been watching my house. If I don't do something soon, if I don't get out, make myself remember something, *anything*, how long is it going to be before he kills again?

22

Jamie

Ian goes mental when I get home. Tail going like a windscreen wiper in a hailstorm, barking his head off, trying to jump up. I ignore him, go straight for the freezer. No ice cubes. No peas. Frozen onion rings it is, then. I slump at the kitchen table, look hard at my mangled knuckles. Damn. Can't believe I did that. Can't believe I was even strong enough. I almost punched a hole through that fence. Wouldn't have been able to do that two months ago. No way.

I read Mum's last message again.

You OK? Don't worry. I'm fine. X

Don't worry? Like hell I'm not gonna worry. I should go home. Now. Just pack my stuff, write Ness a note, and go. Can't let Mum stay with that dickhead. It's one thing to pick on me, but it's another to start on Mum. Someone needs to tell him where to go, and Mum won't do it. She's not strong enough.

What am I gonna do about it, though? He won't listen if I try to talk.

I look at my scraggly arms. I might be stronger than I was, but I'm still weak, pathetic. He'd knock me out in seconds.

I hate that he thinks he can push me around. I gotta keep eating; gotta get the puking under control. Ness is right. If I can force myself not to eat, I can force myself to get better. For Mum. For Myla. For me.

Why did I come last in that list?

God, I'm such a mess. I need to talk to someone.

Myla. I'll call Myla.

Three seconds later, the phone's ringing.

'Hello?'

It's unreal how much better I feel after she's picked up, like just her voice is enough. I let out this heavy, shaky breath.

'Hello? Jamie?'

'Hi.'

'What's wrong?'

I pause. Can't get any more words out.

'Jamie, what is it?'

I open my mouth, and suddenly it's all coming out, all this crap about *him*, about how I abandoned Mum, how I dunno how to make it right. And as I'm saying it, what I should be thinking is how Myla's gonna drop me now she knows what a coward I am, but what I'm actually thinking is how awesome it is to tell someone. And she just listens. Doesn't say a word until I'm done.

'I – don't really know what to say. I'm so sorry. I had no idea you had all that going on. You can't blame yourself for her poor choices, though. And really, what would you be able to do? Like you say, it's not as if you could beat him up, kick him out. It has to come from her. Your mum's got to be the one to stand up to him.'

'But how long do I wait for her to do that? The longer it goes on, the harder it is.'

'God, Jamie, I don't know. I'm sorry. I don't know what the answer is.'

'I wanna see you,' I say straight away.

Myla laughs. 'I want to see you too. Actually, I was wondering if you wanted to meet on the cliffs instead of coming here. Mum can drive me up there.'

'I'm not sure 'bout that.'

'Listen, I just spoke to Lauren. She was chased by someone in the park the other night. It's him. I know it is. I have to do something, get out and try to remember more. If he kills again ...'

'You can't put that on yourself. There's no proof it's the same guy.'

'But I *know* it is!'

'OK, OK.'

'Can we meet near Woolsey's ice-cream van, in an hour?

Mum can park in the car park, so if I have an attack, I won't have to run far to get back to the car.'

'I s'pose so. You sure?'

'I'm sure.'

Lil rings before I leave. Ness chats to her for a bit, then calls me down, says Lil wants a word.

'Jamie, I just wanted to apologise for this morning.'

'S'OK. You don't have to say sorry.'

'No, but I want to. It's a funny thing, grief. Makes you do all kinds of strange things. Sometimes I don't feel like myself. Do you understand?'

Not really, but I say, 'Yeah, I s'pose.'

'I hope to see you soon, Jamie.' Lil sounds all stiff and formal. What's going on with her?

Half an hour later, I'm on the clifftop path that runs next to the car park. The tide's in, so there's not much beach, but that's OK, because the sea is this awesome colour, and it's all flat with hardly any peaks.

Myla's gonna love it. I just need to get her out the car and over here so she can see.

When they pull into the car park, I can tell that Jav thinks this is a bad idea. I can also tell that Myla doesn't give a damn, that she's gonna do it anyway.

I head down the slope that leads to the car park, past the ice-cream van parked up on the grass, thinking I'll have to help Myla out the car, but she opens the door before I even get there.

'The sea!' she shouts. 'I can smell it. Oh my God!'

I grin. 'All right?'

She nods, but now I'm close I can see how scared she is.

'Hi,' I say to Jav.

She gives me a half-smile.

'You ready, then?' I hold my hand out for Myla.

She ignores me, staring straight ahead.

'You can't see the sea from here,' I point out.

'I wonder if there's somewhere else we can park, where we can see the sea from the car.'

'C'mon. It's not the same. You wanna be up there, right? With the wind all in your face, and the view. You can see for miles.'

Myla chews on her bottom lip. 'I'm not so sure, now I'm here.' She looks at her mum.

Jav shrugs. 'I'll take you wherever you want, Myla. I just don't want you pushing yourself too far again.'

'Ness reckons that Woolsey's do the best Mr Whippys. If you get out, I'll treat you.'

I smile. When Myla smiles back, I almost reach down to stroke her chin, before I remember that Jav's sitting right next to her.

Myla straightens her back, claps her hands together. 'OK. Let's do this.'

'Be careful,' Jav says. 'I'll be right here.'

I take Myla's hand. She frowns at my sore knuckles. I

shake my head slightly. Don't wanna talk about it in front of Jav. Don't want her to think I've been fighting again.

I help Myla out the car. I hold out my other hand, but she doesn't take it. 'Let's try to do it normally this time. Let's pretend we're just like everyone else.'

I shrug, squeeze her hand, which is trembling. She moves closer so our arms are touching. I nudge her, nod my head towards them. 'I know I'm pale, but you make me look like a frigging ghost!'

Myla giggles. 'This is pale for me.'

'Better get working on the tan then,' I say, tugging her away from the car.

A middle-aged woman with a dog walks past and gives us this sickly smile. I s'pose we look like a couple. Fine with me. Better than fine!

'So what kind of ice cream d'you want?' I ask, trying to match Myla's pace, not pull her forward. She's taking the smallest steps, her eyes on the ground.

'I – um – haven't had a proper Mr Whippy in ages. I'll have a ninety-nine.'

'Look, the van is just over there,' I say, swinging her arm slightly. 'You can make that, can't you?'

Myla nods. 'I can probably make that, seeing as I've been promised a treat.'

I keep her chatting all the way to the van. When we get there, Myla touches the side, like she needs to prove that she did it. Then she looks up at me, beaming. God, she's beautiful.

Myla doesn't let go of my hand while I buy her ice cream. She keeps shooting little glances back at the car, at her mum. As I pass her cone over, some of the ice cream slops onto my hand. I stare at it, my throat thickening.

'Try it,' Myla says, licking the bits that are dribbling. There's a challenge in her eyes, like she's saying, *I put myself out of my comfort zone. Now it's your turn.* 'It won't kill you,' she points out.

The leeches start to grumble and stir.

I watch Myla's face as she eats. She's so happy. Then her hand whips up and she splodges her ice cream right on my nose. Myla throws back her head and laughs. Anger sparks through me, then disgust, then fear.

What am I so afraid of? Why am I always afraid? Jesus.

Myla's laughter dies down and her eyes grow serious. 'It's only ice cream. Here.' She gives me her napkin, and a look that says I need to lighten up. So I stick my finger into her ice cream, scoop out a bit and land it right on her chin.

'Hey!' she shrieks. 'I can't believe you did that!'

I grin, then lift the napkin to wipe my nose.

'Wait,' Myla says. 'Let's have a picture of us next to Woolsey's. I'll put it up on the blog, tell everyone it's the best ice cream in Stratten.'

I move in close and let her take the shot, then I stare at the mess on my finger. Sod it. Those leeches? They can go to hell. I put it straight in my mouth. It's good. Really good.

We clean ourselves up, then I ask, 'So what d'you think? To the top of the cliff?'

'Well, technically, I can see the sea from here.'

'What? No you can't. You can see a bit of the sea. You could see it all if we go up there. You can make it, I know you can. And I know you want to.'

Myla doesn't reply.

I sigh. 'Do I have to promise you another ice cream on the way back? You're an expensive date.'

She gives me a small smile. 'Who said this was a date?'

'We're holding hands, aren't we? I just bought you food. Date.'

That cute smile again, the sexy look up through her eyelashes. 'I think we might be missing something if we're on a date.'

Myla takes a step closer. I freeze. My breath stops. Another step. So close I can smell the vanilla on her breath. She's craning her head up, about to close her eyes.

I tilt my head down. I'm going for it! I'm gonna kiss her! But then something glints in the car park and I look away, towards Jav's car.

Myla gasps and takes a quick step back. 'Mum,' she breathes. 'I almost forgot she was there. She's probably watching.'

I clear my throat and look away.

'We should try to do this alone next time,' Myla says. 'I'm sick of never having any privacy.'

'But what if someone walks past smoking a fag and you have another panic attack? How am I gonna get you home?'

'Too much for you to handle, am I?'

She's right. I should man-up.

'Besides, I don't think I'm going to have a full-blown flashback every time I smell cigarette smoke. It's just, that was the first time.' Myla sighs, shakes her head. Then she stretches out our arms as she takes a step towards the clifftop. 'Come on, then.'

We start up the slope. I try to talk to Myla on the way up, but she's barely answering. The closer we get to the path, the more her eyes dart left and right along it, trying to see who might be coming.

'It's just around the corner, Heartleas Cove,' she says. 'The place where Asha was taken. I'm glad you can't see it from here.'

I drop her hand, sense her panic, until I wrap my arm around her shoulder, draw her closer. 'You're safe,' I whisper into her hair. 'I won't let anything happen to you. Promise.'

Myla looks up at me, our faces so, so close. 'Thanks.'

We stop at the top of the slope, and everything – the beach, the sea, the sky – opens around us.

There are tears in Myla's eyes as she just stands and stares. 'I want this. I want more than this. I want to come here without needing two chaperones. I'm sick of hiding, sick of being a prisoner.' Her expression hardens and her shoulders tense. 'I'm going to get out. I'm going to find him. And if he wants to come for me, let him come.'

23

Myla

Mum opens the front door and I skip down the hallway, yelling, 'I did it!' I can still taste the salt on my lips, feel the tangles in my hair. I really did it! I want to tell Dad that I went outside and it didn't end with me curled up on the floor, hyperventilating, but he's not back from work. I grab my mobile and fire off a quick text. He's going to be so proud.

My next instinct is to tell Eve, but I'm not sure if I want to talk to her. She really creeped me out the last time we spoke, plus the lack of stuff on her profile page is just plain weird. I suppose the only way to get to the bottom of it is to talk to her. There's no harm in that, is there? I feel like I owe it to her, to try to sort this out before I cut her off.

Mum puts the kettle on and I rush upstairs to open my laptop.

The second I log in, she messages me.

Eve51x: Saffy? My sweet Saffy? Thank God. I've been going out of my mind.

Saffy42: Why?

Eve51x: I haven't heard from you in ages. I missed you. God, I missed you.

I feel a tug at my heart. She missed me that much? Not for the first time, I wonder how deep her feelings are for me, what she means when she calls me 'her' Saffy.

Eve51x: Saffy? How are you? I've been worried.

She's got a nerve, after what she said. It hits me suddenly, just how angry I am with her.

Saffy42: Worried that I was losing sleep because you might be lurking outside my house, watching me? That was a pretty low blow, Eve. Why would you say it?

Eve51x: I'm sorry. I didn't know what I was saying. You're right. You're completely right.

Saffy42: And I want to ask you something.

Eve51x: Anything.

Saffy42: Why aren't you very active on your profile? And why aren't there many pictures? Where are your friends from school?

A pause. I nibble on my fingernail.

Eve51x: I try to keep my school friends separate from this account.

Saffy42: What do you mean? Do you have another account?

Eve51x: This account is just for you, Saffy. You're special. I want to keep you to myself.

I think I'm supposed to feel flattered by that, but I don't. I just feel chilled.

Saffy42: Eve, look. You've been a rock to me. I can't tell you how much it means that you believe me about Asha's killer, but . . .

Eve51x: Oh, I understand. You're going out more now, think you're going to get your old friends back, so you don't need me any more.

I do need you, Eve. I just don't trust you.

Saffy42: I thought you knew me better than that. I am getting better, but you seem to want me to stay trapped in this house. I have to end this, Eve. I'm going back to Heartleas to try to trigger my memory.

Eve51x: Saffy, please don't do this. It's not safe. You don't know what will happen if you go back there.

Saffy42: I'm sorry. It's been brilliant. You've been brilliant.

Eve51x: Saffy, don't. I'm warning you!

Saffy42: Goodbye, Eve. X

I shut my laptop before she can say anything else. I wipe tears from my cheeks, take a shuddering breath, try – and fail – to stop more tears from falling. God, she knows exactly how to push my buttons.

I did the right thing, though. I'll be OK. Eve's not my only friend. I have Jamie, and Lauren's coming back. Like Eve said, once I start going out again, I'll see some of my old friends. Maybe – once this is over – I can even go back to school.

'Myla, your tea's getting cold,' Mum shouts up the stairs.

I nip into the bathroom and splash some cold water on my face.

In the kitchen, Mum has put my tea in the microwave and is watching it spin as if she's hypnotised by it. When she realises I'm here, she turns, smiling, but it drops from her face. 'Are you all right?'

I should have known the cold water wouldn't fool her.

'Er – yes. I'm OK.'

Mum raises an eyebrow.

'Reading! I was reading. I just got to the bit where Boxer is taken away to be killed.'

Mum thinks for a moment. '*Animal Farm*?'

I nod.

She comes towards me with her arms outstretched. I let her fold me up. 'Silly thing. You were so pleased with yourself earlier. You were so brave.'

'I know. Silly.'

I pull away to retrieve my mug from the microwave. 'So I was thinking about trying to have another picnic with Jamie.'

'Nice idea. I'll have another look for those paper plates.'

I pick at a chip in the mug. 'I wasn't thinking of having it here.'

'Okkkaaaay . . .'

'I was thinking of having it up on the cliff, near where we were today.'

'That could work. I could sit in the car park and wait for you.'

I blush, swallow heavily. 'What if you don't? What if you drop me off in the car park, then I give you a call when we're done?'

Mum's lips tighten. 'I'm not so sure about that. Why can't Jamie just come here again?'

Because we want some privacy!

I take a deep breath. 'I want to keep pushing myself. This is one step further, if you're not there to rescue me. One step closer to being normal again.'

And one step closer to Heartleas. If I can do this, I know I'm ready to go back.

Mum eyes a scratch on the table. She won't look at me. 'If it's what you want, you know I'll support you.'

I give her hand a quick squeeze. 'Thanks, Mum.'

'So how are you going to deal with the food thing? You don't want to scare Jamie off.'

'I managed to get him to eat some ice cream earlier. He won't be able to resist if we make a Mauritian feast.'

Mum frowns. 'Just don't push too hard, Myla. Ness says he's been doing well since he got here, and is eating a little more, but you don't want to send him back to square one.'

'He's helped me, so why can't I try to help him?'

'I think you should wait for him to ask for your help. Just be patient.'

Mum and I are making *mine frites* when Dad gets home later.

'Fried noodles!' he says, sweeping Mum up for a kiss and giving me a cuddle. 'Excellent.'

'Someone's in a good mood,' Mum observes.

Dad smiles at me. I grin back. 'You got my text?'

'I did indeed, and I'm proud of you. Really proud.'

That's the first time I've heard him say that for ages.

Dad swipes a noodle from the wok. 'This is a big moment for us. Perhaps we can get on with our lives now.'

I start to lay the plates out.

Dad clears his throat. 'As we're talking about moving on, I was wondering about Asha's room.'

I pause, a plate in mid-air. Mum turns off the heat on the noodles.

'What about it?' I ask.

'Well, as we discussed, I've been talking to my manager about how to find a better work–life balance.'

'And?' Mum prompts.

'And working from home might be a possibility.'

'No,' I snap. 'You can't turn Asha's room into an office.'

'Myla, it's just a room.' Then Dad looks away, his eyes reddening. 'There's nothing left of her in there.'

'Thanks to you!' I shout. 'You couldn't wait to strip that room bare of her!'

'Myla,' Mum warns. 'We've all dealt with this in different ways.'

'Why do you always have to take his side? Are you really saying you're OK with this?'

Mum's eyes blaze. 'I'm OK with having my husband around a little more.'

I bite my lip. Am I being massively selfish? I sneak a glance at Dad. He looks so worn down, almost haggard.

I get up, wrap my arms around his neck. 'I'm sorry,' I murmur. 'I feel like we're losing her again, piece by piece. I hate it.'

'We all do, Myla,' he says, his voice croaky. 'I'm just trying to hold everything together.'

And suddenly I see what a massive responsibility it is. Mum can't work as she has to stay and babysit me. Dad is working too much to pay our bills and all he gets in return is a guilt trip from me. God, I've become so self-centred.

On the table, my phone buzzes with a message. I look over, hoping it'll be Jamie.

It's not. It's Finn.

I snatch my phone up before Mum or Dad can see his name on the screen. What would they do if they knew I was speaking to Si Ashworth's nephew?

'It's Lauren,' I say, slipping away to read it in private.

'I'm dishing up,' Mum calls after me.

'Two secs,' I answer, opening the text.

Saw you on the cliff with lover-boy today.

How did you know I was up there? Have you been following me?

Posted it on your blog, didn't you?

Finn follows my cooking blog? That's weird.

If you can do that, you can go back to Heartleas.
Tomorrow?

I close my eyes. I just want one more nice memory of being outside with Jamie.

Not tomorrow.

When?

Soon.

This has gone on long enough.

Yes, it has. But I'm not the one who ran, who withheld evidence that would've stopped them convicting Si.

You're not bullying me into this.

Soon, Myla. Or I'm coming back, and next time I'll break down the door if that's what it takes.

I sink onto the sofa, my heart pounding way too fast. I have no doubt that he would break the door down. I wonder if I should've told someone that Finn came to the house earlier.

But the only person I could tell is Jamie, and I don't want them getting into another fight. Who knows what Finn would do to him.

Mum and I spend the rest of the evening cooking. We make sweet, buttery *mithai*, aubergine fritters, *dholl puris* (flatbreads) with coconut chutney and Asha's favourites: *gateau patat douce* – sweet potato cakes with cardamom, sugar and coconut.

Just before bed, I check my email. Oh, wow! I've got a response from one of the charities that I contacted. My eyes fly over the text, then I cover my mouth to stop myself from squealing. They're not promising anything, but they're asking for more information, saying they want to interview me. Oh my God!

I know I promised Dad, but I can't take the 'Free Si' site down now – I'm just starting to get somewhere. I'll decide later how I'm going to break it to them, but I've got to put the news on my site straight away. I write a hasty post called 'At last, someone is listening'. I keep the details vague, but try to get across how incredible it feels that someone is taking me seriously. After so long without hope, it finally feels like there's a chance of getting justice for Asha.

I text Finn, tell him to check the site. Then I text Jamie, ask if he wants to meet me on the cliff at midday tomorrow. I don't tell him what I have planned. I want it to be a surprise.

*

Mum and I swing into the car park at quarter to twelve the next day. Mum obviously hasn't seen my post yet as she seems fine. There's going to be a massive fight when she and Dad do find out. I should probably tell them, rather than wait for them to see it online . . .

We sit in silence in the car for a few moments. I stare up at the top of the grassy slope. It's a long way. Longer than it seemed a few days ago. My chest feels fluttery. Mum is looking straight ahead, her hands locked in the 'ten and two' position on the steering wheel.

I clasp my own hands in my lap to stop them from shaking. The smell of food wafts across from the boot and my stomach lurches. I can't do this. I need Jamie!

Mum says, 'What time will Jamie be here?'

My throat is dry. I try to swallow. 'Soon. He said he'd be here at twelve.'

'Shall we go and set it up?'

I give her a brief nod, try to smile.

Mum gets out and heads round to the boot. I just look at my door, willing Jamie to appear, offering me his hand. I try to push down the handle, but my fingers are clumsy and slick with sweat. I sigh, then try again. The sea breeze blusters into the car, almost pushing me back into my seat. Maybe I should just stay inside until Jamie gets here.

'Ready?' Mum asks, her arms laden with the blanket, a coolbag of food, and another bag of sun cream, water and God-knows what else. 'Hope Jamie's not late. I was lucky to get that table at The Vyne – they'd just had a cancellation.'

I close my eyes, breathe heavily through my nose. God, I'd forgotten. She's booked her and Ness a table at this super-fancy restaurant.

Mum tries to juggle stuff so she has a free hand. 'Do you need help?'

The idea of holding my mum's hand in public is enough to get me on my feet. 'No, it's all right, thanks.'

She grins. 'Something special about Jamie's hand, is there?'

I ignore her.

As soon as I shut the car door, I'm aware of all the space around me. This is wrong. It feels so wrong. Mum is already two paces ahead, but she stops. I take a step. My breathing quickens; my chest is contracting. 'Talk to me,' I gasp, thrusting my hand through the crook of Mum's arm.

'Are you all right? I think we should go back to the car.'

My legs are weak, the ground swaying slightly beneath them. 'No. Talk to me. Just talk to me. It's what Jamie does. It distracts me.'

'OK. What would you like to talk about?'

I can barely hear her above the roar of my racing pulse. 'Anything, Mum! It doesn't matter. Just take my mind off it. Please!'

'Right. OK.' She starts speaking, really fast. 'Well your dad and I were talking about taking a holiday next year. We're so pleased with how far you've come and were wondering if you might make it to Mauritius to see some family. Now I know that seems a lot now, but I really think if you can cope with this, you can manage to get on a plane.'

A plane! 'Not . . . helping.'

We're level with the ice-cream van now, though it's shuttered up today.

I blink a couple of times, try to clear my vision, which is dancing with black spots. It's the start of a panic attack. I can't stop it. 'Mum!'

She drops the picnic blanket, the two bags, spins around to face me, grabs both my shoulders and makes me look at her. 'Listen to me,' she says slowly, calmly.

'I can't. I can't!'

'You can. You can beat this. You're safe. You were here just yesterday, and you had a nice time with Jamie and he almost kissed you.'

'God, Mum!'

'And the reason he almost kissed you is because you're amazing. You can do this.'

I'm nodding, drawing in more air.

'Now let's get this picnic laid out.'

I pick up the blanket, Mum grabs the rest and we make our way to the top of the slope. And there it is: the pebbled beach running into the glistening water, the clifftop path stretching for miles either side without a single person in view, the sea rolling lazily towards the horizon. And it's all so big, so beautiful. My lungs fill with the salt-licked air, and I can breathe. I can finally breathe.

'Magnificent, isn't it?' Mum says, beaming. 'The perfect place for a romantic picnic.'

'Will you stop? You've already embarrassed me enough for one lifetime.'

'OK. Let's set everything up.'

By the time we've laid out the food, it's exactly twelve.

'Will you take a picture of me?' I ask. 'I'll send it to Jamie. Might hurry him along.'

Mum takes my phone and stands a few paces away.

'Don't take it from that angle. You'll give me a double chin!'

Mum sighs and crouches down so she's level with me. 'Stop fiddling with your hair. You're on a clifftop – it's bound to look windswept.'

When she's taken a couple and I've chosen the shot I'm happy with, I send a quick text to Jamie.

Hurry up! I'm waiting! ☺ x

I stand back and look at the spread on the blanket. 'I can't believe how much food we made.'

Mum nods. 'Perhaps we did get a bit carried away.'

While we're waiting for Jamie, I post the picture on my blog. I briefly explain what all the food is, promising that recipes will soon follow.

When I look up, Mum's glancing at her watch.

'I'm sure he'll be here soon,' I say, picking at one of the *mithai*. 'He's usually pretty punctual.'

Mum forces a smile. 'Don't worry. Ness will understand if I'm a few minutes late.'

'*She* might. Not sure the snooty gits at The Vyne will.'

Come on, Jamie. Where are you?

Mum sits down to wait. She grabs a corner of the blanket and folds it over, again and again, into a tight little roll.

I sigh. 'Maybe I should call him?'

Mum glances at her watch again. 'We can give him a couple more minutes.'

But I can almost hear her counting down the seconds. This is the first time Mum's been out for lunch in ages. I hate that I'm making her late, stressing her out.

Then I get to my feet. There's a tall, skinny figure in the distance, walking along the coastal path. 'I think that's him.'

Mum stands and squints. 'Are you sure? He's quite a long way away.'

'Yes. It must be. Jamie's got a T-shirt that colour.' I wave. After a pause, he waves back. 'See? Now go. Enjoy your overpriced lunch.'

'I can wait a little longer.'

I laugh. 'Mum, it's fine. I can be on my own for one minute. Go. You're cramping my style!'

Mum squeezes my hand. 'OK. Love you.'

'Love you too.'

Mum actually runs back to the car. She gets in, but doesn't turn the engine on straight away. I gesture with my hands, telling her to leave. After a moment of hesitation, Mum gives me a wave, then speeds off.

I glance along the path, but there's no one there.

Where's he gone? He was there just a minute ago.

My breath stops. What if it wasn't Jamie?

I grab my phone, ring him. No answer.

OK. OK. There's no need to panic. Jamie will be here. And when he gets here, he's not going to find me curled up in a ball and hyperventilating. I'm *not* going to ruin this. I text him.

Where are you? Mum's gone. I'm alone. Trying not to freak out.☹

I focus on the sea, on its ceaseless song. *Shush-shush-shush.* The tightness in my shoulders loosens a little. I tilt my head to soak up the sun.

Something snaps behind me. I gasp, whip around, body rigid with fear. Then I laugh. A seagull. It's just a seagull, eyeing my food.

I turn back to the sea.

And that's when I hear the cough. The phlegmy, moist cough.

24

Jamie

I'm annihilating a zombie, absolutely kicking his face in. A left hook, one in the stomach. He staggers back. I reach for my gun and BOOM, his face is splatted across the pavement. Then one of his mates grabs me from behind, yanks my head back. Sneaky bastard. I move suddenly, nutting him with a reverse headbutt. Sucker!

I pause the game, glance up at the clock on the wall. Five past eleven. I'm good. Loads of time before I meet Myla.

I go back to pummelling the hell outta the undead. A zombie dog leaps out of nowhere. I let rip with my gun. He's gone to zombie doggy heaven now.

I pause again, look up at the clock. Ness forgot to change it at the start of the summer. Then I remember. Crap!

I grab my phone. It's five past twelve.

Myla's sent me a picture message. She looks so pretty. That smile. Killer. God, she's amazing. It's like her worst nightmare, being out there, but she just gets on with it.

I'm grinning like an idiot, until I notice all the food around her.

I put the phone down. I shouldn't have eaten this morning. Should've known that Myla's surprise would involve food.

I can't deal. Not unless Myla wants a repeat of last time. She can't see me spew again. She already knows that something's up, and there's only so long I can keep making excuses.

I have to tell her.

The leeches squirm.

Screw them. I don't have time for this. Gotta go. I start to grab my stuff.

How can I admit it to her? It's so weak. Pathetic. She's gonna despise me.

The leeches open their massive mouths. They gobble up my rancid thoughts, my self-loathing, churn it up with all the other poisonous stuff I've ever thought about myself. There's so much of it, they're bulging, almost bursting.

No! I'm gonna be ...

I grab the bin just in time, hurling up the yoghurt I had for breakfast.

I'm so fucking sick of this!

I stumble towards the toilet, chuck it down the bowl, rinse

the bin in the shower, brush my teeth, spray some deodorant. Now I'm really late.

One missed call and one text from Myla.

I open the text.

What?

Jav's gone? Jav left her! Myla can't be out there alone. Bloody hell!

I call Myla back. It rings and rings. She doesn't answer. I text her.

Sorry. I'm coming now. Ten minutes.

I yank a T-shirt over my head as I run down the stairs. I scoot around Ian, who's winding around my legs, yapping. 'Not now, Dude!' I say.

I head for the garage, for Ness's rusty old bike. I dunno if the brakes work, but that doesn't matter.

I try Myla's number again. Still no answer. She's pissed at me. Must be. That's why she's not answering.

But what if she's lost it? What if she's had another panic attack? What if she can't breathe?

Stop it. STOP IT!

I push the frustration and the fear down through the pedals. I'm hammering along the road, swerving round parked cars, ignoring pedestrians at the crossing.

I'm so unfit. The nausea starts, then the dizziness. But I don't care, just keep going.

Five minutes later, I fly across the empty car park, chuck Ness's bike on the grass, try to start up the slope, but my legs collapse and I fall, hard, forcing all the air from my lungs. All I can do is sit, try to breathe.

Myla's gonna rip it out of me when she sees the state I'm in. I'm sweating, shaking. Honestly, she's gonna find this hilarious.

I stagger up the slope, sometimes on my feet, sometimes with my hands on the ground.

Almost there.

One step. Another.

And then I stop.

No.

No. No. NO!

I'm not seeing this. It isn't happening.

But it is. It's real.

The blanket's all rucked up, food chucked everywhere, plates upturned, a bottle of lemonade on its side. Myla's handbag is there, the coolbag is there, but Myla's not.

She's gone.

25

Myla

My head is murky. I'm swimming up, up, up, searching for the surface. Where is it? Why is it so far away? I'm too deep.

I give up, start to drift aimlessly. Then a thought swims into my mind. I know what I need to do.

I open my eyes.

I see bricks, rubbish, a dark, small space.

Oh, God. He took me. He took me and drugged me and I'm going to die.

I remember that crushing weight of his arm across my chest, pinning me to him. I struggled, kicked. I didn't see his face, didn't see anything before I passed out.

I scream, but something has been rammed in my mouth, pulled tightly around the back of my head. I'm going to die. I'm going to die. Oh God, I'm going to die. I scream and scream again, but the sound is weak, muffled. No one is going to hear me.

A headache pulses at the back of my skull. My throat is dry, scratchy. I really need to wee. As soon as I think this, I almost let go, but then I clench. I won't give him the satisfaction.

My hands have been pulled behind my back, bound with a sticky, strong tape. My shoulders are aching, burning. My ankles are tied. How long have I been like this? I don't even know what time of day it is.

Wait. Light. There's a slit of light. It's still day. Thank God it's not night.

And then I realise where I am. A pill box. If I lie still, hold my rapid breaths for a moment, I can hear the sea. There's sand beneath me, buried under the brittle grass, the crushed beer cans, the scraps of toilet paper. Then I realise what the smell is. Urine.

I taste the sting of acid as it flies up my throat. I roll over as the vomit gushes out, either side of the material in my mouth, flowing down my cheek, into my hair. There's too much! I can't get it all out! Some of it rolls back down. I cough. I'm choking! Can't breathe! I spit. Again and again, forcing it out, my body convulsing with shuddering sobs. Please, no. I don't want to die here.

Is this what happened to Asha? Oh, Asha. Is this where she died? My sister. I can't bear it. I shouldn't have left her, shouldn't have run. This is my punishment. No one's going to find me. Jamie will turn up at the picnic site, realise that something's wrong, but there's no way he'll find me.

Unless he thinks to come back to the place where it all started. I'm sure that's where I am, the pill box on Heartleas Cove. It's almost hidden by one of the sand dunes, tucked away from the main beach. Quiet. Isolated.

If I can move, if I can make it out to the beach, someone will find me, surely. I twist my torso, flick my legs, but they jar. No! Damn him, bastard! Damn him!

There's a metal stake in the ground and he's knotted a length of rope around it and my ankles. I pull my legs, try to yank the stake out, but it must be buried deep as it doesn't even move.

My chest constricts. Oh, God. A panic attack. No. Not here. Not now. I close my eyes, try to breathe deeply, slowly, but there's no coming back from this one. This time, the panic is real. All I can do is lie here, try to manage it, even though I'm convinced that every breath will be my last.

It feels like hours until it starts to ease.

Where is he? Why has he left me? Will he strangle me, like he did Asha? Or will he torture me, get his revenge for making him wait two years?

I remember the smell of tobacco on his hands as he forced something over my mouth. He must've sedated me and then carried me here. He was so strong!

How did he know where to find me? Oh my God. The photo on the blog. I'm so stupid! I practically sent out an invitation for him to come and take me.

At least I'll get to look him in the eyes. I won't have to be afraid any more, because he won't be some faceless stranger chasing me on the beach, or lurking in the shadows outside my house. There will be nowhere for him to hide.

But Mum, oh God, Mum. And Dad. This will break them. I'm sorry. It's my fault. I knew he was out there still, knew it was dangerous, but I just wanted answers. That's all I've ever wanted. To know the truth.

And Jamie. Poor, sweet Jamie. He'll blame himself, wish he'd got there sooner, wish he hadn't told me it was safe to go outside. He won't forgive himself, but it's my fault. It's all my fault.

I scrunch my eyes up really tight, picture Asha stretched out along the sand on our last day together. I can see her halo of shining, black hair, the serene smile on her lips as the sunlight flickered over her face.

Mum believes in life after death. If that's true, it means I'll see Asha again. And I want to, so badly. I want her to be there, waiting for me, to tell me that everything will be all right.

I open my eyes. My heart's racing, mouth thick with the taste of vomit, lips dry and tinged with salt from my tears.

How long do I have? Minutes, seconds? How long before he comes for me?

26

Jamie

Can't believe I'm doing this. Can't believe I'm calling Jav to tell her that Myla's been taken. 'Cos that's blatantly what's happened. Her bag's here, and there's been a struggle.

It's my fault. I was too late. Because I couldn't deal with my own crappy issues.

Ness picks up her phone. 'Hello, Jamie. How's it—'

'Ness, I need to speak to Jav.' My voice doesn't sound right. It's cold, harsh.

'Oh, OK. Sure, just passing you over.'

'Jamie? Is something wrong?'

I dunno how to tell her. I try to hold in a cry, but it bursts out, making this horrible, shuddering, gasping noise.

'Jamie?' When she says my name it's like her voice is sharpened to a point. 'Jamie? What's happening? Has she had another panic attack? Stay there. I'm coming.'

And she hangs up. Didn't give me a chance to explain.

Do I call back? Tell her she's got it wrong?

No. No time. I'll call the cops.

I plug '999' into my phone. The first time I've ever rung this number. What am I gonna say? They won't take me seriously. Why would they? She's been missing for what, half an hour. Jesus. Who the hell am I s'posed to call?

Someone who knows her; someone who knows what happened to her sister. William. He'll understand. He'll help. He'll realise that Myla's been right all along.

Something coils around my chest, pulling it tighter and tighter, until it's crushing my ribcage, my heart. I didn't believe her. Didn't protect her. Said I'd keep her safe, but I didn't.

What if I can't find her in time? What if he's already killed her? It's on me. It's all on me. I can't. Can't even go there. She has to still be alive. I'll find her. I'll hold it together and I'll find her.

I search for the local copshop, get the number and ring. The second someone picks up, I bark, 'I need to speak to William Osbourne.'

'I'll just transfer you.'

A few seconds later, he answers. 'This is William.'

'It's Jamie. Something's happened. I was s'posed to meet Myla on the cliffs by Woolsey's ice-cream van, but—'

'Myla has left the house?'

'Yeah, but I was late, and she's gone.'

'Gone?'

'There's been a fight. All the stuff has been knocked over and ... Listen, someone's taken her, all right?'

There's the longest pause. I can hear him breathing heavily through his nose.

'Are you listening to me? Someone's taken her! No one believed that she was right about Asha's murderer still being out there, but he is. And he's got her. You guys, you messed up. Nicked the wrong man. And you need to help me fix this.'

Nothing.

'William, for fuck's sake!'

'Stay there. I'm coming. Don't call anyone. Understand? I need your line to be open so I can reach you. Leave me your phone number.'

I reel it off.

He says, 'Don't move.' Then he's gone.

This howl of rage erupts out of me. I hoof the bottle of lemonade over the cliff, followed by a plate of food and a Tupperware. I'm screaming and shouting – not even words, just noise – until my voice is hoarse.

There's nothing left to hold me up. I drop and my knees crunch into the ground. How the hell are we gonna find her? What are the chances of getting to her in time? She's gonna die. I'm gonna lose her.

I'm the reason she left the house. Why do I always hurt people? *He's* right. I'm a loser, nothing. No good to anyone.

I run my hand through my hair. I can feel sweat on my scalp, taste it on my upper lip. What do I do now? William and Jav are coming. I just need to wait.

But I can't! Can't just stand here, doing nothing, while this psycho might be hurting her. I need to do something, go somewhere, but I dunno where to start.

I pace up and down, my mind scrambling for the answer. I'm starting to feel crap again. I lift something off one of the plates, shove it in my mouth, then chew without tasting. My stomach gurgles. It's like it's so desperate it's reaching up to grab the food.

I pick up something else, shove it in. I need energy. Need to be able to think. I can't let her down again. I've gotta find her. Where do I start? What about the beach where Asha was kidnapped? Would he take Myla there too? I'm already starting down the slope, faster and faster, until I'm jogging.

Wait a minute. He wouldn't take her out in the open, not in daylight. There must be something else – something I'm not thinking of.

Maybe not something, but some*one*.

Finn's been neck-deep in this from the start. Myla thought someone was watching her house, then Finn broke in. That can't be a coincidence. Was he just pretending to help Myla find the truth so he could keep an eye on her, stay close? What if it was Si Ashworth all along, and he's sent his nephew to finish the job?

Or what if Finn used Myla as bait? What if he was watching, waiting for the real killer to show themselves when Myla was outside?

Whatever the hell is going on, I'm gonna find Finn. And I want answers. Before it's too late.

27

Myla

I've wet myself. I couldn't hold it in any more. It's disgusting – all sticky and damp, my knickers clinging to my dirty skin. I've got vomit in my hair, snot on my face. I don't want my body to be found like this. I don't want Mum or Dad to see me in this state, for this to be their last memory of me.

I've been lying here for ages. I just want it to be over. Why is he making me wait? What's he going to do? Please, let it be quick.

My shoulders have started to throb. I try to move my wrists for the thousandth time, but he's bound them well. I try kicking the stake again, but my shoes just bounce right off it.

Is this what he did to you, Asha? This gag, is it the same one he stuffed in your mouth? How long were you trapped here, terrified, afraid, alone? Did you hate me for not being strong enough to save you? I'm so sorry. So sorry you had to suffer this.

I could've found you, if I'd been thinking straight, if I hadn't been so selfish. I could've hidden in the sea, circled around, followed his footsteps right here to you. But no one came for you. Just like no one will come for me.

I think about all the people I care about, try to remember the last thing I said to them. I told Mum I love her. I love her so much. After everything I've put her through, I never said thank you for all the sacrifices she's made. And Dad. How did I say goodbye to him as he left for work? I was on my laptop, distracted. I don't think I even looked up.

At least Jamie will always have that picture – the one that shows how far I've come, thanks to him. I just hope he'll find a way to forgive himself.

I guess Eve will read about me in the paper. I'll never find out what she was keeping from me.

And Lauren, what about Lauren? What was the last thing ...

Wait. What's that noise? Something is snuffling around outside the pill box. A dog! It's a bloody dog! Which means its owner can't be far away. I start to scream. The noise is almost trapped behind my gag, but some manages to creep out around the edges. I kick the stake again, but my shoes just make a dull thud. Come here. Please, come inside.

God, what if it's Ian? Please, please let it be Ian. I'd give anything to see the top of Jamie's head poking through the entrance. Anything.

The quick, panting breaths get closer. That's right. Good dog. It's coming inside! It even barks. Yes, bark! Bark louder! For God's sake, bring someone here to find me.

A shape appears in the shadows. My heart plummets when I see a small, curly-haired creature. Not Ian, but it'll do. It can still help.

I wriggle from side to side, scattering the pieces of rubbish in the sand next to me. My breaths are steaming out and I'm sweating with the effort. The dog freezes, cocks its head. Then it trots towards me. It barks again. Not a threatening sound. More like an inquisitive one.

Then I hear, 'Chewy!'

I gasp, sob. There's someone out there. They're so close! Please, come and find your dog. Come and find me. Tears are trailing down my cheeks. I try even harder to scream. But my throat is raw.

Chewy comes a little closer. I nod my head, eyes practically popping out of their sockets. Is there any way I can trap him? If I could open my knees, somehow lock them around his head, then his owner would come looking for him. I don't want to hurt him, but he might be my only chance.

Chewy veers off, catching the smell of something in the rubbish. He turns his back on me to root around the empty water bottles and soggy newspapers.

'Chewy!' The voice comes again, closer this time. It's a

woman. Please, you're so, so close. Just in here. Please help me.

Chewy's ears prick up when she calls again, but he ignores her and turns his attention back to me. He sticks his nose right up against mine, then gently licks a bit of the sick off my cheek. I cry out, fresh tears forming. It might be the last time anything living touches me with a bit of kindness.

'Chewy. Come here!'

Chewy's head swings around. He thinks for a moment, then scampers off.

'No!' I wail. 'Please. Please don't leave me.'

But I'm alone again.

28

Jamie

I try Finn's number for the fifth time. Pick up, you prick! But there's nothing. I'll have to find him. I could go to the arcade, or try to find his house. What's the name of the estate where he lives? Ness mentioned it once. It's miles away, though. I'd need someone to drive me. Maybe I should go back to the car park, wait for Ness and Jav, explain everything? No, I can't. Can't wait any longer.

Lil. She's got a car. She'll drive me. It's gonna be OK. Lil will help.

I leap on the bike and hurtle outta the car park.

Five minutes later, I'm a sweating, shaking mess, standing on Lil's doorstep with my finger glued to the bell. Her car's in the drive so she must be around. She's taking too long to answer so I just open the door and go in. 'Lil?' I shout. 'Lil, I need your help.'

She comes through from the living room, clutching a glass. Her face is white and pulled tight, and the ice cubes are rattling as her hand shakes.

I must've freaked her out, barging in like this. 'Lil. Jesus, sorry. Didn't mean to scare you. It's Myla. She's been taken. I need to talk to Finn Ashworth. Do you know where he lives? Even if you don't, we can drive to the estate, knock on a door. Someone will know where he is. He has something to do with this. He knows something. I'm gonna make him talk. Don't care what I have to do. I'm gonna get the truth out of him. Myla might still be alive, if we can just find out where she is, get to her in time.'

Lil just takes a deep drag of her cigarette. 'Good God, Jamie. Have you called the police?'

My phone starts to ring in my pocket. Myla? I grab it. Ness. I let it go to voicemail.

'Jamie, have you called the police?' Lil repeats, her voice clipped.

'Yeah. Course.'

Lil gives me a hard look, then she smiles, her eyes crinkling. 'Sit down, boy. Sit down. Just for a moment.'

'We don't have time for that! Don't you get it? We have to go now.'

Lil closes her eyes, shakes her head. 'Jamie, you're speaking at about a hundred-miles-an-hour and my poor old brain can't keep up. Sit down, catch your breath, and I'll get you a drink. Then you can tell me again, from the beginning.'

'Right. Yeah. In the car. On the way. Please, we have to go!'

Lil sighs. 'All right, all right. Let me just strain my greens first. You'll get old one day. Feels like I have to go every ten minutes.'

She doesn't get how serious this is. Does she think Myla's just done a runner? Does she think I'm nuts? We don't have time for her to pee!

Lil puts down her drink, stubs out the cigarette, and heads for the cloakroom.

I let out a deep, shaky breath, tracing my fingers over my sore knuckles as I wait. Then I realise that I need to go, too. I feel guilty even wasting a second, but if I use the upstairs toilet, I'll be back down before Lil's even finished. 'Going upstairs to the loo,' I shout, taking the stairs two at a time.

At the top, straight in front of me, is Lil's bedroom. Next door must be the bathroom, but there's another room, off to the right. On the door is a sign with the name 'Beth'. God. Her daughter.

I can see an unmade bed, several books, CDs and piles of clothes dumped on the floor. Lil's left the room just as it was. Creepy. Before I know what I'm doing, I'm pushing the door open and going in.

There's loads of dolls, all lined up on a chest of drawers, facing the bed. Babies, princesses, fairies. I look at them for a long time. These are kids' dolls. They don't belong in here.

My skin prickles with cold sweat. The dolls' hair. It's all plaited.

It means something. I can feel it, tugging at the corner of my mind.

'Jamie,' Lil calls.

I jump.

'I thought you were in a rush.'

I sneak along the landing to the bathroom, then do my best not to sound like I'm bricking it. 'Two secs,' I reply, then quietly close the bathroom door.

Something's not right here. Not right at all. That bedroom, it was like a shrine. Why keep it like that?

I stare at myself in the mirror, try to think. I gotta go down soon or she'll get suspicious – but I need more time. What *is* it with the hair?

Lil shouts up the stairs again, asking if I'm all right.

I flush the toilet, run the tap and start to struggle down the stairs. My legs have gone. But I need to keep it together. Need to get outta here, figure this out.

Lil is in the kitchen, a second fag on the go. I look at her broad shoulders, the way she stands, and suddenly see how menacing she is, how powerful.

Wait … she's never smoked in front of me before.

I can't keep up with the speed of my thoughts, can't even begin to process what this means, but everything is telling me that something is wrong. Really, really wrong.

'Didn't know you smoked,' I say, nodding at the burning

fag. How did I not catch that rasp in her voice, notice the faint smell of smoke in the house?

Lil shrugs. 'I don't usually. I have the odd one now and then. William disapproves so I'd given up. But all this with Myla, it's shaken me up. Terrible business.'

What do I do? What the hell do I do? Come on. Think!

'We should go,' Lil says. 'That poor girl.'

She moves towards the door. That's when I see it, leaning against the wall. The canvas shopping bag Lil left on the train the first time I met her. Poking out of it is Myla's top. The green one with the butterflies. What's Lil doing with Myla's top?

And – just like that – it all crashes in on me at once.

'Asha had one just the same. She was wearing it when she . . . when it happened. But they never found it.'

'The man on the beach reeked of cigarettes. All over his breath and his clothes.'

'Asha's hair was in a plait. It wasn't in a plait when I left her. Someone did that to her.'

My stomach shrivels, smaller and smaller, until it's a hard, dry nut. It takes everything I've got not to double up against the pain.

'Are you OK?' Lil asks, narrowing her eyes against the smoke.

I can't answer. This can't be right. Can't be. She's just an old lady. And I hung out with her. I would've known!

Lil frowns. 'You don't look so good, love. Sit down if you need a minute.'

She takes a step towards me. I move back. I have to force the words out. 'Er – I'm OK.' My voice doesn't sound right. I clear my throat, try to act normal. 'It's just getting to me, that's all. Can I – can I have that drink? I'll be quick. Then we'll go.'

Lil smiles, but her eyes are wary. 'Just water?'

I nod.

She turns her back for twenty seconds and I scrabble around for a plan. Something, *anything* to get me outta here.

Just as Lil turns round, I pull out my phone. 'Ness!' I say quickly. 'Ness just texted. She's gonna drive me.'

Lil puts the water down. 'You're sure? I'm happy to help.'

'No, honest. It's fine. I'm sorry for dragging you into this. I'd better go.'

I rush to the door. I've got one hand on the handle when Lil says, 'Wait, Jamie.'

I freeze. She knows! What's she gonna do?

I hear her walking up behind me. I make myself turn around to face her.

Lil puts her hand on mine. I tense, tell myself not to flinch. A curl of smoke wafts through the air between us.

'You'll let me know what happens, won't you?'

I nod. 'Yeah. Course.'

Lil smiles and lets me go.

Outside, I gulp in a massive breath of air, try not to run down the driveway. She's watching. Bound to be watching.

I get on the bike, almost fall off 'cos I'm shaking so much. I manage to wobble around the corner, then the bike tips over and I'm sprawled across the pavement, gasping, crying. Jesus. JESUS!

It takes me a few minutes to get a grip, then I sit up.

I'll call Ness. She'll know what to do. She'll help me figure this out. But her number's engaged. OK, OK. The police? No. Can't trust the police.

I called William! Is he in on it? What have I done? What if he's on his way to Myla now? What if he's gonna shut her up, make sure she never speaks? Is that why he told me not to call anyone else?

I need help. Who else can I call?

Finn. If I'm right about Lil, then his story adds up, and he wants to catch her as much as I do.

I know he's not gonna answer so I send him a text, tell him I know it wasn't his uncle, that I know who did it.

Seconds later, my phone is ringing.

'I'm listening,' Finn says.

'Myla's been kidnapped. And I think I can save her, but I need your help.'

'You what?'

'You need to LISTEN!'

And then I stop, try to slow down, keep my voice level. I run him through the whole damn thing, from start to finish.

When I'm done, we agree to meet at Ness's in twenty minutes, make a plan from there.

I bet Lil's gonna go to the place where she's keeping Myla. Bet she's taking that green top to dress her up or something sick like that. So what now? Can't follow her on my bike. She'll see me. Could me and Finn . . .

And then a car pulls up to the kerb.

Shit.

Lil opens the passenger door, looks down at Ness's bike, then at me, her face full of concern. 'Did you fall off?'

'Er – yeah.'

'Hop in. I'll drop you at Ness's. We're only a minute away.'

'I'm not hurt. Just a bit winded.'

Lil fixes me with a stern stare. 'Jamie, don't be silly. Just get in. Leave the bike. No one's going to steal it. You've got to find Myla.'

What is this? She gonna kidnap me too? I should get on that bike and pedal as fast as I can in the opposite direction.

But if I do that, I might never find Myla.

No. I won't abandon her. No way. If Lil takes me too, least I'll be with Myla.

'Come on, Jamie,' Lil urges.

I stand on weak legs. It's like all my bones have turned to foam.

Can't believe I'm gonna get in a car with the woman who probably killed Asha, kidnapped Myla. Am I really doing this? I almost laugh. But I hold it back. If I start, I won't stop. I'm on the brink, I can feel it. Just need to get a grip.

I drag in a deep breath, take two steps, and get in the car.

29

Myla

How long have I been here? Time seems to be stretching, or is it compacting? How long since the dog came and went? How much more do I have to wait? I just want to find out what he's going to do to me. Make it quick. Please.

My limbs are growing numb now. I'll fight. I'll fight as hard as I can, but I'm weakening, starting to feel lightheaded.

I close my eyes. I wish I could sleep, or pass out, or something to make the time go, to silence the screams in my head, the paralysing fear. My body's shutting down. I try to move, to remind it that I'm still here, still alive.

I open my eyes. Earlier, I counted thirteen cans (six beer, two Coke, five other), seven water bottles and nine plastic bags. What else? Rocks?

The light is suddenly blocked from the entrance. An icy trail of goosebumps sweeps over my body. It's time. He's here.

I writhe and buck, trying to shout behind the gag.

There's the rasping cough as he bends down to walk through the low entranceway, his body filling the space, plunging the pill box into darkness. I scream again, push away into the furthest corner.

His feet brush over the rubbish as he comes closer. My heart sprints. Then he moves to the side and the light floods in again.

I blink. For the briefest moment, I feel relieved. Lil. It's Lil. I'm going to be OK.

Then I see the expression on her face, and I realise how wrong I am.

A scream hurtles up my throat with such force it almost chokes me.

No. No, no, *no!* How? Why? You bitch! You vile bitch!

Lil puts a finger to her lips, tears rolling down her cheeks. 'Shhhh,' she says in a wavering voice. 'Shhhh. Just be quiet now.'

She tries to stroke my hair. I recoil. Don't touch me! Don't you dare!

'I'm sorry. Truly I am.'

I look at her, *really* look at her. She's sturdy, strong enough to be mistaken for a man. All this time, everything I believed was wrong.

'This was never meant to happen,' she says.

Shut your mouth! Don't lie to me! This is what you always wanted, ever since that night on the beach. The night you took Asha. What did you do to her, you sick bitch? What did you do to my sister?

'I'm sorry I left you alone. I had to go home, pick up some things for you. I knew you'd be safe and sound here. All I've ever wanted is to keep you safe, Saffy.'

Keep me safe! By drugging me? Kidnapping me? What are you saying? Do you actually . . .

Wait.

I stop struggling. Everything stills. The roaring rage in my ears quietens, my heartbeat halts, my body stiffens.

Saffy. You called me Saffy. How could you know? How could . . .

Lil shakes her head ruefully, then tuts, like she's forgotten her purse. 'I called you Saffy, didn't I?'

I close my eyes, wish I could close my ears. I don't want to hear this. I can't!

'I just wanted to protect you.'

My eyes flick open, staring shards of ice at her. 'Eve?' I try to mumble.

Lil looks away, nibbles a fingernail. 'I just wanted to be close to you, after I lost Asha. She was only mine for a few days, but I missed her so much.'

She was *never* yours! Never.

My mouth fills with bile. I spit it out and it soaks the disgusting rag. I can't hold the tears back. They explode out in great, heaving sobs.

How is this possible? How was I fooled so easily? Was I

so desperate for a friend, someone to listen to me? Of course she believed me about Si Ashworth. She knew the truth. And I fell for it, let her in, told her my secrets.

'You have to calm down,' Lil says. 'You'll give yourself another panic attack.'

I pour all of my hatred, my venom, into the look I give her.

'I don't want you to die, Myla. I'm trying to save you. I told you not to go out, but you didn't listen. I couldn't let you go back to Heartleas, you understand. Couldn't risk you remembering more.'

I glare, shaking my head. How did I get it so wrong? How could I have got everything so wrong?

Lil shuffles closer. I try to move away. 'Such beautiful hair,' she murmurs. 'My Beth had beautiful hair. I used to comb it for her. A hundred brushes a night, then I'd plait it. It was so long the plait fell all the way to her waist. I used to call her Rapunzel. But there was no prince to save her. Nobody could save her.'

Lil starts to hum. Her breath smells like cigarettes. I close my eyes, try to stop my body from shuddering as her fingers brush against my scalp, then run slowly down the length of my matted hair.

'Your sister had the most wonderful hair, too. You are lucky girls.' She pauses. 'I shouldn't have taken her. Believe me, if I'd known what would happen, I wouldn't have taken her.'

Get away from me. Please, I can't take any more. Please don't.

'I've brought you some clothes. We're going to get you ready. I'll sort your hair out first.'

No. NO!

Lil's trying to turn my head so I'm facing the wall. I lock my neck, struggle, but she's strong. So strong.

'Come on now, love,' she whispers. 'It's going to be all right.'

She wrenches my head around, shoves it against the sand, the scratchy, dry grass. Then Lil parts my hair into three sections and begins to weave them together.

30

Jamie

I dunno how I managed in that car with Lil. Thought I was gonna pass out. My hands were clenched the whole time. Can still see the pits in my palms where my fingernails were digging in.

I was gonna text Ness, try to explain it all, in case Lil was planning on going for me, but when I got out my phone, I saw it. The tracking app. And I had an idea. If I could plant the phone in Lil's car, Finn and I could use the app to follow her without her seeing us. So – just before we got to Ness's – I turned it to silent and slipped it down the side of the seat.

When Lil pulled up outside the house, I couldn't believe she was letting me go, that she didn't know I'd figured it out. But as I left, all she said was, 'You bring that girl back alive, you hear me?'

I almost lost it, then. Almost lunged at her. But I nodded, even managed to say thanks for the lift, and got out.

Now I'm in Finn's car and we're following the red dot that shows where my phone is. He's driving way too fast, almost in the boot of the car in front. He's done two wheel-spins already and run a red light, but I don't care. As long as we get to her in time.

I watched my phone move out of town, but it's stopped now, on a beach. Wonder if it's the same place where Asha was taken. Damn! Why didn't I just go there in the first place? I could've saved her by now. Might already be too late, if William's got there first. No, God. Can't even go there.

I stare at Finn's phone. Wish I knew Ness's mobile number off the top of my head. She's gonna be losing it if she can't get hold of me. What if she thinks I've been taken too? I've tried to ring the home number a couple of times, but there was no answer.

'You sure it's Lil?' Finn asks again.

I grit my teeth. 'I'm sure.'

'I'm gonna take her down!' Finn yells, slamming his hands against the wheel. 'For Asha. And all those months my uncle's been rotting in jail. William must be in on it. Yeah, that explains Asha's body. It was wiped down. Nothing on it. Like my uncle would know to do that.'

I stare out the window as he carries on ranting. I can hardly breathe, like the guilt is wrapped around me, squeezing everything tight. Can't believe how much I've messed up. So many times I should've done something differently. I didn't believe Myla, didn't trust her, even helped her leave the house, played right into Lil's hands. And Lil. I didn't see, didn't wanna see.

Finn says my name. He sounds cross, like he's already said it once and I didn't hear.

'What?'

'We're going to find her. We're going to make that cow confess. We'll sort this, make it right.'

I don't reply.

We start driving down this sandy track, following a wooden sign that says 'Heartleas Cove'.

'There's Lil's car,' I say, pointing. It's the only one in the car park.

I'm out of the door the second we stop, jogging down the path that leads to the beach. Behind me, Finn shouts something like 'hang on!' and runs to catch up.

It's a wide, sandy beach. The tide is out – miles away. I scan left and right, but there's no one around.

'Where's she hiding her?' I mutter. 'She must be hiding her. It's too public.'

Finn shrugs. 'Beach hut?'

'Are there any around here?'

'I don't know.'

I whip round, yelling full in his face. 'Jesus, C'MON! Think!' I wanna grab him, shake him. 'You know the area. Where's she hiding her?'

'How often do you think I come down here? You think I'm a walk-on-the-beach kind of guy?'

'OK. OK. Do we split up, look in different places?'

Finn takes a step back, looks at me. 'Honestly, mate. I'm not being funny but I don't think you'd last long in a one-on-one against anyone.'

'Still got a couple of punches in with you, didn't I?' I say as I turn left along the beach and start to run.

'I let you have them,' Finn shoots back as he follows.

Finn quickly overtakes me. I'm starting to feel a bit faint again. Should've eaten more at the picnic site. We're close, so close, but she could be anywhere. We dunno how far Lil walked after leaving her car. There's nothing here. Just sea and sand and birds and sky. It's hopeless. Myla's gonna die and I can't do anything, can't save her.

Hang on. Footprints. We can pick up her trail from the car, follow exactly where she went.

'Back to the car park,' I bark at Finn.

'You what?'

'Back to Lil's car. We can follow her footprints.'

We charge back. The ground is starting to sway. I stumble, fall onto my hands.

'You up for this?' Finn asks.

'I'm fine. You got any food?'

He shrugs. 'Might have half a Mars Bar.'

My stomach flips. What did I expect, though? He's hardly gonna be driving round with a punnet of grapes on his back seat.

Back at Finn's car, I use his mobile to try Ness's home number again while Finn roots around for the chocolate. I'm just about to give up when she answers, sounding breathless and worried.

'Ness, it's Jamie.'

'Jamie? Thank God. Are you all right?'

'Ness, I think I've found her. Can you and Jav come to Heartleas Cove? Don't call the cops – we can't trust them.'

'Jamie—'

'Gotta go. Just get here.'

I hang up.

Finn comes out the car, waving the Mars Bar. I snatch it and shove it down in two mouthfuls. It's half-melted so I hardly have to chew. Disgusting. I'm disgusting, gorging myself like that. The leeches squeal and scream. They rise up, their stomachs straining as they get ready to release their toxic gas. I close my eyes, take some deep breaths, fight it down.

It's just chocolate, for God's sake. It's not a big deal. My body needs energy, and that's what I'm giving it. Simple. I open my eyes. Why isn't it that simple? Why?

'Here,' Finn says. 'I've got the prints.'

We race along the sand, following the trail. The taste of chocolate is thick in my mouth. Feels so weird. It's clearing my head, though, keeping me sharp.

I stop, look up. The prints are heading for the dunes.

'Over there!' I yell, starting towards them.

As we get closer, I see a block of concrete poking up. It's surrounded by the dunes, tucked away. 'What's that?'

Finn gives me a look. 'It's a pill box, isn't it? From the war.'

There. She has to be there. I hammer towards it.

Outside the entrance, we pause, look at each other. How we gonna handle this? I put my finger to my lips. We don't wanna scare Lil. Dunno what she might do.

Finn crouches, ready to go in, but I grab his arm, shake my head. I have to go first. My pulse is gunning it after the run, my stomach bubbling and boiling.

I bend down and huddle inside, Finn close behind. The smell of piss is the first thing I notice. Then the humming. This low, creepy humming. My eyes are still getting used to the dark so I can't see properly, but I know it's Lil.

The humming stops. 'William?'

I move towards her. 'No. It's Jamie.'

She gasps. 'You shouldn't have come.'

A bit closer. Then I see her. Myla. God, Myla. She's all tied up. Her hair's been plaited, and she's wearing the green butterfly top. She's twisting her head back so she can see me, and the look in her eyes makes me wanna cry. She's not OK. Really not OK, but she's alive. Thank God she's alive.

'Get the hell away from her,' Finn growls, scuttling forward in a crouched position.

Lil wails, 'Stay away!'

But he gets too close. A shriek from Lil, a ticking noise, and

Finn screams as he drops. His head smacks into a rock and, just like that, he's out cold.

What the . . . What the hell just happened? Then I see what Lil has in her shaking hand. Looks like a stun gun. She's staring at it like she can't believe what she just did. Then she looks at me. 'Stay back, Jamie. I don't want to hurt you. I never wanted to hurt any of you.'

I'm on my own now. There's no way I can overpower Lil. Even if I could get the stun gun off her, half a Mars Bar and some fried thing from the picnic isn't gonna undo months of neglect. Why did I have to do this to myself? What the hell's wrong with me?

Enough. This isn't helping.

'Tell me about Beth,' I blurt. 'Tell me what happened.'

Lil lets out this noise that sounds like a dog that's been shot. 'I just want my girl back,' she cries.

'Is that why you took Asha?'

'I wanted to keep her, but she wouldn't stop screaming.'

Myla makes this muffled noise. I can see everything on her face – all the pain, anger, grief. It stabs through me like a knife in the gut. I look at her wide, wet eyes, try to tell her I'm sorry she has to hear this.

'So what happened?'

'No. I can't. Please don't make me.'

'You owe it to her!' I bellow, pointing at Myla. 'You owe it to her to tell the truth.'

'I just wanted to stop her screaming, but it all went wrong.

Everything went wrong. He said he'd handle it. That I wasn't to interfere. But I was sorry, sorry I'd taken Saffy's sister away, and I wanted to try to make it better.'

Saffy? Why's she calling Myla Saffy? Man, she's really lost it.

'How?' I demand. 'How did you try to make it better? What did you do?'

Lil shakes her head, looks away as tears roll down her cheeks.

'What did you do?' I shout.

Lil sniffs. 'I made an online profile.'

What the hell's she on about? An online profile? What's that gotta do with anything?

'I just wanted to be close to you,' Lil says to Myla. 'Eve was the only way.'

Eve? She knows Eve?

'I listened, sympathised. I told you I believed you about the killer when no one else would. I looked after you. Even watched the house sometimes, to check you were all right.'

Oh my God. She *is* Eve! No way.

Lil turns back to me. 'When you came along, I wanted to know more about you, whether you'd protect her. I was so angry that you were trying to help her leave – the one place she was safe!

She was trying to get the investigation reopened: writing blogs, contacting charities. He said – he said we'd need to deal with her if she ever left the house. That we couldn't risk her going to Heartleas and remembering anything that might point to us. I was trying to protect both of them, don't you see?'

Lil pauses, takes a deep, shuddering breath.

Myla is crying. I just wanna reach for her, hold her. I'm sorry, Myla. So, so sorry.

'You think I'm crazy, don't you?' Lil snaps. 'I lost a child. Do you have any idea?'

A cold voice cuts through the darkness. 'That's enough, Mother.'

Lil freezes and mouths his name. 'William.'

31

Myla

Lil looks horrified when she sees her son. 'What are you doing here? How did you know?'

William ignores her and talks to Jamie. 'I'm sorry it took me so long. I had to slip away from my partner.' His eyes flick down to the unconscious Finn. 'I was thinking I could deal with Mother myself, but I can see she's very far gone.'

He edges closer.

Jamie moves as far away as possible, into the corner. 'Bullshit!' he spits. 'You've been in on this from the start.'

A muscle twitches above William's eye. 'I'm sure we can sort this out, just between us.'

Lil moves in front of me. 'She's mine. You can't hurt her, William.'

'Come on now,' William says in the kind of voice you'd use

to talk down a lunatic, a psychopath. 'You're not well. You know you haven't been yourself since Beth. If you give me the stun gun you stole from me, we'll talk about this.'

Lil shakes her head, clutches the weapon to her chest.

William tries – but fails – to hide his irritation. 'I heard what you said earlier. I think you're confused. We all know that the real killer is safely locked away. It's understandable that you blame yourself for Asha, just as you did for Beth, but I can help you sort it all out.'

'No. You said we'd have to get rid of Myla. I didn't want her to get hurt. And I didn't want you to be involved again. Not after you—'

'Be quiet!' William roars, lunging at her.

Lil screams and shoves the stun gun towards William. He tries to twist away, but it touches his arm and he cries out as he drops to the ground.

Lil is so distracted she doesn't see Jamie until he slams into her, knocking her backwards. The stun gun rattles off the bricks and falls behind me. Lil's entire body weight crushes down on me. I can't breathe! I struggle, try to kick Lil off. Coughing and wheezing, she rolls away.

William picks himself up, shaking and sweating. He grabs the stun gun, points it at Lil and snarls, 'Outside. Wait for me there.'

Lil gets up, her shoulders slumping. 'Please don't hurt them,' she whimpers.

William ignores her. God, what's he going to do to us?

Lil starts to shuffle towards the exit, but she stops, looks back at me, her eyes big and mournful. 'I'm sorry.'

I blink. She's sorry? Sorry? After Asha, Eve, what she's put me through today, sorry doesn't even come close.

I turn away until she's gone.

Jamie, William and I stare at each other in silence, wondering who's going to make the next move.

There's no hiding the expression in William's eyes. I can see exactly what he'd like to do to me. Jamie can, too, because he sits up straighter, positions himself between William and me and says, 'You're not gonna touch her.'

William makes a sudden move. Jamie doesn't flinch, holds his ground. 'Ness knows where we are. She's called the cops. Your partner? He'll be here in minutes.'

William thinks for a second.

I hold my breath. Please, just leave. Leave us alone.

William makes a small 'hmm' at the back of his throat, turns around and heads for the exit.

My breath swoops out in one big rush. Jamie is at my side in an instant, his trembling fingers brushing my face. He pulls the gag out. For a second, my jaw won't move. Then I gasp and start to cry.

Jamie looks like he wants to say something, but nothing comes out. He just stares at me like I might still be snatched away from him. Then he bends down and kisses my forehead. My disgusting, vomitty forehead.

I cry even harder. I can't stop.

'Shhhh,' Jamie says. 'Don't.'

He starts working on my hands, untying the tape, and all the time he's telling me it's OK, that I'm going to be all right.

But it's not OK. It's not over.

'What are we going to do?' I say in a voice that's cracked and dry. 'They'll be waiting for us out there. We're trapped.'

Jamie pats down Finn's pockets, pulls out his phone. He looks at it for a moment, then swears and slams it into the sand. 'No signal.'

I want to get out of this hole alive. I just want to see my mum and dad. My body shakes with great, heaving sobs.

Jamie wraps his arms around me and pulls me into his lap. I cry out, my muscles cramping, the blood trickling back into places that had gone numb.

'Do we just stay here, wait for the police?' I ask.

Jamie shakes his head. 'I told Ness not to call them. Told her we couldn't trust them.'

My heart drops. 'So they're not coming. But Mum and Ness are? We've got to get out of here.'

Jamie nods. 'Let's go. You all right to move?'

'I'll have to be.' I start to lift my head from his lap, but I freeze. 'The plait.' I reach back and try to undo it, but it's woven tightly and my fingers are clumsy and weak. 'Get it out!' I shriek, yanking and tugging at it. 'Get it out! I don't want Mum to see.'

'OK, OK,' Jamie says, gently taking my hands.

I sit in silence while he works, starting from the bottom.

Within seconds he's nearing the top, and I feel the sweep of the thick braids moving over and under each other. Then Jamie's running his fingers through my hair, teasing out the curls, and it feels so good, and he's so careful, it makes me want to cry again.

Jamie looks over at Finn. 'We'll have to leave him for now.'

'Leave him on his own in here?' I shudder.

'We'll come back for him. I can't drag him. What if they're waiting to jump us as soon as we get out?'

I bite my lip. I can feel a swarm of hysteria gathering in my stomach like wasps. I try to bat them down, stop them from overrunning my whole body.

Jamie grips my hand, gives it a squeeze. 'Don't worry. I'll go first.'

'Jamie?'

'Yeah?'

'Thank you. For finding me. For coming for me.'

He blushes, runs his hand over his head, and turns towards the exit.

I follow him down the low passageway, scrambling out on my stomach. It feels like I'm crawling through tar. The exit seems to stretch out, further and further away.

I don't know what's waiting for me outside, don't know if William is going to be poised, ready to slam the stun gun into me, or if Lil is going to smother me with another drug-soaked rag. But whatever's out there, I'll face it with Jamie. I focus on his shoes in front of me, clench my teeth and wriggle faster.

It's dark outside. I feel the space open up as Jamie gets out. I stop, listen. He's shouting. Is he grappling with someone, trying to fight them off?

Suddenly, strong arms hoist me up and out of the passageway. Someone is wailing, putting their hands all over my face. I scream and try to push them away. Get off me! Don't touch me!

Then I hear their voice, make myself stop.

Mum. It's Mum. And ... oh God, Dad. He's crying, checking me all over as he murmurs, 'My girl. My poor baby girl. I thought I'd lost you too.'

I look around. My head feels like a kaleidoscope, spinning with all these garish colours.

The person Jamie is yelling at is a policeman. Ness must've called them after all. Or is he William's partner? Did he realise something was up, follow him here? Jamie's pointing at William, trying to explain that Lil confessed to killing Asha, but William cleaned up after her.

Ness is behind my parents, pale and anxious as she looks at Lil, who is crying and rocking on the ground. 'What's going on?' Ness asks her. 'Why are you here? Why are you handcuffed? I don't understand.' Lil doesn't answer.

'Look Aidan,' William says to the other policeman. 'You're my partner. You've got to trust me on this. I've explained why I had to come alone. She's my mother. I thought I could diffuse the situation. Now, there's a boy unconscious in there. Why don't I go and retrieve him and wait here for the paramedics? You can walk everyone else back to the car park.'

No! If we leave, he'll run. I can see that Jamie's thinking the same thing. Everyone is looking at Aidan, whose eyes are boring into his partner's. Aidan shakes his head. 'I'm sorry, Will. I have to take you in for questioning.'

Nobody says anything. It's like we're all suspended, just hanging there.

William glances down at his stun gun. The second he goes for it, Aidan's on top of him. I scream, stand back as they wrestle in the sand, grains flying up around them. First Aidan's on top, then William. I can barely keep up – they're almost a blur! Then someone else wades in and delivers a short, sharp punch that sends William sprawling. My mouth drops. Dad?

Aidan handcuffs William. He talks into his radio, asks the backup to get a move on, then tells the rest of us to wait for him at the car park.

We move as one solemn party along the deserted beach. Ness is clinging to Jamie's arm, dabbing her eyes with a tissue. Mum and Dad are propping me up. They've given up asking questions. I can't. I just don't have the words. Everything hurts. Everything.

I look out across the ocean. The same ocean I plunged into that night to hide from Lil. Oh, Asha. My sister. My beautiful sister. Tears spill down my cheeks. I don't wipe them away, don't try to stop them.

I let Mum and Dad guide me, let foot follow foot follow foot, in time with the *shush-shush-shush* of the sea. I hear her voice, teasing me about the Smarties. I smell the citrus and green tea on her skin, feel the cool metal of the bangle around her wrist.

By the time we reach the car park, there's an ambulance trundling down the rutted road, followed by several police cars, sirens blaring.

Is that it? Is it finished?

My legs drop beneath me. I'm on the sand, grabbing fistfuls of it like it's the only thing connecting me to reality. Then Jamie's on his knees next to me, holding my hand, and Mum's sinking down beside us, throwing her arm across my shoulders.

Jamie finds my eyes and smiles and says the best two words ever. 'It's over.'

32

Jamie

I've got my eyes closed, the sun pounding down on my face. There's a bee buzzing around the flowers at the back of the garden. I run my fingers through the grass. It's clipped short and it smells good, like summer.

I open my eyes when I hear the door open. Myla comes out of her house, wrapping the ugly throw around her, even though it's boiling. I smile. She smiles back. 'Hi, freckle-face. Working on your tan?'

Myla looks better than she did yesterday, but she still walks slowly, hunching a bit. She was well grumpy about being in hospital, made such a fuss they agreed to discharge her early. Not sure it was a good idea. When she sits next to me, cuddling against my side, I feel her shivering.

'You're hot,' she says.

'It's you. You're cold.' I wrap my arm around her, pull her closer. 'You all right? Been eating?'

Myla raises an eyebrow, as if to say: Really? Coming from you?

I let out this surprised laugh, stare at her for a moment. I should tell her. Be honest about everything.

So I do. I explain why I started being weird about food. I describe how much I liked the feeling of power. But I say how scared I was when Myla was taken, afraid that my body would let me down, that something might happen to her 'cos I wasn't strong enough.

'And now?'

I sigh. 'I s'pose I was just being an idiot. I wanted to hurt *him*, show him that I was in control. Truth is, he doesn't give a damn whether I eat or not. All I was doing was beating myself up. And hurting Mum.'

Me and Mum have talked a bit over the last couple of days. It's been all right. She didn't mention *him*, was too busy flapping about me, asking me to come home early. Told her I had to stay, see it through to the end, check that Myla was OK.

'I wanna get better, wanna be strong for Mum, help her to ditch him.'

Myla smiles and squeezes my hand. 'I'm here. I'll help.'

And – for the first time – it feels like maybe I can do it.

We sit in silence for a bit. Then Myla says, 'The police called yesterday. They found Asha's bangle at Lil's house. I can't have it back because it's evidence. I think they're going to charge Lil with manslaughter, abduction and harassment; William with perverting the course of justice. I suppose they'll release Si soon.'

'Jesus.' I dunno what else to say.

Myla looks up at me. 'So they'll be calling you back to be a witness, which means I'll see you soon, right?'

I nod. 'Definitely.'

The word hangs in the air. Neither of us says anything. Myla shifts a little, sighs.

This is the thing. The thing we can't talk about. I mean, it's too soon, right? We can't talk about what happens next with us, not after everything.

I've only got a week left. Myla's not ready. I know she's not ready for anything more. What she's dealing with ... it's huge. She doesn't have space to think about me. I mean, I'd be a dick if I asked her to be my girlfriend, try to make it work long distance.

But then I look at her body curled against mine like it's meant to be there, and all I wanna do is kiss her. What if this is my only chance? What if I leave, come back and she's found someone else? I guess she'll go back to school. Boys will be sniffing around her, and it would be easy, much easier than trying to go out with a bloke who lives a hundred miles away.

'What's the matter?' Myla asks.

'What?'

She pulls away so she can look at me. 'What's the matter?

You've gone all tense.' She nods at my hands, which have stiffened into claws, digging into the ground. 'What are you thinking about?'

I shrug, try to smile. 'Everything.'

Myla settles back down against my side. 'Me too. It's going to take years to sift through all the stuff in my head. Dad's on about trying another counsellor. I think it would be a good idea.'

I dust off the soil, run my hand up her arm, then down again, grinning as I see a trail of goosebumps following it.

How would it even work? I dunno if she'll ever be up for going out alone, even now it's all over. I won't be able to afford to come and see her every week.

'Have you heard from Finn?' Myla asks.

'Nope. Not since the hospital.'

He was a couple of wards away from Myla. While she was asleep, I went in to see him. He was weird. Seemed different. Probably the painkillers.

'Listen,' he said. 'I know I was a bit, you know, heavy.'

I snorted. 'Heavy?'

'All right, well I want to say . . . '

'Seriously, man. Don't.'

'You've got to know how much it was eating me up, knowing that Asha's killer was still out there, that my uncle was locked away and it was my fault. I was desperate.'

'Honestly, don't. You're freaking me out. Did that bump on the head loosen something in there?'

Finn laughed. Held out his hand. I shook it.

A cat walks across the top of Myla's fence. We both watch it. Pretty cool, how it balances like that. So precise. The sunlight is bouncing off Myla's hair. I lean down, almost kiss the top of her head, then pull back.

'She fooled me,' Myla says. 'She knew just what to say, exactly what I wanted to hear.'

I nod. 'She got close to me, too.'

'Dad's lawyer says she probably won't go to prison, that her defence will plead insanity.'

'Like Lil said, you can't live through what she did and stay normal.'

'I do feel sorry for her. She knows what it's like to lose someone. That's why she could get so close to me.' Myla pauses, then says, 'Jamie?'

'Mmmm?'

'Will you kiss me?'

I freeze, heart speeding. She sits up, faces me, her expression all hopeful.

'You sure?'

Argh! I didn't mean to say that. I'm trampling all over the moment. I want to, so bad. But . . .

'Listen,' I say. 'You've got a lot to deal with. I don't wanna, y'know . . . '

Myla rolls her eyes. 'Shut up, Mr Nice Guy. I'm giving you permission to take advantage.'

And then she leans in, going for it. And I dunno what to

do. I mean, I've kissed girls before. Myla's not just any girl, though.

This feels wrong. She's not thinking straight.

But she's not stopping, and I want her. I *really* want her.

I tilt my head, but I go the wrong way and our noses bump, then we both smile and our teeth almost clash, and it's not s'posed to be like this. I feel like a complete arsehole who's making a move on this fragile girl. And we try for a couple of seconds, our lips squashing together, but she knows I'm not feeling it, and she pulls away, tears in her eyes.

Myla blushes. 'I thought you liked me. I totally misread the signals, didn't I?'

'No, Myla, please!' I say as she gets up. 'I do like you. I really, really like you, but this – it feels wrong.'

'So you thought you liked me but kissing me felt wrong?'

'It's not like that. Not at all. Can I just explain?'

She gives me this sad smile. 'Not now, Jamie. I'm pretty tired.'

And like an idiot – a complete idiot – I watch her head into the house. I don't follow. I just let her walk away.

By the time I've let myself out the garden gate and onto the street, I'm pissed off. So pissed off my blood is fizzing with it. Why did I do that? Why do I have to overthink everything? That was it. My chance. Blown.

The leeches start to churn up everything in my stomach. They can't wait to spew out all their toxic mess. But I've had enough. I'm not doing this any more. I tell them to fuck off and die.

I wrench my phone out of my pocket and find Kai's number.

I called him yesterday, told him everything about Myla and Asha and Lil. Took ages to go through the whole thing, though I reckon he'd already read some of it in the papers. He just listened, didn't say a damn word until I'd finished. He was awesome.

'Jay! How's it going?'

'Dude, I messed up.'

'What? You spill your guts to a reporter?'

'Worse. I screwed things up with Myla.'

Kai sighs. 'You're talking to the wrong man, my friend. I told Isma last night I thought her boobs looked bigger. Apparently that means I'm saying she's put on weight.'

I roll my eyes. 'You're such a fool.'

He laughs. 'I know, right? She loves it, though.'

'God knows why.'

'Listen, about Myla. Don't sweat it. Just give her some space.'

'That's what I was trying to do. Seems like that was the wrong thing.'

'Isn't it always, my man? Hey, when you coming home? Nana Bo's been asking after you. You are coming to see her, right?'

Ah, crap. Nana Bo. I should've told him this ages ago. 'Yeah, about that . . . '

'Was starting to seem like you was dissing her, not coming round no more.'

I never meant to disrespect Nana Bo. I frigging *love* Nana Bo.

'I wasn't dissing her, mate. It was nothing personal, I swear.'

'So what was it, then?'

'It was . . . the food thing,' I mumble.

'You need to tell me straight, 'cos it still sounds like you're dissing Nana Bo. You don't like her food?'

He's really gonna make me say it. I s'pose that's fair. 'You know I've been having a hard time with eating and stuff. I couldn't deal with her trying to shove food down my throat the second I walked through your door. I'm sorry, yeah? Tried to tell her to stop, but she didn't listen.'

'You know she's just being polite, right? That's what it's like back home. Everyone feeds.'

'Course. I get it. It was me. Not her.'

'Why didn't you just say? I thought you had some beef with Nana Bo. I was getting ready to bust your skinny arse!'

I smile. 'Yeah? Well this skinny arse isn't going to be so skinny for long. Tell Nana Bo to get some of that coconut rice on.'

'Yeah, man! Sounds like you're doing better. I've got to go, but call me when you're home. Later.'

'Bye.'

I hang up and call Mum.

'Hi, sweetie. How are you?'

'Listen, Mum. We need to talk before I come home. About *him*.'

Mum takes a breath. 'OK.'

'You say he's been putting you down? Well he was putting me down for months before I left.'

Mum gasps. 'Why didn't you say?'

'Didn't think you'd believe me. You were so wrapped up in him. But if he's treating you bad, then you've gotta get rid of him.'

She lets out a shaky sigh. 'Jamie, I don't know if I can.'

'Trust me. You can.'

'But I – I love him.' Her voice is trembling, like she knows it's not true.

'Really? Do you? 'Cos he's a bully. Just a little man acting like a big man.'

'I don't know what to think. But I do feel like he's . . . '

'Like he's what?'

'Come between us. I've missed you.'

'I'm gonna help you. I'll come home tomorrow and we'll face up to this – to *him* – together.'

I say goodbye, then hang up. Did I just say that? Did I really just say that? That was . . . wow!

At Ness's, I start to pack. She's gonna be gutted that I'm leaving early, but I gotta go, take care of Mum. And Myla doesn't wanna see me again.

I work really slowly, folding and refolding. Feels weird 'cos I'm not bothered about stuff being neat, but I don't wanna think about everything else.

When I finish packing, I eat a banana. Me and Ian, we're gonna take one last walk. We catch the bus to the place with the boardwalk, the place with the amazing beach, if we can make it that far. I stop at the ice-cream van, buy a lemonade and a bottle of water for Ian.

We start to walk. I grab massive lungfuls of air, knowing that tomorrow I'll be breathing in the crap in London again.

Either side of the boardwalk, fishing boats lean on their sides in the muddy flats. There's even a wreck, really close to the path. Me and Ian jog down to get a better look. It has sunk into the ground, with grass growing in the middle. One side of the boat is intact, the other rotting, with bits of wood sticking up like rib bones. Most of the paint has chipped off, but there are still patches of bright blue. Bit like a necklace that Myla . . . No. Don't.

Ian's sniffing around like mad. I pull on his lead, tug him away from a pool of water he's got his eye on. I open my can, start to drink the lemonade. I'm not used to the sugar but it's all right.

We head back to a bench on the main path. I pour some water in my hand for Ian. He slurps quickly, only pausing to pant a bit. I stroke his hot ear, just where he likes it. 'We can do this, mate. We're gonna make it all the way this time.'

We stop about half an hour later so I can eat the cereal bar

I stuffed in my pocket at Ness's. Instead of bolting it down, swallowing the guilt, I chew slowly, actually taste it.

We're pretty close to the dunes now. There's fewer people, just like Myla said. A couple of birdwatchers tut and glare as Ian trots past, but I ignore them.

As I trek up the sand dune, my legs are shaking, my T-shirt sticking to me. I'm muttering that this better be worth it. But then I reach the top and I can see everything . . . literally everything.

The beach is massive. I can look both ways and see it disappear into the distance. The sand is fine, white and soft. The tide is out. It's miles away. I'd have to walk for another ten minutes just to get to it. There's no one around. Just me and Ian, who's pulling on the lead, desperate to charge across the sand towards the water.

I bend down and unclip him. He shoots away.

I kick off my shoes and run down the dune after him.

33

Myla

I check the clock by my bed for at least the fifth time. It's 1 a.m. I can feel the pull of tiredness at the back of my eyes but I shake my head and take a big gulp of tea, grimacing at its sweetness. I hate sugary tea, but I'll do anything to stay awake; anything to keep the nightmares away.

I was prescribed sleeping pills at the hospital. I took some the night I was discharged. When I started to dream about the pill box, started to feel hands around my neck, choking me, I couldn't wake up. I was trapped.

When I eventually managed to rouse myself, I was caught in a full-scale panic attack. I scrabbled around for the light, unable to scream. I sent my bedside lamp crashing to the floor. Seconds later, Mum was in my room, like she had been listening out for me.

My head nods and my eyes flip closed. I force them open again. Jamie. I'll think about Jamie. That'll definitely keep me awake. My whole body flushes. God, it's all so cringey. Maybe it's just as well he's leaving in a week.

What am I saying? I can't believe he's going. We have to stay friends. We have to! I can't imagine him not being in my life. I just hope I haven't ruined everything.

I'll wait a couple of days for things to calm down, then I'll give him a call, sort this all out before he leaves. It was just a misunderstanding, that's all. I mean, it was hard not to get carried away. I thought he was giving me the right signals. He did almost kiss me on the cliff, until he realised Mum was watching. Or was it all me? I was the one who made the first move. Perhaps he was just using Mum as an excuse.

I'll get over it. That's what I'll tell him, anyway. But I feel bruised, and it's close to the surface, painful. It's weird that, given all the other crap I have to deal with, the one thing that really stings is the fact that a boy doesn't want to kiss me.

He's not just any boy, though.

I think I make it through most of the night without sleeping. I definitely drop off a couple of times, but it's not deep enough for me to dream. I'm going to need a lot of caffeine and sugar today. I think I'll make cupcakes. For medicinal reasons.

I get out of bed before Dad leaves, so we can all eat breakfast together. He took a few days off work, but today's his first day back. He cooks pancakes, saying he doesn't care if he's a few minutes late.

After he's gone, Mum sits at the table while I'm whipping up the cupcake mix. She makes a special request for lemon so I grate some zest in, the kitchen filling with its tangy scent. We try to talk about normal stuff. We've spent enough time talking about all the other stuff, going over and over it. Mum apologised so many times for not believing me that I ended up snapping at her and telling her to stop.

We have a cup of tea while we're waiting for the cupcakes to cool. Probably my sixth tea of the day.

'So when's Lauren coming round again?' Mum asks.

'I don't know. We've been texting, though, and she's left a couple of comments on my blog, which is sweet. The whole thing with Albie really shook her up, but I think she's feeling better now that he's locked away.'

'You said you thought it was all related, that Albie might have been the one who . . . '

'I didn't know what to think. I'm just glad the police caught up with Albie. I couldn't believe it when I mentioned him in my interview and they said they'd already arrested him for hassling those girls.'

I poke one of the cupcakes. It's almost cool so I start to mix up a lemon buttercream frosting.

'So what's next for the blog?' Mum asks.

'I was thinking a couple more vegetable cake recipes. They seem to be quite popular at the moment. Beetroot, courgette . . . '

Mum pulls a face.

I laugh. 'What? You'd eat carrot cake.'

Mum's mobile rings in the other room. She heads off to answer it, and I start to pipe the icing on top of the cakes, listening to the gentle murmur of her voice through the walls. I move the icing around in slow, careful swirls. This is nice. This is normal.

Mum comes back in. 'You didn't tell me that Jamie was leaving today. I thought you seemed a bit quiet yesterday. Was it awful saying goodbye to him?'

'He's not going today. It's next Thursday.'

Mum puts a hand on my arm, stops me mid-swirl. 'Ness just called,' she says gently. 'She's taking him to the station today.'

I put the piping bag down. 'What? No. It's Thursday. We have until Thursday.'

'Myla,' Mum says, but I'm already running out of the kitchen, heading for my room, my mobile. He wouldn't have changed his plans without telling me. I know yesterday was awkward, but he wouldn't do that to me. He wouldn't!

I snatch my phone off the bed. No texts. Mum must've got it wrong. I check my emails too. Nothing.

Unless he's left me a video message? I quickly sign in to the app we use. One message from Jamie. My hand shakes a little as I press the play button.

There he is, smiling his shy smile, sitting on his bed, leaning against the pink wall.

'Er, hi,' he says.

'Hi,' I reply, even though I know he can't hear me.

'I wanted to leave you a message to – er – explain about yesterday and to tell you not to feel embarrassed.'

At this point, he blushes, then looks away for a moment. When he looks back, he's staring straight down the camera, as if he's looking right into my eyes. 'I really like you, Myla. More than you know. You joked about me taking advantage, but that's what it felt like, like I was doing something wrong, 'cos you're still dealing with everything else.'

Jamie sighs, runs his hand through his hair like he always does when he's stressed. 'God, this is weird, not telling you face-to-face. I thought it would be easier. Thought you'd still be cross so you wouldn't wanna see me, but this is just … weird.'

I laugh. I love it when he gets all awkward and tongue-tied. Then I let out a little gasp because he says, 'I've wanted to kiss for you for so long, and I just wanted it to be, well, better than that.'

'Oh, Jamie,' I murmur.

'And now I gotta go, and I know it's a bit sudden and it probably seems like it's 'cos of you, but it isn't. I gotta go home and help Mum. I don't wanna leave you, but I'll come back, if you want me to.'

There's a pause. 'OK,' he says, nodding. 'Bye.'

The screen goes black.

My heart's beating way too fast. I have to see him. I have to see him *now*.

'Mum!' I yell as I fly down the stairs. 'When did Ness say they were leaving?'

'I was trying to tell you. His train's booked for half-two. They must be about to leave.'

I glance at the time on my mobile. 'I can make it. I just need to see him for one minute. That's all.'

Mum grins. 'I'll just find my keys. I'm not sure where I left them.'

I shake my head, rushing into the hallway to grab my shoes. I don't want Mum looking over my shoulder when I do this. 'No time. I'll go on my own.'

'On your own? Absolutely not, Myla. Just wait for me. I know the keys are around here somewhere.'

I charge back into the kitchen, give her a peck on the cheek, swipe a cupcake from the side and say, 'I love you, Mum.'

Thirty seconds later, I'm out of the door and sprinting down the road.

34

Jamie

I'm standing by Ness's car, waiting for her to finish locking up, when my phone rings.

'Jamie?' Mum sounds all breathless.

'What's the matter? What happened?'

'Nothing.' And then she laughs and I realise it's an excited kind of breathlessness.

'Seriously, what's going on?'

'I didn't want you to come home to this ... horrible situation with me and Damian. So I sorted it out myself.'

'No way. You ended it?'

'I – I did!' She actually sounds surprised.

'That's frigging awesome. Seriously, Mum, that's awesome.'

'So if you want to take the extra week, stay in Norfolk, I understand. I'll be all right.'

But I can hear the wobble in her voice. 'Mum?'

'I'm fine. It's just … hard, you know? It was so quiet last night, I almost called—'

'Mum, I'm coming home now. I'm about to catch the train. We've got this. We're gonna be fine, you and me.'

'Yes, OK. Just you and me.'

'Listen, I gotta go. Ness is coming. I'll see you in a couple of hours.'

'Can't wait. Bye, sweetie.'

I hang up, put my phone away.

'What are you grinning about?' Ness asks.

'Mum. She kicked him out.'

Ness claps her hands together. 'That's wonderful. Good for her! I always knew he was trouble. I told Angela she was better off without him.'

Mum's blatantly gonna get a big 'I told you so' next time she speaks to Ness.

Ness opens the boot. Ian jumps straight in and she slots my case next to him. He wags his tail and licks her arm. 'Poor old thing. You're going to miss your new friend, aren't you?'

I stroke his head. 'I know, buddy,' I whisper, leaning down so he can lick my face, covering me in meaty drool.

'Are you all set, then?' Ness is trying to sound all right, but I can see how much she's struggling.

She's had a hard time these last couple of days. Said she knew something wasn't right after Lil lost Beth. Thinks she should've known. But any of us could say that. Me, her, Myla. Lil fooled us all.

'Have you got everything?'

I nod.

'Did you see that I'd left a bottle of shower gel in your bedroom? It was half price, and I know you like that one.'

I say yes, then thank her.

'And did you pick up your DVD from the lounge? That awful one with all the violence and the silly alien things?'

I roll my eyes and nod.

'I washed your jumper as well. Did I remember to give it to you?'

'Yep. I've packed it. We should go, shouldn't we?'

Ness sighs. 'Yes, I suppose we should.'

I head around to the passenger side, but stop when I hear footsteps running towards us.

Myla's breathing heavily, hair all messed up and sticking to her forehead. 'Myla?' I say, moving towards her. 'What you doing here on your own?'

'I came ...' She gasps. '... to give you ... this.'

And she holds out a cupcake. It's a bit squashed and some of the icing has smudged and dribbled off the top. I laugh, then look up. She's laughing too.

'It's a peace offering. But it can be a symbolic peace offering. You don't have to eat it if you don't want to.'

'Why don't I get a sandwich bag for that?' Ness says, taking it from Myla. 'We don't have long, I'm afraid. It's the last train today.'

I nod. Can't stop staring at Myla. She came all this way on her own!

'Thought I'd do the whole dramatic "turn up at the last minute" thing,' she says. 'Maybe it would've been more dramatic if I'd rocked up at the station just as your train was about to leave.' She pushes my chest gently and pouts. 'I can't believe you were going to go without a proper goodbye. I only just got your message. I wanted to say—'

But she doesn't get to say it 'cos I'm grabbing her waist, pulling her towards me, and my lips are on hers, and her hands are all over the back of my head, stroking my hair, tickling my neck, and I kiss her harder, and she gasps and smiles and I smile back but we keep on kissing and I don't even care when someone drives past and beeps their horn, or when Ness comes back and clears her throat.

Myla must still be outta breath from the run – or is it from the kiss? – 'cos she pauses, her chest heaving. Then she grabs me in this hug, her fingers digging into my back.

All this warmth spreads through me, like bright light, and it's filling me up. Feels incredible.

Ness taps her watch. Now? We gotta go now? What about all the stuff I gotta say?

But it's OK. We don't need to say anything. And Myla doesn't. Not even goodbye. She just watches me get in the car, giving me a small wave and a quick smile. I fight with the lump in my throat. Is she crying? I don't wanna know. I don't turn back.

As we pull away, Ness checks her wing mirror. 'It's all right. Jav's just pulled up.'

I let all my breath out and sink into the chair, looking at the cupcake in a bag that Ness has put on my lap.

I kissed her! Yeah! I kissed her. Now *that* was a proper first kiss. Man, I'm still shaking from it.

Ness hurtles down the road, the engine roaring in second gear. There's a breeze coming from her window, which still only winds down a couple of inches. Ian's panting in the back. I don't smell him any more. Must've got used to him. Or maybe he was having an off-day when I first got here.

Ness swerves slightly as she takes one hand off the wheel to reach for me. 'I'm really going to miss you,' she says, her voice about to break.

'Thanks for everything. You've been brilliant. Honestly.'

'Well at least I know you'll be coming back. Not necessarily to see me, but I'm pretty sure I'll see you again soon. I'll try to keep the clutter out of your room.'

'Yeah, right!' I say, laughing. 'I saw that stack of stuff on the landing. You're gonna stash it in my room the second you get home.'

Ness smiles. 'Just as long as you remember that it is *your* room. Well done for helping your mum get sorted. I'm proud of you. I bet she's proud too. You stay strong for her. She's going to need you.'

'I will,' I promise.

We say goodbye in the station car park. Ness gives me a hug. She's properly crying now.

Ian lunges for my face when I bend down to get my case. Another lick.

'Thanks again,' I say to Ness. 'Gotta go. Literally got two minutes.'

I wave at her, then run up the steps, squinting at the screen to check my platform. I just make it through the train doors before they close, then I head down the aisle. I keep going through the carriages until I find a pair of empty seats. I lift my suitcase into the luggage rack and shuffle over to the chair by the window.

I put the cupcake bag on the table. The icing has smeared all over the inside. I grin, take the cake out and start to pull down the wrapper.

Acknowledgements

Thank you to Mum for that wonderful weekend of barbecuing and brainstorming, for being one of the first readers of *Consumed* and for commenting so honestly.

To my editor, Sarah Castleton, for her support and encouragement, for delving into the edits with such a keen and practised eye, and for making me want to tell the best story I could.

My gratitude, as always, to my writing group, WordWatchers, for helping me pull together the plot in the early days, for keeping me on track while I was writing and for critiquing in such a thoughtful and valuable way. Special thanks to the lovely Daddy Hoggy for always being on the end of an email and for coming to the rescue on more than one occasion.

Many thanks to my other writing group, Swallows, for

their excellent feedback and enthusiasm for the story, especially Kersti Worsley, for letting me pick her brilliantly creative brain.

I'm also grateful to Derek Kevern for sharing his wealth of knowledge about the police force and firearms.

Most of all, massive thanks to my husband, Nick. Thank you for never complaining, for your constant love and support, for being everything I needed to get this book written: editor, idea generator, research assistant, cook, cleaner, tea-maker extraordinaire . . .